BLOOI

By Kim

INDEX

AUTHORS OTHER WORKS

WHATEVER IT TAKES
EAST END HONOUR
TRAFFICKED
BELL LANE LONDON E1
EAST END LEGACY
EAST END A FAMILY OF STEEL
PHILLIMORE PLACE LONDON
EAST END LOTTERY
FAMILY BUSINESS
A DANGEROUS MIND
FAMILY FIRST
A SCORE TO SETTLE (BOOK ONE)
A SCORE SETTLED
A DANGEROUS MIND (TWO)
BODILY HARM
SINS OF THE FATHER
GREED
EYE FOR AN EYE
CRIME DOESN'T PAY
FORBIDDEN FRUIT

Web site www.kimhunterauthor.com[1]

1. http://www.kimhunterauthor.com

QUOTES

Revenge is barren of itself: it is the dreadful food it feeds on; its delight is murder, and its end is despair.

Friedrich Von Schiller

1759 – 1805

MAIN CHARACTERS

Nicky Stanton is now the head of a notorious firm of London villains. A chip off the old block, he was prematurely forced to take over the business when his father suffered a massive stroke. Nicky didn't resent being pushed to the fore; he would do anything for his family, but it wasn't what he really wanted from life. It had long been his ambition to leave the life of crime that the Stanton name carried, or at least detach himself from it as far as was possible. Nicky has always had the dream of being a club owner, but he was forced to put his plans on hold when his father became ill. A determined man, one way or another, he would eventually make his dream come true, of that he was sure. Not marrying until he reached his early thirties, Nicky wasn't what you would call faithful. Oh, he loved his wife, but women had always been his weakness, and for that weakness, he would soon pay a heavy price.

Diana Stanton, who everyone called Dodi, was a stay-at-home wife. For some, she was living the dream, but that wasn't the case for Dodi. Falling in love with her husband years earlier when they were still in school, she dreamed of motherhood and being the perfect wife with the perfect

family, but sadly, that wasn't to be. Nicky had postponed their wedding again and again, but finally, she had pinned him down just before his thirty-third birthday, and she had planned to get pregnant as soon as she could. Unfortunately, fate took a cruel hand, and the outcome would turn out to be heartbreaking.

Chief Inspector Anna Draycott, is a high-flying, recently promoted and recently widowed member of the Metropolitan Police Force. Fresh from the successful closure of a high-profile murder case, she is transferred from Tottenham to Charing Cross police station when a case being worked on has come to a standstill. The public is up in arms, and the top brass needs the case solved as soon as possible. Anna insists that her team go with her as the pressure to get results is huge, and she knows it could ultimately make or break her career.

Detective Cherry Graham, a respected undercover officer, works mostly in the vice squad, but Cherry isn't the normal kind of detective that Anna Draycott is used to dealing with. Cherry takes her roles seriously and completely immerses herself in the characters she portrays. Newly assigned to the case, Cherry takes on the persona of a prostitute. She is so good and so convincing in her role that she is unrecognisable.

PROLOGUE

Nicky Stanton woke to the sound of his mum's voice down in the kitchen, and the delicious smell of bacon wafting up the stairs was mouth-watering. It was the first time he'd slept at his parents' home in years, and he'd only agreed under pressure from his fiancé. Descending the luxury mahogany staircase, Nick entered the kitchen to be greeted by the sight of the farmhouse-style table groaning with the amount of food his mother had prepared.

"What! You feeding the fucking five thousand mum?"

"If I can go over the top on the day of my only child's wedding, then I don't know when I can. You reckon Diane's mother is spoiling her? On second thoughts, don't answer that. Linda Smith has always been a right tight bitch, so I expect there won't be much more than cereal on offer for the poor bride to be."

Nicky sighed heavily and hoped beyond hope that this wasn't how the rest of the day would continue.

"Mum! Now come on, you promised that for today at least you'd behave."

As Nicky took a seat, his mother, Monica, bent over and placed a kiss on the top of his head.

"Sorry, son, and yes, I did, so from now on, not another mean word will leave my mouth

regarding that bitch Linda, at least not for today."

Nicky found that hard to believe, but he let the matter drop as arguing the point would only put his mum in a strop, something he hated dealing with at the best of times. At the other end of the table and seated in a wheelchair was Nicky's dad, Bernie. A severe stroke a year earlier had robbed the once proud man of most of his mobility and had instantly promoted his only son to the head of the firm. Father and son had previously been close, and Nicky now struggled to see his hero and mentor, resigned to living like a baby.

"Morning, Dad."

Bernie could no longer speak but slowly nodded his head in acknowledgement. Nicky began to help himself to bacon and eggs, and at the same time, his mother sat down and started to feed her husband. It was something Nicky couldn't bear to watch, but neither could he leave the room, so he averted his eyes and concentrated on the offerings in front of him. Pushing the food around his plate didn't go unnoticed.

"You okay, son, not like you to refuse food. What's troubling you, or is it just nerves?"

Placing his knife and fork down, Nicky leaned his elbows on the table and clasped his hands together.

"I don't think it's nerves, Mum, but I am anxious."

“About what?”

Nicky could feel his dad's eyes boring into him, and when he looked up and saw the runny yellow egg slipping down his old man's chin, he felt like crying.

"I'm almost thirty-three years old, so why the fuck I'm getting married, I don't know. What if it's a mistake? What if Dodi isn't the one? What if I fucking hate it?"

"You soppy sod, of course, she's the one. You've been together ever since you were at school, and if that don't speak volumes, I don't know what does. Everyone gets the jitters before they tie the knot, and I'd be worried if you didn’t have them. Look, you've been living together for years, so all you're really doing is getting a piece of paper that makes it official."

"It's not that mum and don't get me wrong, I do love Dodi, but you know I've always played the field."

"Of course, I know, but has Diane ever let on if she knows or not?"

"If she does, she's never said a word, but to me, it hasn't really felt like cheating, but when I'm married, it will be a different story. She will have power over me, and I fucking hate that."

"Doesn't have to be like that, love, you just need to be more discreet. What the eyes don't see, the heart can't grieve over, or at least that's what I used to tell myself. Do you think your dad has always been true to me? Of course, he hasn't,

and you ain't any different from this one, to any man come to that."

“You mean my dad played away!?"

"Of course he did, they all do sooner or later. Start off with their undying love, but that soon changes. All men eventually get fed up with fillet every night and fancy a bit of scrag end, but I must say that your dad was the epitome of discretion and never brought any trouble home; he knew I would have chopped his balls off if he had."

Suddenly, the conversation stopped when Bernie began to choke on the piece of toast his wife had placed in his mouth. She hadn't been concentrating; it was too big, and Bernie had tried to swallow. Furiously, Monica began to beat on his back and seconds later, the piece of bread shot out of his mouth like a rocket and landed on the table.

"There you go, my darling, all sorted."

The sight made Nicky feel like heaving, and when he looked in his mother's direction, she smiled at him.

"I don't know how you do it, mum, honestly, I don't."

"It's simple; I love him, always have and always will, no matter what that brings."

Nicky could see the tears rolling down the side of his dad's face and didn't know if they were due to the choking or the complete helplessness his father must feel locked inside his own broken body. It was like a living hell and one he wouldn't wish on anyone; if he ever suffered the same fate, he knew he would rather be dead.

"I'm going to pick Robbie up from the station, and I can't wait. It'll be like having the old team back again, you know, he's only been home three or four times since the engagement, and I want him to have a good time today. Maybe one of Dodi's bridesmaids will give him a good seeing too; God knows he must need it. Anyway, I'll see you later, mum."

"Okay, love, tell Robbie the spare room is made up and all ready for him. Well, go on then, or you'll be late!"

Nicky grabbed his car keys from the hall table and set off to collect his best man. Robbie Evans had been at school with Nicky and Diane, and even though Robbie had enlisted in the army as soon as he turned eighteen and his best friend Nicky had joined the family firm and now lived a life of crime, the two men had retained a strong friendship. Their conversations were now mostly carried out over the phone, and Nicky Really missed the closeness they once shared. He knew Robbie loved Diane dearly, but his loyalty would always remain to his best friend, and Nicky was hoping that the tin pot soldier, his nickname for Robbie, could offer some words of wisdom regarding how Nicky was feeling and convince him he was doing the right thing. Robbie's train had already arrived, and when his

friend pulled up at the station, Robbie was sitting on a bench outside. Standing up, he hauled up his Barrack rucksack and threw it onto the rear seat of the car.

"Didn't think you was coming; thought you'd changed your mind."

Robbie laughed at his own words, but stopped as soon as he noticed the solemn look on his friend's face.

"What's up?"

Nicky slowly shook his head as he pulled out into the traffic.

"Oh, I don't know, I just got up this morning with the feeling I'm making a mistake. What do you think, Rob?"

Robbie puffed out his cheeks. What a fucking question!

"How should I know, but if you've got doubts, then it would be fucking cruel to Dodi if you go through with it."

“Guess I’ve got some thinking to do.”

"Well, you'd better think fast, pal."

CHAPTER ONE

(2018) 4 Years later

Diane Stanton woke with a searing pain in her stomach. Jumping out of bed, she raced to the bathroom, and when she'd finished on the toilet, she looked down to see a pan full of blood. Tears began to stream down her face as once again the realisation hit her that yet another failed pregnancy had happened. It had been the same scenario since the day she had married, when the couple had decided to try for a baby straight away. Nicky refused to see a doctor; his male pride wouldn't allow him to even contemplate that the trouble might lie with him. Diane or Dodi, as everyone called her, had been through a barrage of tests which had all drawn a blank. She loved her husband with every bone in her body, but it hadn't stopped her, if only fleetingly, from thinking about sleeping with someone else, anything that would get her the child she so desperately craved. Nicky had already left for work, so, climbing back into bed, she thought about her past and all that they had been through. Nicky had purchased the house on Greenham Road in Muswell Hill eighteen months before they got married, and up until then, they had rented. It was a bargain price at six hundred and fifty thousand pounds, even though it needed a complete renovation. Together, the couple had consulted with the

builder regarding what they both wanted, and Nicky had given her free rein when it came to the decoration and furnishings. Dodi had impeccable taste, and by the time she had finished, the house resembled something you'd see in a high-end magazine. It was now a fantastic property worth almost a million and a half, with four large double bedrooms, a state-of-the-art kitchen and two spacious reception rooms. Furnished with nothing but the best, Dodi knew she was the envy of a lot of people, and that included her mother. Linda had only visited once, and after seeing all that her daughter had, she was envious beyond belief. Out of nowhere, the tears again began to fall, but this time they were even heavier, and Dodi didn't seem to be able to stop them. It all now seemed such a long time ago from her days living in the flats, and as her mind drifted to an earlier time, a part of her wished she could turn the clock back, if only for a while.

Linda Smith and her hen-pecked husband, Wally, had lived with their two daughters, Emily and Diane, in a three-bedroom post-war flat in Levita House in Sommers Town. Wally was a cab driver, and Linda worked part-time in the local betting shop on Marchmont Street. They weren't wealthy, but neither were they poor; even so, when they were in a position not to want for much, Linda was extremely tight with money and thought nothing of dressing her daughters in clothing from charity shops. Emily was eight years older than her sister Diane and was very studious, so much so that she gained a scholarship at Sidcup County Grammar School for Girls at the age of eleven. Lodging with a local family in Kent, it was a fight to get her to come home in the holidays, and she would eventually move out of London completely by the time she was seventeen. Diane didn't know her sister that well, as she'd only been three when Emily had first left, so it had always felt like she was an only child, except for Christmas time when her sister would return for a few days, but it was always under duress. For some reason, Linda Smith thought she was better than her neighbours and looked down on anyone else in the block. She treated her husband, Wally, like a second-class citizen, so when he wasn't out on the cabs, which he did for seven days a week, he was also a frequent drinker in the Jubilee on Polygon Road. Diane wouldn't say that her childhood was happy, but then it wasn't bad either, and compared to some of the stories she'd heard from friends, she knew she'd been lucky.

St Aloysius Catholic Primary School in Camden had been the first place Diane Smith had set eyes on Nicky Stanton and his sidekick Robbie Evans. At the tender age of five, Dodi had been a shy child, and when Nicky Stanton had pulled her hair in the playground, within a few minutes of her arrival, she had vowed never to be his

friend, but secretly she liked him, liked that he didn't give a damn about anything. The two boys were constantly in trouble with the teachers, which also included the Nuns, and Nicky was forever being told, especially by Sister Hildegard, a particularly vicious Nun, that he was bound for hell if he didn't change his evil ways. Nicky would just laugh, even when he received the slipper or cane as punishment. His dad was Bernie Stanton, and anyone who was anyone in the area knew not to mess with the son of a gangster. That was apart from the Nuns, but Monica Stanton soon put them straight, and it was agreed that Nicky would be left alone and his parents would only be contacted if it was something very serious. Luckily, Sister Hildegard never found out about his little protection racket that saw many pupils left hungry at lunchtime. By the time they reached secondary school, everything changed. Haverstock Primary School at Chalk Farm wasn't Catholic, wasn't segregated by gender, and the pupils felt free for the first time.

Suddenly, it was 1993, there was a youth club, and Nicky Stanton felt like he was king of the hill. The night Dodi realised that she truly loved Nicky occurred at the weekly disco. A group of lads from Walthamstow had turned up uninvited, and the ringleader, Trevor Fish, was giving it large and even though she had tried to resist, he had pulled Dodi onto the area used for

dancing. He was like an octopus; his hands were all over her, and she desperately struggled to get free of him but was failing dismally. Out of nowhere, Trevor was grabbed by the scruff of the neck, yanked backwards and with one punch from Nicky, was now lying flat on his back. Thankfully, old Freddy Montgomery, who helped to run the place, had seen what happened, and the Waltham lot was swiftly thrown out. Nicky was allowed to stay as he wasn't seen as the instigator, but it wouldn't have made any difference, as knowing just who his father was, allowed him special privileges whenever he went out in the manor. The boom box started to blare out 'Now That We Found Love' by Heavy D & The Boyz, and Nicky took her by the hand as they smooched to the tune that quickly became their song. That summer was a hot one, and the couple and Robbie spent their days down at Parliament Hill Lido in Hampstead Heath. It was open air, and the water was always freezing, but it didn't bother the trio, who were now coming of age, an age where sex was constantly on all of their minds. Robbie never seemed to have a girl, and it had crossed his pal's mind that he might be queer, especially after what had happened with Mandy Spooner. A quiet girl with spectacles but not unattractive, Mandy had moved into a flat two doors down from Dodi. She hadn't gone to the same school as the three of them, but Dodi had

still struck up a friendship with her new neighbour when they had both stood out on the landing one hot summer night. Thinking of Robbie, Dodie had asked Mandy if she would like to make up a foursome. The new girl jumped at the chance, and a date had been made for the following afternoon down at the garden in plot 10. Built by volunteers on an old bomb site in the 1970s as an area for children, a community hub was soon erected, but that wasn't used by the teenagers, who all preferred to lie around the garden during the hot summer months. Dodi had arranged to meet Nicky, and as usual, Robbie was in tow like a second skin. As soon as he saw the stranger, he went on the defensive, and no matter how hard Mandy tried to chat, he either blanked her or gave only yes and no answers. After a while, Nicky led Dodie over to one of the trees for shade and a kiss and cuddle, but just a few seconds later, a scream rang out. Mandy was then seen running home, and when the couple reached Robbie, he was pacing up and down and at the same time, Nicky noticed a few spots of blood on the concrete.

"What the fuck happened, Rob? What did you do?"

"It was that dirty bitch; I don't know why you brought her along, Dodi? She's a slag, tried to put her hand down my trousers. I told her to stop, but she wouldn't and kept slobbering all

over my face, so I fucking lumped her one."

"Oh no!"

Dodi couldn't believe what she was hearing, and when she returned to the flats later that evening, she knocked on Mandy's door, but there was no answer. When she did finally see the girl again on the street, Mandy Spooner walked straight past Dodi as if she didn't know who she was. From then on, Nicky had concluded that his pal batted for the other side, but it didn't worry him; he just wished sometimes that he and Dodi could be alone more. Robbie lived on the same estate as Diane, but his flat was situated in Walker House. Not much was known about his family except that the man thought to be his dad had been banged up for most of Robbie's life and wouldn't be around for a lot longer. His mum would often turn a trick to put food on the table, and she didn't care who knew. Robbie wasn't open about his family and Nicky,

and Dodi imagined that he must have been very embarrassed; still, they respected his privacy and never questioned him.

Nicky's family resided in a nice four-storey Georgian terrace on St Pancras Way in Camden. The house was huge and decorated luxuriously, something neither Dodo nor Robbie were used to, but they were never made to feel uncomfortable, and Nicky's mum, Monica, always made them feel welcome. Monica would often cook for them all as she had a feeling

Robbie Evans didn't get a square meal that often. Aware that Dodi and Nicky were sweethearts, in the beginning, she didn't read too much into it; they were both young and would probably go their separate ways at some point. As the years passed and they were still together, it was accepted that they would one day get married, and from then on Dodi was included in any parties and family get-togethers, though no business dealings were ever discussed in front of her. Bernie Stanton was a private man, and he was always on his guard regarding what people knew about his firm.

When their school days came to an end, it was time to find work, and Nicky immediately joined the Stanton empire. Dodi joined a local firm of solicitors as a junior receptionist. She'd never had any aspirations of a career, and Nicky's mum had told her that once she married Nicky, she would be expected to give up her job so she could devote all of her time to her husband. Too many, the suggestion would have pissed them off, but not Diane; she loved her man completely, and she would always put his happiness above her own. On her eighteenth birthday, he proposed with a massive diamond solitaire and a party was hastily arranged at the Stanton house, much to Linda Smith's annoyance, but at least she wouldn't be expected to contribute, so she supposed that was at least one good factor. On the night, the house shone

like a new pin, and outside, caterers had been brought in. The food was fabulous, and Wally Smith couldn't believe his eyes. Rare roast beef and lobsters were in abundance, and he stuffed as much as he could into his mouth until Linda nudged him hard in the ribs.

“Wal, you look like a fucking pig, and you're showing me up!"

"Oh, sorry love, but ain't it bleeding lovely grub?"

“You make it sound like I don’t feed you.”

"Well, no, I didn't mean that, but there ain't any supermarket reductions on offer here, is there?"

Linda's pursed lips spoke volumes, and Wally knew he was in for an ear-bashing when they got home.

Dodi looked radiant. Her olive skin and raven hair were complemented by the expensive jade-green sequined gown that

Monica had helped her pick out; she had also paid for it as a present to her future daughter-in-law. Just after nine, Bernie addressed the room and began his speech. As she looked around, Diane realised that apart from Robbie, her parents and Nicky's parents, she didn't know a soul. The house was full of Bernie's employees and other known London faces, many of whom looked like the stereotypical gangsters portrayed on television, and they made her feel uncomfortable. Still, she knew better than to complain, but as the wine flowed, Linda Smith didn't hold back, and it

didn't take long before she started to embarrass the family with her dancing, loud voice and insinuations as she spoke to anyone willing to listen.

"Look at her, that's my daughter. I never thought she'd end up marrying a bloody gangster!"

Diane didn't know where to look or what to do, but things were taken out of her hands when Monica grabbed Linda by the sleeve of her dress and almost dragged her into the kitchen. One look told the caterers to disappear, and when the door was closed behind them, Monica turned on Linda with a vengeance.

"I don't know where the fuck you get off, lady, coming into my house and making the most of my hospitality and then fucking bad-mouthing us."

"Bloody cheek! I have done no such thing."

"You what? Your old man has stuffed so much grub in his cakehole it's a wonder he ain't burst by now, and your mouth has done nothing but spout fucking slander regarding my family. Get your coat and fuck off out of here before I do you some serious damage."

"You and who's bleeding army?"

"I don't need any army, sweetheart, and just to confirm, you do know who my husband is?"

"Can't be fucking off of it. He's a gangsteeer!"

Her sarcastic elongation of the word made Monica's blood boil.

"Remind me again what your old man does, oh yes, he's a cabbie, ain't he? Well, that can instantly change, sweetheart, and then where would you be with no fucking money coming in? Your snooty fucking ways would have to end, Madam and if you think I'm joking, just fucking try me."

Linda stormed out of the kitchen and, grabbing her coat, called over to Wally, who was just about to shove another prawn vol-au-vent into his mouth.

"Wally! We're leaving."

Linda didn't even bother to look in her daughter's direction, and before the front door had slammed shut, Dodi ran up the stairs in a flood of tears. Nicky went to go to her but was stopped when his mum placed her hand on his arm.

"Let me son."

Monica found her future daughter-in-law sitting on Nicky's bed with tears streaming down her face, and when she saw Monica enter, it made the tears fall even harder.

"I'm so, so sorry. You have given us a beautiful party, and I am so grateful and so heartbroken that my own mother could be so rude and spoil it all."

"Don't be silly, love; it would take a lot more than that jealous, spiteful cow to ruin things. Remember, some of the people here tonight are the hardest, most vicious bastards you will ever

meet. You may have thought it strange that Nicky's dad invited them, but it's like a rite of passage for our son and you as well. They have welcomed and accepted you, Dodi, and you will never need for anything or fear anyone ever. It's almost as if you are now a part of their family as well, and within the community we live in, that is always a good thing. Now, I have had a good talk with your mum, and I don't think there will be any more trouble. She might give you a bit of an earache later, but I know you can handle her. Come on, let's fix your makeup and get back down to the party."

A week later, and on the day of his eighteenth birthday, Robbie Evans enlisted in the army. Nicky wasn't happy about it when he found out, and it would be strange not having his best friend always by his side, but Robbie didn't want to join his friend in the Stanton business and as he told Nicky, there wasn't anything to keep him in London anymore.

The wedding took fifteen long years to come to fruition, much to Dodi's disappointment. Every time they were about to set a date, Nicky would come up with some reason why their plans had to be temporarily put on hold. When she finally gave him the ultimatum that he either marry her or they would go their separate ways, he caved in and agreed. Robbie came home on leave to be the best man, and after the ceremony had taken place, it was then a much similar affair to the

engagement party with the reception being held at her in-laws' house. The same faceless guests were in attendance, but at least this time, Linda Smith was on her best behaviour. Nicky Stanton had been generous, not only paying for the wedding, but he had been slipping Linda a fifty whenever he saw her. To him, it was worth it just to keep the old bag on side. Dodi looked stunning in her ivory silk designer gown, and after a week's honeymoon in Greece, the couple soon settled into married life. Dodi smiled when she thought back to that day, the happiest day of her life. Suddenly, the searing pain started again, and she rushed back to the toilet. This felt different to the last few times when her disappointment had been at the sight of her period. Groaning in agony, she heard a plop in the toilet pan, and when she stood up and looked down, she began to sob. Maybe it was just a big blood clot, but then again, maybe this had been a true miscarriage, and the mass in the toilet was her longed-for baby. The realisation that she really could have been pregnant this time broke her heart all over again.

CHAPTER TWO

1976

The Stanton family firm of today is a far cry from its humble beginnings. Back in 1968, at the age of fifteen, Bernie had begun to work full-time on his father's fruit and veg stall in Walthamstow market, but being an East End barrow boy didn't faze him in the least. The days were long and the work backbreaking, but he loved the camaraderie with the customers and other stallholders. He had a roguish face with a glint in his eye and was loved by everyone except for his father. The youngest of five, Bernie was the result of a drunken night of passion, and he hadn't been wanted from the off. His parents had struggled to raise their previous four children, and Bernie was seen as just another mouth to feed. When he was strong enough to lift a cabbage, he was set to work, and education took a back seat. By the time he came of school leaving age, he could barely read and write, save for his name, but he had a brilliant brain for figures and reasoned that would be enough to see him through. His father, a tall, strong-built man who went by the name of Shaffer, was overly tough on his youngest, and it had caused arguments in the market when other traders had been witness to the severity of his tongue and, on occasion, even his fists. The only day off young Bernie was allowed was on Sundays, and

no matter what the weather, he would leave the house at first light and not return until it was dark. He had no real place to go, but the less time he spent around his parents meant the less likely he was to receive a beating. It wasn't as if he was missing a nice family roast as food always seemed to be thin on the ground, especially where he was concerned, and portions had strangely reduced even more when one by one his siblings had left home.

Eight years later, after a chance meeting on a quiet Sunday afternoon in the Crooked Billet pub, Bernie began a conversation with a slightly older man he came to know as Dusty Houseman, someone who would quickly change his life forever. Sitting at the bar, the two men chatted about their lives, hopes and dreams. Bernie revealed what his life was like on the stall and what a wicked cunt his old man was. It hadn't shocked Dusty as he'd come from a very similar background. Dusty, his real name being Nigel Houseman, went on to reveal that he was now part of the criminal fraternity and loving every minute of it. He didn't usually share anything about himself, but this young bloke was easy to talk to, and the several pints they had drunk had loosened his tongue. Bernie was intrigued and couldn't wait to find out more.

“Don’t you worry about the Old Bill and getting banged up?”

"Comes with the territory, sunshine, but the rewards far outweigh the risk, and besides, I'm careful. You know what car I drive?"

Bernie shook his head; this man’s life was really starting to grab his interest.

"A brand-new Jag, top of the range no less, with full leather, the works in fact. I have a flat in a nice area, and I'm about to buy a pad on the Costa del Sol, just for holidays like. Oh, and I didn't mention the birds, like flies around shit when they see my motor. I reckon I've got my leg over at least a dozen times in the last month. So?"

“So What?”

“Fancy joining me? You said you're twenty-four? Don't you think it's about time you broke away from your old man’s apron strings and begin to live a little?"

Bernie thought for all of five seconds. This stranger was offering him the chance of a lifetime. Suddenly, he stopped. This was all too good to be true; maybe it was a wind-up, or maybe this bloke was a bit of a storyteller, after all, the city was full of them.

“For real or are you taking the piss?”

Dust momentarily looked offended, but then he realised that it all must sound a bit far-fetched.

“For real. Look, don’t decide now. Come round to my place of business tomorrow morning and have a butcher's for yourself.”

Bernie smiled, and after Dusty handed him a slip of paper with an address on it, he headed home.

The walk cleared his head, and he realised that there was no way his old man would let him take time off tomorrow. Mondays were always busy as Shaffer went to Covent Garden in the early hours to stock up for the week. After that, he stopped off for breakfast, and as he didn't get back to the market until well after eleven, it was always down to Bernie to set up and run the stall.

The next morning, Bernie opened up as usual, but the closer it got to nine, the more agitated he became. He could be missing out on the opportunity of a lifetime, and all because he was too scared of his dad, and the realisation that thought brought made him feel like a complete pussy. Franny King, who ran a lingerie stall opposite, had always had a soft spot for Bernie and seeing his long face, she called over.

"You alright, babe? Looks like you have the weight of the bleeding world on your shoulders."

It was quiet for a Monday, and with no customers at the moment, Bernie walked over to the woman.

"I should be somewhere else about now, but there's no way the old man would give me any time off. I met this geezer yesterday who offered me work, better than this shithole."

"Oh, thanks a bunch, sweetheart."

"No, I didn't mean the market, Franny; I meant working for my bastard old man."

There was no further explanation needed, as Franny hated Shaffer almost as much as Bernie did. The man was a bully who seemed to put down everyone he came into contact with, especially women. His mouth was foul, his sexual innuendos were legendary and not funny in the least, and she had witnessed how nasty he could be firsthand.

"Look, if you shoot off now and be back by ten thirty, then he won't ever know. I'll keep my eye on the stall for you, darling."

Without another word, Bernie kissed the woman on the cheek and ran down the High Street and out of the market as fast as his legs could carry him. Dusty had a small unit on Coppermill Lane that backed onto the reservoir. With traffic and people, it took Bernie eight minutes running flat out to reach the address. In his naivety, he tried the door and was surprised to find the main entrance locked. Glancing around, he noticed a bell, above which sat a CTV camera. In 1968, closed-circuit television had just started to be trialled and was only really available in the UK to the Metropolitan Police, but there wasn't anything Dusty couldn't get his hands on. Bernie thought it was a bit over the top, but maybe it made Dusty feel more important. A minute or so later, the door was opened by a huge, mean-looking man who seemed to tower above Bernie.

"Yeah?"

Bernie fronted it out and, standing tall, no one would ever have known how scared he was feeling inside.

"Oh, hello. Dusty is expecting me."

The man, whom Bernie would come to know and love as Big Willy, held the door open. When Bernie stepped inside, he couldn't believe his eyes. Wall-to-wall racking went from floor to ceiling, and the shelves were filled to capacity with boxes of all different shapes and sizes. When they reached the far end of the unit, Bernie saw Dusty taking inventory with a clipboard in his hand and a pen tucked behind his ear.

"Mr Houseman, this geezer said you want to see him."

Dusty looked up with a broad grin on his face.

"Bernie, my old sunshine! You came; I was doubtful, to be honest. Come on through to the office, and we'll have a chat. That's all, Willy, and can you make sure rack seven is ready to go this afternoon? Spader is expecting it, and you know how fucking arsey he can get if he doesn't get what he paid for."

Willy Fox nodded his head and then turned and walked away.

"He's a bit fucking scary, Dusty."

"And just the kind of bloke I need working for me. You'll soon see why if you decide to join me."

In the small back office, the two men sat down,

and Dusty immediately began to explain what his business entailed. He explained about the regular long firms he set up and the kind of merchandise they handled, which was anything you could imagine, from high-end designer clothes to DIY power tools.

"I must say I'm a little surprised you're sharing this amount of information, my friend. I mean, I could be the Old Bill or something."

Dusty laughed and slapped his newfound friend on the knee.

"Don't you think I did a bit of investigating? I have a man who finished checking you and your family out shortly before you arrived. If there had been anything suspicious, then Willy would have dealt with you in the appropriate manner. I must say, your old man sounds a right cunt."

"You ain't wrong there, Dusty."

Dusty's words had been spoken with a smile, but there was something in his eye that told Bernie he meant every word. The meeting went well, and by eleven, the two men had agreed that Bernie should join the firm. Saying their goodbyes, Bernie set off for the market but hadn't realised the time. When he reached the stall, he looked over at Franny, who silently mouthed the words 'Sorry'. Walking to the rear, Bernie was about to put on his apron when he felt a sudden thud, and a searing pain ran through his head.

"You little cunt! You have one fucking job to do,

and you balls that up. I'm breaking my back getting fucking stock, and you piss off to God only knows where. Well, I'm fucking docking you a day's pay, you little wanker!"

Shaffer was about to deliver another blow when Bernie suddenly stood tall. Throwing his apron down onto a crate of cabbages, he grabbed Shaffer's wrist, twisted it and at the same time glared at his father. In that moment, Shaffer saw something in his son's eyes he had never seen before: strength.

"Hit me again, you cunt, and it will be the last thing you do, now stuff your fucking job where the sun don't shine."

"You leave now, and that's fucking it, you little bastard!"

"Suits me fine, you cunt!"

Walking away, he unexpectedly heard the sound of clapping begin and, looking over, saw Franny beaming from ear to ear. A few seconds later, more joined in, and as Bernie left the market with his head held high, there was now a continuous round of applause. Making his way home, he grabbed a bag and stuffed in his clothes and the few measly possessions he owned.

"Where are you off to?"

Turning, Bernie came face to face with his mother. Joanie Stanton was all red lipstick and no knickers, and Shaffer had only married her when she got up the duff. Somehow, the

marriage had endured, but neither she nor her husband was cut out for parenthood.

"Out of this fucking shit hole as fast as I can."

"Your father will have something to say about that!"

"He already knows. I would say see you around, mum, but I really hope I don't."

"Why you little..."

Slamming the front door behind him, Bernie marched off down the road, but having balls was one thing; now he had to find a place to stay, and the only person he knew who would help him was Dusty. By the end of the day, he was safely installed in the spare room of a very smart flat in Camden. It was clean, and the fridge was rammed full of food and beers. Within the first eighteen months, Bernie had a place of his own, which was swiftly followed by a new car and his prowess at getting women into bed soon became legendary among the London underworld. Bernie not only had all the trappings of wealth, but he was tall, dressed impeccably and was as handsome as any man could be. The two men worked well together for the next few years, and Bernie was eventually made a partner. Money was plentiful, and he quickly gained all the trappings that Dusty had told him about. Having played the field for several years, it all abruptly stopped the night he met Monica Graves. He was in his early thirties and not looking for anyone serious, but she was

unlike anyone he had ever known. Monica didn't fall for his smooth patter, and she wasn't the least bit interested in his car or the amount of money he had. There began the chase, and Bernie was determined to have her, but he hadn't yet realised that for the first time in his life, he was starting to fall in love. Within the year, he had proposed, and the couple were swiftly married in a registry office ceremony when Monica revealed she was pregnant. With the birth of their son Nicholas, something changed in Bernie. He now wanted more from life, more for his family, and that wasn't about to happen if he carried on working with Dusty. The two men had a meeting, and both put their cards on the table. Bernie explained how he was feeling, and Dusty shared that he had no interest in stepping up from what he was doing now. There was no argument, and the two would always remain friends, but it was agreed that they would divide what they had and then go their separate ways. Their friendship had grown so much that Big Willy Fox asked permission from Dusty to go with Bernie. Dusty would be sad to see the man leave, but he was also astute enough to know that refusing wouldn't do any of them any good. To Dusty, loyalty was everything, and if a man in his employ wasn't happy, then he would never be truly loyal.

Twelve months later, Bernie Stanton had set up

his own firm and quickly gained the respect of most of the serious players in London. Unlike Dusty, Bernie would deal in anything. The drug trade was lucrative, as was armed robbery and after hiring several good men who were adept at violence and persuasion of the serious kind, it felt like nothing could touch him. The years passed quickly, money was plentiful, and the family now had a very nice house in Camden. The couple, though they tried hard for several years, were never blessed with any other children, so Nicky became their main focus, and he was spoiled beyond belief, especially by Big Willy Fox, who had now gone into retirement but had kept in close contact with his former employer. When Nicky left school, it was a foregone conclusion that he would join the family firm, something he was happy to do for a while at least. Starting at the bottom by running errands and then going out on jobs, he slowly worked his way up to becoming his father's right-hand man. Dodi had been on his case to finalise a date for the wedding, but he was in no hurry and had used the ruse of wanting to be at the top of his game before he settled down. She wasn't best pleased, but loving him with all her heart meant she had to go along with whatever he wanted. He cheated on her regularly, and deep down, she knew even if she had no proof. It broke her heart, but so long as he always came home to her, she could live with it if she had to,

anything rather than lose him.

A year before Nicky's wedding, he had been carrying much of the burden of running the business, so it was a natural rite of passage that when Bernie suddenly suffered a major stroke at the age of sixty-four, his son would take over. It would take at least six months of rehabilitation if Bernie was ever to regain any mobility, so Nicky had stepped up to the plate without question. He was nervous at first as he'd always had his old man to fall back on, but now the decisions were solely down to him. He needn't have worried; everything he touched and every decision he made seemed to see money rolling in, and he now had a new expansion idea. It was a suggestion he had mentioned a couple of years earlier to Bernie, but his father had dismissed the idea of a club out of hand. Recently, the family had been advised by several doctors that Bernie would never improve more than he had so far, so all permanent decisions moving forward would be completely down to Nicky, and a club was definitely on the cards. Not just any old club, this was going to be the envy of Soho, and as Nicky had always been a sucker for a pretty face, women would soon be added to the menu as well.

CHAPTER THREE

Mary O'Toole stepped off a plane from Belfast early one cold January morning. A small holdall carried the few possessions and clothes that she owned, and with just thirty pounds to her name, she was ready to take on the world. Her life in Ireland had been hard. At fourteen years of age, she had been forced to help raise her four younger siblings after her mother, Reena, passed away shortly after her last child had been born. Paddy O'Toole was a brute of a man who regularly beat Rena and had moved on to his oldest daughter after his wife's death. The beatings were violent to the degree that on one occasion, his oldest daughter had received a broken arm. He showed no mercy and would launch his assault for any reason he could find, and at times even when there was no reason. The beatings Mary could handle, but when eight years later he viciously raped her, Mary knew she had to get away, or he would probably end up killing her. It broke her heart to leave her four little sisters, but she had no choice. Before she left, she composed a detailed letter to her maternal grandparents in Cork. Due to her father's behaviour, they had been estranged since her mother's death, but with God's will, when they read what had happened to their oldest granddaughter, they would step in and take the little ones into their care or, at the very

least, notify the authorities. It was the best Mary could hope for, and now she had to make a new life for herself, but in all honesty, she didn't have a clue about where to start. After catching the train to King's Cross, she walked around for a few hours, but by lunchtime, she was freezing cold, her feet were killing her, and she was desperate to sit down. Spying Ronnie's Café on Euston Road, Mary reasoned she could at least afford a cup of tea, and if she took her time and made it last, she would be able to get warmed up.

For the past week, Nicky had two of his men trawling the areas where runaways were known to arrive, but it had been slim pickings.

Davey Melton and Gary Smith had been with Bernie for several years, and when his son had taken over, they were given this latest task, it hadn't gone down well, but they knew better than to complain. The Stanton's paid very well, so when the new boss said jump, you said 'how high' and you did it with a smile on your face. There was no way Bernie was ever coming back, so they just had to do what they were told. Entering the café, it was Gary who spied Mary first and, nudging his colleague, whispered in his ear 'Thank fuck! It finally looks like we've got a live one. Not wanting to scare the girl away, it was Gary who took a seat opposite her while Davey went and ordered the tea.

"Mind if I take a seat here, sweetheart?"

Mary looked up from the mug she'd been nursing for the last twenty minutes, and which was now stone cold. The stranger scared her, but she wasn't about to show her fear and instead nodded her head.

"Free country."

She was hostile, which wasn't good, but glancing at the bag resting on her feet, Gary could tell she had only just arrived in the city.

"No need to be like that, love, I'm only being friendly."

"In my experience, people are never friendly, not without wanting something in return."

"Maybe not where you're from, sweetheart, but in good old London we welcome newcomers with open arms."

Mary rolled her eyes upwards; did he really think she believed him? When Davey joined them, he placed three mugs onto the table, and as he pushed one in Mary's direction, she finally smiled.

"Thanks."

"You're welcome, I'm Gary, and my partner in crime is Davey. Are you looking for work?"

Mary's eyes narrowed; she was suspicious, as back home she'd read about this type of thing in the newspapers. She'd read stories about men who preyed on lone women, women who were strangers in a city and also vulnerable. The concern on her face was evident, and it didn't go unnoticed by Gary,

"You ain't got anything to worry about, darlin', I swear. We work for a local firm, and our Boss has asked us to find girls who would be interested in hosting in a new club he's opening."

"Hosting, really?"

"That's right, kind of meeting and greeting the customers."

"Yeah, yeah, I know what you're talking about, and it isn't just meeting and greeting. I ain't as green as I'm cabbage looking, so you can just feck off right now."

Gary stretched out his arm and touched her hand, but instantly she pulled away. Nicky had warned his men not to come on too strong; the women had to want to work for him or not at all.

"Don't be like that, sweetheart. I mean what I say. If you choose to add that service onto the menu, then it's up to you, but that's not what we are offering. For a start, it's against the law."

Davey, who had just taken a gulp of his tea, almost spat out the mouthful as he fought hard not to laugh. Gary ignored him and, handing over a business card, told her there was no pressure and to be at the club tomorrow at ten if she was interested. That night, a night of thinking and walking the city streets as she had nowhere to stay, finally made up Mary's mind. She knew the kind of work that the man was talking about; she might have been Irish, and to a lot of people, that meant she was thick, but Mary was far from thick. She wasn't a virgin

after what her father had done to her, but to sell her body went against everything she believed in. There was just one glaring problem: principles and morals didn't put food in your belly or a roof over your head. There were only two choices: go back home with her tail between her legs and face the wrath of her father with a future of nothing but beatings and rape, or take a chance and see where life led her. To Mary, there really was no choice.

Nicky had recently taken over a very long lease on the Triang Club on Romilly Street in Soho. It wasn't as busy as Old Compton but had direct access from Shaftesbury Avenue, meaning he would be the first stop for tourists heading from Leicester Square and Chinatown, with the added fact that the location was a little more discreet for customers not wanting to be seen entering. Now named Nicky's Place, the former Triang had been empty since the punk era, when it had showcased up-and-coming bands. It was an easy negotiation as the owner, Bobby Trent, was old, tired and scared of the villains who in the past had given him nothing but trouble, wanting protection money even though the club had ceased trading. Its bare walls, still daubed in the graffiti style of the seventies, were soon painted a rich crimson red. A raised dance floor with a pole was erected in the centre of the main room, and after the bar was given a good clean and restocked, the place was ready to open. Door

staff were hired along with a woman older in years who would be seated just inside the entrance to take the ten-pound entry fee. Nicky had borrowed four girls from his dad's old mate, Stan Jackson, who owned Secret Pleasures on Glenthorne Road. It was only temporary, just until he could hire his own girls, but Stan had said it was no big issue, and Nicky could keep them for as long as he wanted. Nicky knew he had to have something to lure in the punters, and even though he would earn well from the exorbitant prices he charged for drinks, the big money would be made with the Toms he was going to hire.

The day after, Gary had given Mary his business card, Nicky was waiting in his office, hopeful that at least a couple of skirts would show their faces today, when there was a knock on the door. Maxi Willmore, one of the new doormen, popped his head inside. The man had skin as black as the night, his size was so big that he almost filled the doorway, and he was as tough as they came, with a face only a mother could love.

"Bit of skirt outside, Boss, asking if there's any work going?"

"Then show her in Maxi, my man, show her in."

Jojo Johnson sauntered into the office with more bravado than she actually felt. Residing in London since she was sixteen, Jojo had struck lucky, and by the time she was twenty, she was

turning tricks in hotels, meaning she still looked good, unlike some of the women who worked the streets and now appeared far older than their years. Her blonde hair and blue eyes were an instant attraction to Nicky, and all thoughts of his doting wife instantly disappeared.

"Hello, Sweetheart, I understand you're looking for work?"

"That's right, Mr Stanton, and I won't waste either of our time by beating around the bush. I'm a Tom and a fucking good one. I heard you're looking for girls, and you won't get better than me."

Nicky beamed from ear to ear.

"I certainly am, but I've always been a try-before-you-buy sort of guy."

Jojo walked over to the door and turned the key. He was good-looking, so this was going to be fun. Ten minutes later and after a lengthy blow job, Nicky had emptied his sacks and was once again seated behind his desk.

"So tell me your story, darling?"

Jojo kept it short but went on to explain that she had been on the game for over ten years and mostly worked out of hotels, but that she was tired of it and wanted a change, wanted to be with other women and not be alone so much.

"In that case, sweetheart, you're hired. Actually, I need someone to be in charge of the other girls as well, so if you're interested and it will obviously come with a wage, the job is yours. I also plan on having a couple of pole dancers, but no private rooms, and I will expect my girls to cover if the dancers are sick or take a day off?"

"Sounds good. By the way, if you want me to recruit for you, it's no trouble, I have quite a few contacts and the girls are all decent."

Could the day get any better? Just then, Maxi knocked on the door again. Nicky signalled for Jojo to leave, and as she unlocked and opened the door, Maxi explained that there was a woman named Mary looking for him.

"Show her in and Jojo, leave your contact details with Maxi, and I'll be in touch."

Mary O'Toole sheepishly stepped into the office and nodded her head in Nicky's direction.

"Hello, Sweetheart, you must be the young lady Gary told me about. Well, come on in then, don't be scared."

Even if Mary had been willing, Nicky didn't have the energy to give her a try, so, pointing to the chair, he asked her to take a seat.

"So how much did Gary tell you about the job, darling?"

"He said it was a meet and greet kind of position, but I'm not naive, Mr Stanton, and I know it will involve a lot more than that."

Nicky slowly nodded his head as he weighed up the situation, and at the same time, also tried to weigh up the woman sitting in front of him. She was slightly overweight, but not enough to stop him from hiring her. Rosie cheeked, she had

that homely look that a lot of men liked.

"Well, Gary was partially right, and as you've said, it does involve more. I want to have the best stable of girls in the city, but at the same time and unlike most of the pimps around here, I will not force anyone into anything they are not comfortable with. I want to attract wealthy punters, but I won't allow, for want of a better phrase, business on the premises. That will be down to the girl, and any money earned will be taken on trust, so you give me a cut when you return."

That wasn't completely true, as Nicky had also hired a woman named Rosie Goodson, who was well-known in the area for being able to physically take care of herself and had at times beaten several men to the ground. A married mother of two, Rosie was employed to sit at a desk near the side door, the only exit and entry allowed for the women to leave and ply their trade. Each time one of his girls left and then returned, their name and the time would be logged, so he knew whether he was being shafted from the off. In her time, Rosie had also been on the game and knew all of the tricks, so none of the brasses would be able to pull the wool over her eyes.

"Tell me your story."

Mary explained about all that had happened in Ireland; she even told Nicky that her father had raped her. He didn't bat an eye. Over the years,

he'd heard many stories, and some of them were far worse than this. Hearing that she had never worked the streets before, had him grinning on the inside. The punters loved fresh meat and being untouched; her father didn't count, which meant she could charge top rates, but there was also the chance that she might back out.

"There is a flat rate of a hundred per trick, but in your case, as you are new to the business, it would be quite a lot more, let's say one forty. If you don't know, that's a fucking good amount when a punter can get his leg over for thirty nicker out on the street. That said, my girls will all be lookers, clean, well-dressed and polite. If you choose one hook-up a night or ten, it will be up to you, and anyone who treats my girls with anything but the utmost respect will be given a life ban, which will be made clear on their first visit. There's a small guest house at the end of the road where I have seven rooms permanently rented out to me. The rooms are cleaned, and the sheets are changed daily, so it's not like I'm expecting you to drop your drawers down some dirty side alley. I will also require you at times to cover the pole slots, but it won't be that often. So, Mary, what do you think?"

Mary took a few moments to mull over the offer. It certainly wasn't what she had wanted out of life, but that said, the money was good and would mean she could get a place and have a decent standard of living for once. Another

thought crossed her mind; if she had stayed in Ireland, she was in no doubt that her father would have continued to rape her, so she would have been giving it away for free anyway. Regarding the dancing, she had always liked

music and messing around in her bedroom, and they always say 'practice makes perfect', so she could give it a try, she supposed.

"I would like to take your offer, Mr Stanton, please."

Mary was given a start date for the following week, and Nicky loaned her enough money to get a room and a few decent clothes. By the end of the day, he had also employed Sheila Mason, a Tom, who, though older in years, still looked good, and Nicky reasoned that there were also punters who liked an experienced woman. He had also taken on Lulu Low, an Asian girl who had been trafficked but had managed to escape several years earlier. That was about as much information as Lulu was willing to share, and after she had shown papers to prove she was now legal, Nicky was happy to hire her. Swearing to be just twenty-three, it was difficult to tell Lulu's real age, as with most women from that part of the world, she was wrinkle-free, and her skin was unblemished. After calling and giving her a start date, his stable now stood at four girls, but Nicky still didn't have a full house, and he planned to take on another four or five women as soon as he could, but he at least

had enough to finally have a formal opening night. The place had already been trading to drinkers for a couple of weeks to iron out any teething problems, and so far everything was running smoothly, but now it was time to become Soho's hottest night spot. Later that evening, he talked over the event with Dodi, as his wife had good ideas and excellent taste. Dodi hadn't told him about losing the baby six months ago, nor the one that followed it only last week; he had enough on his plate, and besides, there was nothing he could do about it but feel sad for her. That said, Nicky wasn't stupid; with so many past disappointments, he recognised the empty look in her eyes, but rather than upset her further, he didn't mention anything.

"Why, don't you organise the whole thing for me, babe?"

"Really? Oh, Nicky, I would love that."

"Great, and you've got free range on any additional decorations you want to add."

It was agreed that she would have seven days to make all of the arrangements, and silently Nicky knew he could go that length of time without shagging any of the staff. He wasn't sure if Dodi knew about his antics, but either way, you shouldn't shit on your own doorstep, and he would never rub her nose in it. The next week passed in a blur, but at last they were ready to officially open. Invitations had been sent out,

posters had been plastered throughout the area, and the place had been decorated with a gold theme, which complemented the crimson décor. Dodi looked stunning in an off-the-shoulder black dress, and all of the Toms had gone the extra mile to look good for their new boss. It went without saying that the night was a resounding success, and the next month passed by quickly as mounds of cash rolled in from all avenues, but none more so than the earnings from his girls.

CHAPTER FOUR

Opened in nineteen sixty-three by Benny Gayle, Drummonds restaurant on Romilly Street served high-end British cuisine. Over the years, the place had won many awards and attracted upper-class clients, who didn't complain about the hefty-priced menu. Drummonds had been Benny's pride and joy for years, so much so that he didn't even contemplate settling down until he was forty-five. Marrying Rosa Talbot, a waitress twenty years his junior and who had adored her boss from afar since the day she started working at Drummonds, swiftly saw the arrival of the couple's only child in nineteen seventy-eight. Now, forty years after first opening the doors, Benny's health began to decline to the point where even turning up at the restaurant became a daily struggle. After a lot of nagging from Rosa, he accepted defeat and admitted that it was finally time to retire. A family meeting was held, and it was agreed that he would pass the reins down to his son, Martin. Benny would soon be celebrating his eighty-third birthday, and, realising that he didn't have that much time left on this mortal coil, he owed it to Rosa to devote what little time he had left to her. Martin Gayle, or Marty as everyone referred to him, loved Drummonds as much as his father. From the age of twelve, he had worked at the restaurant evenings and

weekends and then at sixteen had started full-time. His father hadn't given him an easy ride, but after beginning with pot washing, he gradually worked his way up through the ranks and had even excelled at his stint of cooking in the kitchen. Marty hadn't been at the front of the queue when God dished out the looks, but it didn't bother him, as just like his father had been in the early years, he didn't bother much with women and preferred to concentrate on business. When Drummonds was finally signed over to him, the only stipulation had been that he didn't remove the favourites from the menu or change the restaurant's name. Marty was happy with that, but he did have grand plans for the interior, and after a large investment, courtesy of the bank, the work had begun in earnest.

Six months later, the amount he borrowed had escalated, and now that the renovations were complete, he needed to start earning revenue to pay off his debts. Classically understated décor with sumptuous seating saw Marty swiftly gain rave reviews, and he even managed to get articles into several of the top newspaper Sunday supplements. Soon, the place was full every night and at times, there was even a waiting list. The menu, much to Chef Raymond's pleasure, had also been upgraded, but Drummonds still offered all of the classics, though they were now served on designer

tableware with the addition of micro herbs and an array of modern veloutés, foams and fresh sauces. The portion sizes were reduced, which increased the takings, but no one seemed to notice, or if they did, it wasn't mentioned. At the end of the first month of trading, the takings had doubled and the profit margin, which had always been good, had increased by twenty-five per cent. Marty felt like the cat that had got the cream; he was riding high on the crest of a wave, but that wave, out of nowhere, was about to come crashing down.

On the opening night of Nicky's place, Drummonds, as usual, was busy, but with the added bonus of pre-club diners, and Marty realised that the new place could be good for his business. That notion lasted for less than a fortnight. Suddenly, numbers began to drastically drop, and for the life of him, he couldn't work out why. There wasn't anything wrong with the food, and Marty thought that Chef Raymond, since the renovation overhaul, had actually improved the menu, if that was at all possible. Finally, after one of his regulars telephoned to cancel their booking, Marty took the bull by the horns and asked why. It was out of character, but he just had to find out why the restaurant, which had been a hotspot only two weeks earlier, was now dying a sudden death.

"I'm sorry to hear that you will not be joining us this evening, Mr Beaumont. May I inquire if

there is some kind of problem?"

There were a few seconds of awkward silence on the other end, but finally, after a time of feeling embarrassed, Kenneth Beaumont nervously coughed before he went on to explain, and it was an explanation that shocked Marty to the core.

"As you know, Drummonds has always been our favourite place to dine. And as you also know, my wife Miriam and I have celebrated birthdays and anniversaries with you for many years, but now, well, now, it just feels unsavoury being so close to, well, the only way I can describe it is a brothel."

“Excuse me?”

"That new club, it's nothing more than a glorified knocking shop, and the prostitutes can be seen coming in and out with men, and it's not something I wish my wife to be witness to. The last time we dined and decided to take a stroll after our meal, I was accosted by one of the so-called women right in front of Miriam. I have never been so embarrassed in my life, and I can tell you my wife was quite upset. I am sorry, Marty, but until things change, we won't be dining with you again."

With that, the line went dead, and Marty just stood there for several seconds with the receiver glued to his ear. It was Friday, usually one of the busiest nights of the week for the restaurant, but as yet they had fewer than twenty covers booked. Realising he had only two choices, sit

back and do nothing and watch his business crumble around him, or do some investigating and see if there was anything he could do to change things.

Just before ten and when the last of the guests had eaten, Marty slipped out of Drummonds and, tightly pulling up the collar of his overcoat, he began to walk along the street. As he neared Nicky's place, he slowed his pace. For a moment, everything appeared alright until a woman walked out arm in arm with an older man who was slightly the worse for wear. Crossing the road, he watched the couple, and just when he thought they were about to turn the corner, he was surprised to see them enter old Myrtle's bed and breakfast. Myrtle Skinner had owned the building for years and had catered mainly for the construction crews who were always building at some site or another in the city. After she had passed away two years ago, the business had for some time remained closed. Then Marty had heard whispers that it had been purchased by an Asian family. When the guest house still didn't reopen its doors, he had assumed it was just idle gossip, but not now, as it was obviously being used by the tarts to carry out their trade. Lurking in the shadows, he felt like a bit of a pervert, but within the hour, he saw several other women exit Nicky's Club with men and then walk along to the bed and breakfast. When the first woman returned and

within minutes came back out again with another punter, Marty accepted that Kenneth Beaumont had been correct. With his shoulders slumped and a heavy heart, Marty headed back to the restaurant. He had a lot of thinking to do.

The following morning, and after a sleepless night of tossing and turning with his thoughts going in all directions, Marty decided the first thing he had to do was call in at old Myrtle's place and see if he could find anything out. It was still early when he arrived in Soho, and as he climbed the four stone front steps of the old Victorian house, he had a feeling of foreboding. As with most guest houses, the front door wasn't locked and walking into the long, barren hallway, he stopped at a small mahogany makeshift reception desk. The foyer had been painted in a cheap magnolia, and it hadn't been done very well, but then he supposed it didn't need to be. Pressing the brass bell, he was only kept waiting for a few seconds before a door at the rear opened and an Asian-looking woman, wearing a dowdy sari, approached.

"Yes?"

"Oh, hello, my name is Martin Gayle and I own Drummonds restaurant just over the street."

"Yes."

"Do you own this place?"

"Yes."

Suddenly, the rear door opened again, and this time a younger man came over.

"Mummy, get back in the kitchen."

The man then turned to Marty and introduced himself as Ahsan Abbasi.

"I'm sorry about that, but my mother doesn't speak a word of English, well, not apart from the word yes. Thirty years in this country and still all she can say is yes. I heard you mention that you own Drummonds?"

"That's correct, but I'm not sure for how much longer."

"I'm sorry to hear that. Well, how can I help you today?"

Marty didn't really know how to begin without offending the pleasant young man, but begin he must if he was ever to save his restaurant.

"Well, I won't beat about the bush. Since the new club opened, it has hit my place hard, and bookings have dropped beyond belief. I've heard a few unsavoury rumours, so last night I watched the club for myself. I saw women, many women in fact, coming in and out of there with an assortment of men who they then brought back here. Now I wasn't born yesterday, and it's obvious that the women are Toms and are using this place for sex."

"I'm sorry, but that's none of my business; all I do is rent rooms. What goes on inside is the business of the occupants. We all have to make a living, Mr Gayle. Now, if you'll excuse me, I have many tasks to complete today."

"So, what about my fucking business? I wonder

what the Old Bill will say if I phone them? I don't know about where you come from, sunshine, but prostitution is still fucking illegal in this country."

Marty was about to apologise regarding his language as he would never normally swear, but was instantly stopped when seconds later, Ahsan was on the other side of the desk and staring menacingly down at Marty. He didn't like people sticking their noses in, and he'd also taken the man's last sentence as a racial slur.

"You need to learn to keep your fucking trap shut, Mr, if you know what's good for you. Do you not know who Nicky Stanton is?"

Marty wasn't stupid; the Stanton's were notorious in London and especially in the Soho area, but what option did he have? Fight and try to sort this out and save his business, or give up and lose everything?

"Of course, I know who he is."

"Then watch your mouth, now, as I said, I have work to do."

Marty returned to Drummonds feeling lower than ever, but he hadn't lost the battle just yet, and tonight he would pay Nicky Stanton a visit and plead his case in the hope that the gangster would help him, but deep down, Marty wasn't holding out much hope.

That evening, when he'd given the club time to get up and running, Marty once again set off. Standing in the shadows as he had before, this

time he removed his mobile, and for a little over thirty minutes, he snapped away whenever the prostitutes came out of the side door with a punter. When he was confident he had enough evidence, he crossed the road and entered the club. Standing at the back, he took in all that was going on, the women hanging around the bar area obviously waiting for punters to hook up with, and the scantily clad dancer gyrating around a pole on the dancefloor. Marty soon noticed Maxi Willmore standing guard beside a highly polished mahogany door at the far end of the room. Swallowing hard as he was more scared than he'd ever been in his life, he slowly made his way across the room to approach the man.

"Excuse me, I am the owner of Drummond's restaurant down the road, and I would like to have a word with Mr Stanton if that is at all possible."

Maxi looked the man up and down and contemplated for a few seconds whether he should just tell the visitor to 'fuck off!' Deciding that maybe this had something to do with his boss's business, he tapped on the door and popped his head in.

"Sorry, Boss, but there's a geezer outside who wants a word, says he owns that posh nosh joint up the road."

Lulu was under the desk giving her Boss head, and Nicky had been just about to cum when the

knock at the door had put him off.

"Give me a few seconds and then show him in. Lulu, it's okay, sweetheart, you can't get blood out of a stone, and I ain't in the mood now anyway."

Lulu Low stood up and pushed her small breasts back into her bra. Smiling sweetly at the man she really couldn't stand, but who she would do anything for, as this was the best job she had ever had, she sauntered over to the door and walked out as Marty walked in. Nicky stood up and offered his hand.

"Nicky Stanton, Mr?"

"Gayle, Martin Gale."

"Nice to meet you, Martin. Now, how can I help you?"

"I take it you know my restaurant?"

It was a rhetorical question, but Nicky spoke before Marty could continue.

"I do indeed and have dined there several times, but that was back when your old man was at the helm."

"Well, I have a problem, Mr Stanton. Since you opened this club and the women you employ began to ply their trade, my business is rapidly going down the pan. I mean, who wants to enjoy fine dining in the middle of a red-light district?"

The man's words had Nicky's hackles up in seconds, and he didn't hold back.

"As you well know, Soho has been a red-light

district, as you put it, for years, so who the fuck do you think you are, you jumped-up little cunt! If your shitty café can't work alongside other businesses, then that's down to you. Now sling your hook and don't come fucking winging to me again. Maxi!"

The door opened, and Maxi Willmore appeared wearing his most menacing expression. He knew through recent experience when the tone in his boss's voice meant trouble.

"Boss?"

"Sling this cunt out, will you?"

Maxi grabbed the collar of Marty's coat and, frogmarching him through the club, proceeded to throw him out onto the pavement. For a few seconds, Marty lay dazed and was stepped over by a couple of laughing punters. Finally, he pulled himself up and slowly walked back to the restaurant. Once in the solitude of his office, he mulled over all that had been said, and a rage began to build up in him, a rage like he'd never felt before.

The next morning, Marty marched straight down to the council offices, but he seemed to hit a brick wall with every department he tried. Next, he contacted his local member of parliament, Jasper Remington, who just happened to be holding a local surgery later that day, but that was just as bad. While his MP was sympathetic, he didn't think it was something he could get involved in, as it could appear that he was taking sides with one business against another. There was also the added fact, though unbeknownst to Marty, Jasper himself regularly frequented many of the clubs in Soho. The only avenue now left open to Marty was to seek out the help of the police. Situated on Agar Street, Charing Cross station was an imposing five-storey converted Georgian building. Just the thought of going inside scared Marty as he'd never received so much as a parking ticket. Approaching the front desk, he was asked what the problem was by the desk Sergeant, so he quickly laid out the basics of his complaint. As soon as he mentioned Nicky Stanton, he was swiftly shown to a side interview room. Ten minutes later, and sitting with a smile on his face, confident he was at last going to get somewhere, the door opened, and Detective Colin Hull entered. What Marty didn't know was that Nicky Stanton had several police officers and three or four detectives working for him, and Colin Hull was one of them. It had begun years earlier with his father, and when one officer retired, another would be groomed to take his place. It made anything the firm dealt in pass under the radar, and it was well worth the hefty monthly payments that were paid out. Marty wasn't threatened as such, but he was firmly told that if he didn't drop the matter, his own business could be made to suffer, and the police couldn't guarantee his safety. When he

was back out on the street, he stared up at the building, not quite believing what had just happened. Well, he wasn't going to leave things like this; he would have to grow some balls and take matters into his own hands if Drummonds had any chance of survival.

CHAPTER FIVE

A week after the formal opening, the club was going from strength to strength, but there was just one problem: as hard as the girls worked, they couldn't cover the number of customers wanting their services. It was truly a case of demand outstripping supply, and Nicky realised he had to sort something out and do it fast before the biggest spenders went elsewhere. Sending out the same two men he'd trusted before, they were to spread the word by any means necessary. Gary Smith and Davey Melton were both now so good at it that Nicky Stanton was soon interviewing a new batch of women.

Jeanie Lovell was nineteen years old and desperately trying, and dismally failing, to pay her way through university. She came from a single-parent family, so there was no chance of any help from her mother, and she was desperate not to rack up more student loans than she already had. Jeanie had a part-time job in a coffee shop, but it just wasn't cutting it, so when she was approached in broad daylight by Gary Smith, which was risky on his part, she took the details and gave the offer some serious thought. Jeanie weighed up the risk of infections, not to mention punters who could cut up rough. Then she reasoned that her Uni friends gave it away for free most weekends at the numerous campus

parties, so why shouldn't she get paid for it? Having decided to accept but also to keep working at the coffee shop for the time being, which would give her a legitimate cover, Jeanie paid a visit to Nicky's club. He asked her the basic questions, and when she told her new boss the reasons she was prepared to turn a trick and that it was her only option or she had to give up her education, Nicky was grateful that there was no heart-wrenching tale to be heard this time. Some of the women he employed had led horrific lives, but he didn't feel guilty; as far as he was concerned, he wasn't forcing anyone, and the money they got for a few minutes of physical contact was very good.

"Sweetheart, it might not be your chosen career, but you'll earn in one night what it would take you a week to accumulate in a shop or a care home. I reckon you won't want to give it up, I mean, who would, no matter what letters you have after your name."

"I appreciate that, Mr Stanton, and thank you."

Strangely, Nicky didn't ask for a sample; the girl was genuine, not to mention very young, and somehow it just didn't feel right. Hiring Jeanie on the spot, it was agreed that she would come in that evening, just to see the setup and watch how the other girls operated. Next to be approached was Josette Solomon, a six-foot-tall woman of Nigerian descent. Josette was a mother of three children, all under the age of ten.

Arriving in the United Kingdom eight years earlier with her eighteen-month-old son, it had been agreed back home that she would, by way of payment, marry a British-born man of Nigerian heritage. Within a week of her arrival, the ceremony had taken place at Tower Hamlets Registry Office on Cable Street. Josette wore the only decent dress she possessed and hoped that she wouldn't disappoint her husband, as she was very attracted to the handsome stranger. With a cheap ring on her finger and the licence tucked safely in her handbag, Josette knew that she could now stay in the country, and she was hoping for a bright future for herself and her baby. Sadly, things for Josette didn't work out as she had dreamed. Akin Solomon didn't like his bride one bit. He'd been born and bred in London, and most of his girlfriends were white, skinny with blond hair and not someone who had the same skin colour as his mother. There was just one problem; he desperately needed the money that Josette, or at least her father, was willing to pay. Regardless of the fact that he didn't fancy his wife, within a year, she was pregnant again, and ten months after the birth of her second son, her third arrived. Life was sad, and she was always living on the breadline as Akin gave her very little money and was rarely at the family home. When he did show his face, it was usually on a Friday or Saturday night, but only then if he hadn't been able to pull a bird of

his liking to get his leg over. If Josette refused his advances, he would beat her into submission, and sometimes it was so bad that she could hardly see out of her bruised eyes for a week. Akin couldn't stand the kids screaming and always left the flat before they woke up, so they hardly knew their father. His family were no better; his mother looked down on her daughter-in-law and didn't want to know or help her grandchildren in any way. Finally, when Josette couldn't stand it any longer and after a particularly nasty beating, she gathered up her children and fled to the London Black Women's Project on Barking Road. From there, the family were housed in a secure refuge in Bethnal Green. Josette needn't have worried as Akin didn't even try to look for his wife and children, and when he realised that they were gone for good, he breathed a sigh of relief. After six months of sharing a small room with just one double bed, the family were at last given a two-bedroom maisonette on Tolmer Square in North London. The rent and utilities were paid for by the borough council, but the measly amount Josette was left with from her benefit didn't cover the basics, such as food and clothing. Attending an interview for a cleaning job at the Premier Inn, Soho, and when she came out crying in the knowledge that she hadn't got the job, Josette was stopped by Davey Melton. He showed a fake interest in her distress and then went

straight in for the kill. Surprisingly, the woman hugged him; she knew what was on offer, but right at this moment, she would do anything to bring money home. Nicky had listened to her story, but it didn't move him in any way, and he was relieved that the interview was swiftly over when Josette accepted on the spot. She didn't appeal to him personally, but there were a lot of blokes out there who loved a bit of black, so she would be a good addition to his stable.

Taking a break as Dodi wanted him to join her for lunch at the Ivy, Nicky was full when he returned to continue vetting the last girls, and he wasn't much in the mood for it, let alone trying before he bought as he usually did. There were two others to see that afternoon, the first being Lucy Barber. This one was elf-like in her build and young, very young, and Nicky wanted proof of her identity before he would continue. Unlike a lot of the other players in Soho who would supply anything for the right price, he wasn't into providing fresh meat for kiddie fiddlers. Lucy saw the look on his face, but she was savvy and more than a little street-wise. Removing the gum from her mouth and after placing it under the edge of his desk, she flipped open her small clutch, swiftly pulled out her birth certificate and handed it to Nicky.

"I know I still look like a little kid, but I left home a year ago when I turned sixteen, and I've mostly been on the streets ever since then. My

old man was helping himself to what's in my knickers, and the old lady did nothing to fucking stop him. I mean, what woman lets her husband do that to their daughter? The dirty cunt!"

"And this is the kind of life you want, darling?"

"Mr, I might be young, but I ain't fucking stupid, what else is on offer for someone like me that at least pays a decent wage?"

Nicky nodded his head as he studied her. When word got out, she would certainly bring in the punters.

"I'm prepared to give you a trial, but there are rules. Firstly, stop with the swearing. I want my girls to be respected and to some degree, classy. You get checked out by my doctor every week, keep yourself clean and dress smartly. Lastly, you do not do a single thing to bring my place into disrepute."

Lucy smiled but then looked down at her shabby clothes and frowned. Nicky knew the score and, removing a wad from his pocket, peeled off six fifties.

"This is purely a loan, and it will be paid back weekly. If you've done your due diligence, you will know who I am and that it would be very fucking silly to try and rip me off, sweetheart."

Handing Lucy a card, he held onto it as she went to take it.

"This is the address of a woman who works for me. Rosie has agreed to provide a bed for anyone in need, but it's only for a few weeks until you can afford a place of your own. Don't for a second contemplate messing her about, or Rosie will put you in an early fucking grave and I ain't kidding when I say that. Get some new clobber and come back tomorrow night at seven."

Lucy Barber couldn't believe her luck, and the money she had gripped in her hand was starting to burn, but he was right, and she had checked him out. If Lucy was ever going to try to rip off Nicky Stanton, it would be for a lot more money than the three hundred he'd given her.

"Oh, and by the way, you will be known as little Lucy. It will bring in punters who like young pussy."

His words didn't bother Lucy, and after peeling off the hidden gum from under the desk, she placed it back into her mouth, smiled and nodded before closing the office door. Glancing at his watch, Nicky sighed heavily. He was tired, and when he felt like this, it was a part of the job that he disliked, and he still had to call in and check on his parents. Dodi also wanted him home early, but at this rate, that wasn't about to happen. Since he'd first told her about the club, she had made him promise that he wouldn't spend more than two evenings a week at the place, and reluctantly, he'd agreed. Standing up, he stretched his arms and ran his fingers through his hair in an attempt to liven himself up. A couple of minutes later, Maxi knocked on the door and popped his head inside.

"Last one is here, Boss."

"Thank fuck for that. Show her in Maxi, and then you can get off home for a break."

"You back later, Mr Stanton?"

"No, not tonight, the little woman wants me at home, and you know what they say, 'a happy wife, a happy life', though how much longer that will be the case remains to be seen."

Maxi grinned and then, holding the door open, motioned with his hand for the girl to enter. As Janice Connolly walked in and offered her hand, Nicky felt as if fireworks had started to go off in his brain. She wasn't the most beautiful girl in the world, but the instant attraction was undeniable.

"Thank you for seeing me, Mr Stanton. My name is Janice Connolly."

"No problem, and please, call me Nicky."

There was an awkward silence for a few seconds as their eyes locked until Nicky pointed to the strategically placed chair and then took a seat behind his desk.

"So, Janice, what makes you want to work here?"

Janice neatly crossed her legs and smoothed down her skirt. Everything about the woman was classy, classy without trying too hard, unlike most of the women he knew, and that included his wife. Her clothing was smart casual, and her dark hair was cut into a flattering bob.

"My mother died a couple of years back, so I moved here around six months ago with my father. Since the move, Dad has met someone, and his partner isn't keen on having an extra person in her flat. So, I'm left living in the two-bedroom place in Paddington we rented when we first came to London. I don't mind living alone, but it means I will soon be struggling to pay the rent, and I still have another ten months left on the lease. When my dad signed it over to me, I didn't think much about the implications, but obviously, he did. I'm a qualified nurse and work at The National Hospital for Neurology opposite Queen Square Gardens."

"So why don't you get someone to do a flat share?"

"I am in the process of doing that, but it still won't be enough. That's why I hoped that a couple of shifts here would help make up the shortfall."

Nicky leaned forward and placed his arms on the desk, smiling as he spoke.

"I admire your strength and determination, but have you ever done work like this? I take it you do know what would be required of you?"

Her dark hazel eyes never left his as she slowly nodded her head, and Nicky felt as if he was swimming against a tide of emotion he had never experienced before.

"No, I have never done this sort of work, and yes, I understand what goes on here and what

would be expected of me. Given a, of course I wouldn't even consider going down this route, but the point is, I don't have a choice, Mr Stanton."

"Please, Mr Stanton makes me feel fucking ancient. Everyone here calls me Nicky, well, all except Maxi, but he's another story."

Sitting back in his chair as he thought, he joined his hands together and rested his index fingers under his chin. There was no way he was going to let this beauty turn a trick. She was clean and pure, and he would never forgive himself if he allowed her to be defiled by some sick cunt just so they could get their rocks off. If he was being honest, and even though they had only just met, he didn't want anyone else touching her.

"How about you come and work behind the bar?"

Janice smiled. He was so handsome, and now he was being kind and protective, something she hadn't expected.

"Could I ask what the pay would be?"

"A ton a night, sounds fair, I think."

The amount was absurd, and normally, he wouldn't pay half that amount for a bar worker, but there was just something so special about this woman. Janice couldn't stop her eyes from opening wide in shock.

"Well, that's far more than I thought, and yes, I would love to."

Janice was far from stupid, and she could see

that he was attracted to her. If it came to it and she had to spread her legs for her boss, it would still be better than having a host of strangers pawing at her. It was agreed that she would start the following night, and as he saw her to the door, Nicky knew that his promise to Dodo to only work two nights a week was soon to be broken. As he closed the door and leaned back onto the woodwork, a smile spread across his face. He couldn't wait.

Calling at Camden to check on his Parents, Nicky spent half an hour with them, and after a quick cup of tea, he got back to Muswell Hill a little before six-thirty. Dodi had made her special casserole, and she was pleased he had kept his word.

"Hi, babe. Do you want to take a shower? Dinner will be ready soon."

Smiling, he nodded. She was so sweet, but the feeling just wasn't there anymore, if in all honesty it had ever been in the first place, and for that, he felt guilty. The food was good as always, and tonight they would snuggle up and watch a movie, but little did she know that nights like this would become few and far between. Her husband would continue to break his promise just as he had always done throughout their marriage.

CHAPTER SIX

Born in 1994, Jamie Brewer was adopted at birth by Ralph and Jenny Brewer. An only child, Jamie led a charmed life and didn't want for anything. Even when he went off the rails at sixteen, his elderly parents could still see no wrong in him and had supported Jamie completely until, thankfully, he got back on track. After getting his act together, he went on to university and gained a degree, but just before his twenty-fifth birthday, his world came crashing down around him with the death of both his parents within a few months of each other. His mother and father had always been truthful with their son, and by the age of five, Jamie knew that he was adopted, but it hadn't changed the way he felt about Ralph and Jenny, and he'd had no interest, even when Ralph gave him the option, of finding his birth mother. His biological father was listed as unknown, so he had a suspicion that things may have been tough for his mother. After the second funeral had taken place and while he had been clearing out his parents' belongings, he came across his birth certificate and adoption papers. Something began to stir in him, a feeling he had never felt before. Maybe now was the right time; perhaps he could find her and fill the void that losing his parents had left. He felt so alone now and without love in his life; little else mattered. The

house in Leicester sold within a few days of being listed, and as the purchasers were cash buyers, the sale went through quickly. Jamie made up his mind that with the large amount of money he had inherited, he could begin his search without worry or hindrance. The first step should have been to contact social services, but Jamie wanted to do it all himself. Using the government's general online register, he searched to see if his mother had died. There was no record, so Jamie decided to head for London. Named as Daphne Hammond, his mother had resided in the Borough of Islington, and it hadn't taken him long to realise that, as the address was included on his birth certificate, it meant that he had been born at home.

Travelling to London on a cold Monday morning and exiting at the Angel underground station, Jamie found a small Bed & Breakfast close by on Duncan Street. Run by Wilma Claxton for the last thirty years, the place was old school in its décor but still warm, clean and friendly. Jamie and Wilma had hit it off instantly, and he had been welcomed into her inner sanctum kitchen, which was normally strictly off-limits to guests. Over several cups of tea and slices of Wilma's home-made fruit cake, Jamie revealed his life story to the woman.

"Looking for your old mum could be opening up a can of worms, sunshine."

"I know, but what choice do I have? If I give up,

then I'll spend the rest of my life wondering. I mean, maybe she won't want to know me, but what if for all these years she's been wondering and worrying about what happened to me?"

"Where did you say she lived, darling?"

"Ritchie Street."

"I know it well, though most of the old houses have now been turned into flats. Can I offer you some advice?"

"I would welcome it, Wilma and thank you."

Getting up to refresh the pot, she continued to talk as she did so.

"Rather than go in blindly knocking on doors, try one of the locals. The Tap or the Pig & Butcher, as it's now known on Liverpool Road, would be your best bet. It's been there since Adam was a boy, but it wasn't called The Pig and Butcher until recently. I'm sure you'll find someone in there who remembers your mum. If not, there are plenty of other old pubs in the area."

Jamie was smiling. What a brilliant idea. He didn't want to embarrass his mother by just barging into her life, as she may have another family that didn't know about him. Wilma's suggestion was a perfect way to start.

"So, how long are you staying, sweetheart?"

"That's a good question and one I can't answer at the moment, but at least four or five days."

"Then I'll book you in until Friday, and then if you need longer, we can take it a day at a time.

I've put you in room six, it's one of my biggest and has a private bathroom, so it's very comfortable. Turn left at the top of the stairs, and it's the first door on your right. Breakfast is between seven and nine thirty, and you get a full English included in the room rate."

Jamie thanked the landlady and then made his way upstairs. The room was decorated with bold floral wallpaper, and the same theme was used on the bedding, but the patterns didn't match. It still somehow worked, and the bed was the best he had ever sat on. The small shower room situated in the corner meant that he wouldn't need to leave the room again until the morning, but after a short nap, he decided to go out, grab a bite to eat and at the same time do a recce on the pubs in readiness for the next day.

After a brilliant night's sleep and a belly full of Wilma's delicious food, Jamie set off at just after ten. He wasn't in too much of a hurry as the pub didn't open until twelve, so he walked the area, wondering what it would have been like to grow up here. It wasn't a patch on his home area in Leicester, which was green with open leafy spaces, but here, everything seemed so cold and grey. It was a few minutes after noon when he reached his destination, but strangely, he didn't feel nervous. A four-storey building, Jamie had guessed that the pub was one of the new trendy places with lots of polished brass and overflowing colourful floral displays in the

window boxes. It turned out that his assumption was correct. Stepping inside the foyer, there were doors on either side of him. To the right was the main bar and restaurant, but to the left was a small door with a sign saying 'SNUG'. Choosing the main bar, Jamie ordered a pint and glanced all around as he waited. The previously dark wood bar had been stripped and was now a mellow golden colour. All the seating and curtains were covered in a luxurious gold fabric, and the framed prints on the walls were all of local scenes. Thankfully, as the place was yet to get busy, the barman had time to chat.

"Not from around these parts, are you?"

"No, how did you guess?"

"You look too fucking healthy, sunshine."

Jamie laughed, and the barman smiled as he busied himself wiping glasses.

"I'm here trying to locate some long-lost family, but this doesn't really look like the kind of pub that could give me any information."

"I wouldn't be so sure about that."

"Really, why?"

"Back when this place was modernised in two thousand and twelve, a stipulation was put on the old pub that the snug had to remain for the old-timers. The landlord wasn't too happy, I can tell you, but not a lot he could do about it. Take a wander down to the snug; there are some right old characters that fill that little room every day. They're all born and bred on the manor and

there ain't much they don't know about. Personally, I think they come in here to keep warm and not have to pay for any heating, it certainly ain't for the booze as they can make a half a stout last for bleeding hours."

Again, Jamie laughed. The barman was funny without even trying.

"You should try stand-up, mate."

Draining his glass and then ordering another pint, Jamie picked up his drink and walked back to the main entrance and entered the SNUG. The room wasn't much more than twelve feet by twelve feet, but there were already eight or nine old people sitting around the four tables, which were situated in each corner. It was obvious that when the pub was remodelled, no money had been spent on this area. The ceiling was still heavily nicotine-stained, and the furnishing looked ancient, but it didn't seem to bother the occupants, and in all honesty, they looked very comfortable. When he walked in, the conversation stopped dead, and all eyes were suspicious as they stared at the stranger. Jamie ignored this and took a seat opposite an old timer who was smoking a roll-up despite the ban. Smiling, he nodded his head.

"May I sit here?"

"Free country, son. So, you're new to the area?"

"Well, yes, but I'm just visiting, actually."

The two men talked about the weather, the state of the country and life in general, but the man

knew there was another reason for Jamie being there.

"So come on, son, what's the real story? Why would you want to spend your time with a load of bloody old codgers like us?"

"Honestly? I'm here trying to find my mum or any details I can about her."

"How come?"

Jamie leaned in closer and, taking a sip of his beer, placed it back down onto the table.

"I was adopted as a baby. The people who raised me were great, but after they both recently died, it kind of got me thinking, and I would like to meet her before it's too late, if it's not already."

The old man nodded his head sagely.

"Makes sense, I suppose. I've lived in this shithole all of my life, sunshine, as have most of these good people. One of us must be able to help you. What's your old mum's name?"

"Daphne Hammond and I was able to find out that she never married, and she hasn't died. She would be about fifty-five now. The lady who I'm staying with said the houses on Ritchie Street had all been converted into flats, so I don't think she will still be living there."

The old boy that Jamie would come to know as Harold held his hand up to stop Jamie from continuing and then stared across the room.

"Kath? Kath love, you remember anyone called Daphne Hammond, who lived over on Ritchie

Street?"

The petite grey-haired woman with a deeply wrinkled face, who was nursing half a pint of Guinness, furrowed her brow; she didn't like being interrupted.

"Come on, Kath love, you're like the fucking oracle of Islington and what or who you don't know ain't worth knowing anyway."

Kath took a moment to think as Jamie waited with bated breath. Harold was as sharp as a knife and noticed when her eyes widened slightly, but then she shook her head.

"Nah, don't ring any bells."

"Go and wait outside, son, there's definitely something in the old bird's memory bank, but she obviously ain't comfortable sharing it in front of a stranger. I'll get her to spill her guts and then come and find you."

Jamie thanked the man and then placed a ten-pound note on the table, telling his newfound friend to treat himself to a drink. Living on the pension was a struggle, and the offer only had to be made once as Harold quickly grabbed the note and stuffed it into his pocket. With the stranger now gone, Harold turned to the old woman.

"Come on then, Kath, spill your guts. I know you know something. Tell me, and I'll treat you to another half and a feel-up round the back if you're lucky."

Kath Smith giggled like a schoolgirl and, picking

up what remained of her Guinness, sauntered over to Harold's table.

"I'll take you up on the drink, but you can forget about the other; my days of drunken fumbles are well and truly over. Now, let me think. Well, she was a brass and if I remember correctly, worked around the back of Angel station. Everyone knew her as Dirty Daphne. By all accounts, a right slut, she wasn't choosy when it came to her punters, or so I'm told."

Harold was well aware that Kath had also turned a trick or two in her past, but there was no way he would ever raise the subject.

"You little minx, so you did know her. Well, come on out with it, what happened to her?"

"By all accounts and from what I was told, mind you, that was years ago now, she got herself a dose of syphilis, but the poor cow didn't know, and by the time they got to her, it had spread to her brain. They were able to cure her but not reverse the damage, so the old Tom is now in a care home and, from what I've heard, is not quite the ticket."

"Why didn't you tell him?"

"Not my story to tell, sweetie and besides, who wants to receive news like that?"

"No one, I suppose, so you know what home she's in?"

"Dame Street, or so I was told, but that was a couple of years back; she might even be dead by now."

"Wait there, and I'll get you another half."

Harold slipped out of the front door and walked to the corner where Jamie was seated on a low wall.

"Anything?"

"Yes, but it ain't good son. Seems your old mum ain't too well and she's in a care home."

Harold felt heartbroken for the young man when he saw Jamie's expression go from happy to sad in seconds.

"Do you know where it is?"

"I know where she was, but if she's still there? Who knows? That ain't all, son and don't shoot the fucking messenger, but Kath reckons your mum was on the game, that's how she got sick."

"Aids?"

Harold was shocked at Jamie's words and spluttered slightly as he spoke.

"No, no, nothing like that. Apparently, she caught syphilis and didn't know it, so by the time they were able to treat her, and I might add, cure her, the damage had been done to her brain, which was irreversible."

Jamie felt sick and, leaning forward, began to retch, but nothing came out. Harold placed his hand on Jamie's shoulder as the young man dry heaved.

"I know it must be a bit of a shock, sunshine. So, what are you going to do now?"

"Not sure, I think I need to take a bit of time and give it some thought. The last thing I want to do

is upset her. Thanks, Harold, for your help, and I really mean that."

"You're welcome, Son, and I hope things turn out well for you and your old mum."

The two men shook hands, and then Jamie headed back to Wilma's. If anyone could give him good advice, it would be his landlady, and he wasn't wrong. After listening without comment to all that her lodger had learned about his mother, she thought for several seconds before she commented.

"Sweetheart, you need to see her, or you'll never have any peace. I suggest that you don't judge her until you've heard her story, that's if she's able to tell it to you."

Jamie smiled, he knew she was right, and deep down he had already decided, but he just needed another opinion that what he was about to do was the right thing.

The next morning, after breakfast, Jamie set off for Dame Street. It was only a three-minute walk, and he couldn't believe his real mother was so close to him. Stopping in front of the double-fronted detached Victorian property, he took a few minutes to study the place. Large and imposing, it was obvious that it had been a private dwelling at one time. Finally, he plucked up the courage to ring the bell, and thankfully, he wasn't kept waiting. A portly woman with a stern face, dressed in a navy uniform, opened the door and peered at him.

"Yes?"

The carer who had answered was not polite, and her abrupt tone instantly got Jamie's back up.

"I'm here to see my mother, Daphne Hammond."

"Daphne doesn't have any kids, so if you're here trying to rip off any of our old people, you can sling your bleeding hook. Now, who are you really?"

"I can assure you that Daphne is my mother. I have my birth certificate, but I'm not showing it to you. Now, if you're not going to let me in, then please call your manager so I can file a formal complaint."

The expression on Paula Wilmot's face instantly changed; she'd already had one warning this month and couldn't afford another. Opening the door wide, she motioned with her hand for the visitor to come inside. Paula didn't speak again, and Jamie had to pick up his stride as he followed the woman down a long, dimly lit corridor. The home was magnolia floor to ceiling, it smelled strongly of urine and old people, and it saddened Jamie to think that so many of the older generation ended up in places like this. Stopping outside room five, Paula pointed and then walked off in the opposite direction. Jamie could feel a knot forming in the pit of his stomach as he tapped on the gloss-painted door that had long since turned in colour from brilliant white to cream. When there wasn't an answer, he slowly turned the handle and went inside. The room had an unwashed smell, and the curtains were still closed. Making his way over to the window, he pulled the fabric to the sides, allowing sunlight to instantly flood the room. As he looked around, his eyes stopped at the bed, where a frail-looking lady was propped up to an almost sitting position. Her hair was greying, and she was dressed in a nightie and some kind of knitted bed jacket.

"Hello, handsome."

Jamie smiled, and taking a seat on the side of the bed, took his mother's hand in his.

"Hello, mum."

Daphne looked confused, and as she started to get frightened, she sharply pulled her hand away.

"You ain't my son, my boy died years ago."

Jamie again took hold of her hand, but this time his grip was a little firmer. She tried to pull away again, but couldn't, as well as her cognitive skills being damaged, she was also physically disabled and exertion of any kind was difficult and drained her.

"You had me adopted when I was a baby, don't you remember?"

Daphne frowned. Somewhere deep inside, a memory so deeply embedded slowly began to surface, and as tears streamed down her face, she turned and nodded her head towards the

bedside chest. Jamie opened the top drawer, and sitting there, untouched for a long, long time, was his mother's diary. As he lifted out the small blue book, locked with a tiny padlock, Daphne turned her face away from her guest, and Jamie realised she wanted him to leave. Tenderly kissing her head, he did as she wished, knowing that there was a good chance he wouldn't return.

"Take care of yourself, Mum."

He didn't look back as he made his way out of the room and headed to the main entrance. Deep in thought, Jamie just walked for several minutes with no destination in mind, but he somehow ended up on Noel Road. When he walked past the Island Queen pub, he decided it was as good a place as any to hole up and read. An hour later, he finished the pitiful diary and was now raging at the life his mother had been forced to lead. Her mother had put her to work on the street at the age of twelve, so there had been no real education. By the time his grandmother passed away, Daphne was a seasoned prostitute with no chance of escape. When he returned to Wilma's, he shared what he had found out, that his mother had been put on the game by her own mother. She had also been raped by numerous pimps, bullied by the older Toms, and had been forced to give away the only child that she would ever have and then to top it all off, was infected with syphilis. She

would later learn, though far too late, that one of the other Toms had infected one of Sheila's regulars, and that's how she had gotten sick.

"That's a very sad tale, love, but sadly not an unusual one."

Wilma didn't really know the young man sitting opposite her, but the change and anger in his voice were evident in his next sentence.

"Those dirty bitches need to pay Wilma; they ruined her life in more ways than one. No one gave her a chance, or me, come to that, because if they had, she might have been able to keep me."

Wilma knew that probably wasn't the case, but she also knew better than to add fuel to the fire. Her guest was hurting, and to comment further would only cause him more pain and achieve absolutely nothing.

"So, are you going back to Leicester now?"

His reply was swift and sharp and took her by surprise.

"Didn't you hear me? They need to pay, all of them!"

CHAPTER SEVEN

Janice had now been working the bar at Nicky's club for almost two months, and to say she loved the work was an understatement. The working girls were all friendly, and it was a laugh a minute when the punters came in and gave their chat-up lines, all of which had been heard a million times before. Since she'd started, Nicky had been at the club every night, and it hadn't taken long before the two became close, but it was far more than sex; they had a connection that neither of them had ever felt before. They both tried to back off when they realised what was happening, but it was futile. Late one Friday afternoon, when Nicky had finally gotten out of bed, he made his way down to the kitchen to find his wife, stony-faced and sitting at the breakfast bar, filing her nails. Nicky bent to kiss her cheek, but Dodi pulled away sharply.

"What the fuck is wrong with you?"

"Wrong with me? You selfish bastard, when you started that club, you promised you wouldn't be there more than two nights a week, but you ain't been home for one night in almost a month. I'm your wife, Nicky, in case you've forgotten, but lately, I've started to feel like a single woman. Maybe I should start joining you, at least that way I'd get to see you."

Dodi could see the panic in his eyes; he was up to his old tricks again, of that she was sure.

"You wouldn't want that, would you?"

"What the fuck are you on about?"

"I ain't stupid, Nicky, so don't treat me like a bloody fool."

Since meeting Janice, Nicky hadn't given much thought to his wife, but now that he was being forced to, he realised that he felt very little for the woman sitting before him. Dodi had been in his life for as long as he could remember, but he wasn't in love with her; never had been if he was brutally honest. He had married her as it was the right thing to do, and everyone had been expecting it. She was okay as a wife, but she had a charmed life that she now didn't seem grateful for, and he had already begun to compare the two women, which was never a good idea. Janice was winning hands down, and suddenly Nicky became angry.

"I work my fucking arse off so you can have all of this, and all you do is fucking whinge!"

Nicky surveyed the beautiful house with his open hand. The decor was all top-notch with expensive furnishings; in fact, anything she wanted, she just went out and bought, no matter how expensive it was, and he never complained when the credit card bills came in, as long as she was happy. Now, when he thought of Jan, who didn't ask him for a thing, he realised that Dodi wasn't as nice a person as she tried to make out.

“You don’t have to work, you spend money like fucking water, and still you moan.”

He stared as if he was boring through her and didn’t notice the pools of tears in her eyes.

"I'm lonely, Nicky, don't you get that? I can't have a baby, or we can't, but you won't have any tests to find out which one of us has a problem, so I sit in this fucking prison all day, every day, alone. I don't give a shit about all of this so long as I'm with you, but that isn't what you want, is it, or at least not any more it isn't."

“Fucking Prison!?”

“There might not be any bars, Nicky, but it feels like a prison all the same.”

“I ain’t got time to listen to this shit, I have work to do.”

With that, he grabbed his keys and stormed out. Dodi burst into tears. In all the years they had been married, all he'd cared about was making sure she was happy, but now it was obvious that he wasn't bothered anymore. Suddenly, it hit her like a bolt of lightning: he had another woman, he must have, as he'd changed so drastically.

Oh, she knew about the one-night stands and had accepted them long ago, even though it hurt deeply, but this was different, and for the first time, she felt threatened. Well, if he thought he could do that to her without paying the consequences, he could think again. From now on, she would gather as much evidence as she could because he was going to pay dearly, and the best way to hurt her husband was in the pocket.

As he walked into the club, Nicky's mood was still dark until he saw her standing behind the bar. Just the sight of her made him feel warm inside. It was still early, but the place was in full swing, and music being played by the in-house DJ, bleared out from the speakers. Walking over, he politely asked for a scotch, and when she heard his voice, Jan turned around with a broad grin on her face.

"Good evening, Boss."

"Janice, everything okay?"

"Great, no trouble yet, though no doubt that will change as the punters get rat-arsed."

Winking and then nodding, Nicky picked up his drink and headed towards the office. They had agreed that while at work, they would both act professionally, but the other staff had still guessed what was going on. Nicky Stanton was a hard man and a real task master, but it was obvious what he was up to as the boss seemed to come alive whenever Janice was around. When she took her break, Janice made her way to Nicky's office, and once inside, she locked the door. In a matter of seconds, the two were all over each other, but with her, it felt different to when he shagged the other girls at the club, which had come to an abrupt halt as soon as Janice had begun to work behind the bar. The sex was also different from that with Dodi; with his wife, it had turned into a duty in her quest to get pregnant and for the last few weeks, he had been avoiding it as much as he could without giving the game away. With Jan, it really felt like making love, something he hadn't experienced before.

As soon as Nicky had left the house, Dodi ran up to her bedroom and picked out the sexiest outfit she possessed. Her makeup was perfectly applied, and with her long black hair piled high on her head, there was no denying that she was stunning. Pulling on her flat shoes and with her four-inch Louboutin heels in her hand, she drove over to Soho and parked up in the small side street at the rear of the club. After she exited the car and swapped her shoes, she headed for Romilly Street. Maxi Willmore, who was on door duty, spied his boss's wife. He ran inside the club, knowing full well what was happening in the office. Rapidly knocking on the door, he tried the handle, and surprisingly, the door opened. Nicky was sitting at his desk, and his face spoke volumes when he looked up.

"What the fuck! Never heard of fucking waiting to be invited in?"

"Sorry, Boss, but I thought you were entertaining."

"Well fucking good job I'm not, or are you into that kinky shit of watching people shag?"

"No, no, nothing like that. I've just seen Mrs Stanton heading this way, and I didn't want you getting caught out, that's all."

Nicky was angry, as a few minutes earlier, and

that's exactly what would have happened. After apologising, he thanked Maxi for looking out for him and then instructed his employee to show his wife in when she arrived. As he left the office, Maxi spied Dodi marching through the club, and she didn't look happy. A couple of the girls tried to engage in conversation with her, but she point-blank ignored them and only stopped when she came face-to-face with Maxi.

"Mrs Stanton, nice to see you."

"Where's my husband?"

"In the office."

"Who's he got in there?"

"No one, Mrs Stanton, he's alone."

Dodi studied Maxi's face, and it was obvious he was telling the truth, so instead of going to see Nicky, Dodi took a slow walk around the club looking for the kind of woman that she knew her husband would be attracted to, big tits, big lips and dressed trashy. No one seemed to fit the bill, so when she reached the bar, she took a seat on one of the tall chrome stools and scanned the room.

"Good evening, Madam, what can I get you this evening?"

Dodi studied the woman; she was rather plain, and she didn't seem like Nicky's type, but then nothing would surprise Dodi as far as her husband was concerned. Knowing that the Toms often served drinks, Dodi jumped to conclusions and wondered why this young

woman would choose to be on the game, but she didn't ask.

"Gin and tonic, please. So, how long have you been working here?"

"Only a couple of months, but Nicky, I mean my Boss, has been so nice to me, and the other girls are very friendly."

"Are the girls getting many punters?"

"Excuse me?"

Janice didn't know who this woman was, so she was on her guard; maybe she was Old Bill.

"Forget it!"

Inside, Dodi was raging and downing her drink in one, she slammed her glass down onto the bar and stormed out of the club. A few minutes later, Nicky appeared, and he seemed to be on edge as his eyes scanned the room, looking for someone.

"Is everything okay, Mr Stanton?"

"I'm not sure, Jan. Maxi said my wife was here, but I can't seem to see her."

"A lady was sitting there a few minutes ago, a very beautiful lady, I might add, but she had one drink and left. Actually, she asked if the girls were busy, which I thought was a bit strange."

Nicky started to panic. What was that devious cow up to?

"Jan, you didn't say anything, did you, about us, I mean?"

Janice was hurt that he gave her so little credit, and his worry, which was evident, made her

wonder if he was just with her for a leg over and if his wife got wind of the affair, he would dump Jan in a heartbeat. She studied his face. Did he really care about her at all, and why was he with her when he had a real beauty waiting for him at home?

"No! Of course I didn't, and if you're that bloody panicky about her finding out, well, it doesn't say much for our relationship, does it?"

Nicky reached over the bar top and took hold of her hand.

"Don't be silly, sweetheart, you know how I feel about you, and if we go the distance, then I will leave her, I promise, but it's early days yet, so why rock the boat?"

Janice didn't reply, and pulling her hand away, she turned her back to him and began to wipe down the optics. He realised he'd pissed her off, but as with all women, he knew to leave her alone to calm down before he tried to continue the conversation.

Outside and not wanting to take any chances, Dodi had moved her car further out of sight and now just sat there. She had several hours to wait until the club closed. Back to wearing her flats, and after she'd retrieved her puffer jacket from the boot, she set her phone alarm for one fifty am. Reclining the seat, she snuggled down and tried to get some sleep, but it was difficult. She must have managed to drop off as she sat bolt upright when the alarm went off. Dodi climbed

out of the car and walked to the back of the club to where her husband's car was parked. The empty barrel store was open fronted, but she was still able to hide out of sight in one of the dark corners. Just after two, Dodi heard footsteps and laughter as they came around the corner, and her heart sank. Nicky walked the woman from the bar to the passenger side of the car, and before she got in, the couple shared a long, lingering, passionate kiss, and Dodi felt her heart break into a million pieces. Watching from the dark, she saw her husband, the love of her life, kissing a woman the same way he used to kiss her and the deep pain she felt was almost physical. Closing her eyes, she couldn't bear to watch, but she had no option but to stay where she was until the car pulled away. Back at home, Dodi showered, removed her makeup and climbed into bed, but sleep evaded her for most of the night. Once again, she must have finally drifted off because when she woke later that morning, she felt beside her, and the spot where her husband should have been was empty and stone cold. He hadn't come home, and it was the first time in their entire marriage that it had happened. Getting up, she pulled on a robe and made her way downstairs. An hour later and after several cups of strong coffee, she at last heard his key in the lock; at least he had come home to her, so maybe it was just a fling after all. Grabbing something to read so she didn't appear

bothered by his absence, she slightly turned her head so she could glance out of the corner of her eye into the hallway.

Earlier at Janice's flat, Nicky had stirred and looked over at the bedside clock. Seeing it was just after six, he knew he was in trouble, but strangely, he didn't care. When the door opened and Jan came in carrying a tray of tea and toast, he knew this was where he wanted to be; he didn't care that the place was rundown and that Jan didn't have much. What was lacking in that department was more than made up for with love and laughter.

"Morning, babe, thought you might like a bit of brekkie before you get off."

Jan climbed back into bed and, resting the tray between them, picked up her mug and took a large gulp.

"Ahh, that's better, can't beat the first one of the day."

Nicky propped himself up against the headboard; unlike Dodi, there was no fancy coffee in fine bone china cups, and she wasn't fully made up. Her hair was messy, and she wore an oversized sweatshirt that kept slipping off her shoulder, which he found to be incredibly sexy.

"I know it's early days, Jan, but I also know how I feel about you."

She placed her mug on the bedside table, now fearing that he was about to end their

relationship, but remaining silent, she waited for him to continue.

"Well?"

"Well, what?"

"How do you feel?"

Janice sighed heavily. Why, when things were going well, did something always have to rear its ugly head and fuck it all up?

"That's not important if you're about to end things, is it?"

Nick sat bolt upright and turned to face her. His expression was deadly serious.

"End things? You soppy mare, I'm trying to tell you that I love you and want to be with you permanently."

Janice could feel the tears as they trickled down her cheeks; this all felt so surreal, like she was dreaming.

"I love you too, but what about your wife? I don't want to be the reason a marriage ends."

"Sweetheart, meeting you made me realise that my marriage was over a long time ago, and if I'm brutally honest, it should never have happened in the first place. I thought it was love; we'd been together since we were kids, but I now know it was nothing more than a lifelong friendship. I'm going to leave soon and go and face the music; the sooner I come clean, the sooner we can all move on with our lives."

When Nicky walked down the hallway of his soon-to-be ex-marital home, he saw Dodi sitting

in the kitchen reading a magazine, and as she looked up and smiled at him, he felt as if a knife was being plunged into his heart. She didn't mention him not coming home last night, and that surprised him as he'd been expecting, actually hoping, for her to go off like a bottle of pop; it would have at least made leaving her easier.

"We need to have a chat, babe, and you're not going to like what I have to say."

Dodi didn't comment and waited for her husband to take a seat opposite her at the breakfast bar.

"I'm so sorry, and there's no easy way to say this, but I've met someone else."

"You mean the whore who was serving behind the bar last night?"

For a few seconds, he just looked at Dodi in shock. He didn't like her reference to Janice, but he supposed his wife at least deserved to slag off the woman who would be taking her place.

"She's not a whore, but that's beside the point. Now I will make sure you are provided for financially, but eventually, I will want a divorce."

Instantly, Dodi was on her feet, and her next sentence came out with venom.

"And I will take you to the fucking cleaners, you bastard. I've been reading up, and I'm sure the Courts will give me at least half of what you've got, and if I can get more, then I will, and it has

nothing to do with the money. If I can ruin you, I will, let's see how much longer the slut stays around then!"

Nicky knew that when she was like this, there was no point in trying to talk to her, so going upstairs, he packed a bag and then walked out of the house and his marriage. Standing in complete silence, Dodi broke down and sobbed so hard that she made herself vomit into the sink. Finally, when she'd composed herself, she ran upstairs, quickly dressed and pulled on her coat. Grabbing her car keys, she drove straight round to her in-laws' house. Using her key, Dodi entered the hall and, popping her head into the front room, she saw Bernie positioned in front of the television. Continuing down the hallway to the kitchen, she found her mother-in-law standing at the sink. Monica Stanton turned when she heard footsteps, and when she smiled in her daughter-in-law's direction, Dodi couldn't stop herself from breaking down again.

"Oh, sweetheart, what on earth is the matter?"

“He’s cheating with one of the Toms from the club.”

Monica’s brow furrowed as she slowly shook her head.

"What! You must be mistaken, love, no, it's silly, he loves you, darling."

"He didn't come home last night, and then an hour ago he walked in, told me he didn't love me anymore and then packed a few things and

left."

Usually, Nicky could do no wrong in his mother's eyes, but this was a different matter altogether.

"Leave it with me, sweetheart. I'll go and have a talk with him. Will you sit with Bernie for a while?"

Dodi nodded her head and tried to smile at her mother-in-law. As Monica pulled on her coat, she was seething, and as she spoke, her words sounded so angry.

"Those fucking whores have a lot to answer for, and if one of them dirty sluts thinks that she can ruin my family, she has another thing coming. I'm a force to be reckoned with, Dodi, so don't you worry, my son will soon be back in your arms, or that bitch will pay for what she's done. I'll be back as soon as I can; Bernie's had his breakfast, so you don't need to do anything for him. Just sit with him and keep him company."

When she heard the street door close, Dodi walked into the front room and took a seat on the sofa. Her father-in-law didn't seem to know that she was even there, but it didn't matter, as her mind was filled with heartfelt prayers, in the hope that Monica could work her magic.

CHAPTER EIGHT

By the time Monica reached the club, she was furious. Storming past Maxi, she marched straight into her son's office and found him deep in conversation with a young woman, who she guessed was the tart he was carrying on with. Just seeing them together made her blood boil, and she slammed the door behind her as she entered. The noise instantly startled Nicky, and to say he was shocked was an understatement. He was out of his seat in seconds.

"Mum! What on earth are you doing here? It's not, Dad, is it?"

"No, it bleeding well ain't. So, I suppose this is the little slag, is it? What the fuck are you doing, son? You've broken Dodi's heart. I never thought you would do such a thing. That girl has done nothing but bleeding love you for years, and I might add, even when you didn't deserve it."

"Jan, go and stock the bar, love, while I have a chat with my mother."

Janice bowed her head and didn't look in Monica's direction as she passed; if she had, then she wouldn't have liked the look of daggers that the older woman was giving her. When the door was at last closed, Nicky turned on Monica like never before.

"Don't you ever fucking storm in here, laying the law down again. This is my club, and what goes

on here is my business."

"Your club, is it? And just who paid for it, because if it wasn't for your poor old dad, you wouldn't have a pot to piss in. I know for a fact that if he had his capabilities, he would knock you to kingdom fucking come for what you're doing."

"Look! I can't help how I feel, and I ain't staying in a fucking dead marriage because you want me to!"

Monica could feel the tears as they welled up in her eyes, tears of rage but also of heartbreak. Her family was falling apart, and there wasn't a damn thing she could do about it.

"Want you to! Nicolas, you took vows in a church, before God, and you need to honour them."

"God? Don't make me fucking laugh. Oh, it's okay to suddenly be all religious and moral, is it, but when my old man was beating and doing God only knows what to people, that was okay, was it?"

"I didn't come here to get into a judging match regarding what your dad may or may not have done in the past, so stop trying to bloody turn the tables because it won't work this time. I'm ashamed of you, son, something I never thought I'd say."

"Dodi isn't innocent in all of this, you know."

"Don't you dare! That girl has done nothing but love you for years, and this is how you treat her?

Don't forget, I know all about your cheating before you got married and probably after and no doubt Dodi had an idea of what's gone on in the past, but she stayed true to you. Now, since you opened this shag palace, you've hooked up with some slut and broken your wife's heart. Well, I just hope Dodi has the sense to get tested because God only knows what you could have given her. You've gone too far this time, Nicky."

"This time, mother, it's different. I've never felt like this in my life, and there is no fucking way I'm giving Jan up. I tried to be gentle with Dodi when I told her, and I assured her she won't want for anything. Do you know what she said to me? She will take me for every penny I have, the greedy bitch!"

"Can you blame her, Nicky? You've hurt her beyond belief, but she'll calm down, she ain't got a mean bone in her body, bless her little heart. Don't ever expect me to accept that Brass into my home because it won't happen, and like I said, if your dad still had his faculties, he would have hit the bloody roof, you know he would, but then maybe you wouldn't be doing this at all because of what you know he would have said."

"Well, he hasn't got his faculties, has he and I can't do anything about that but just let me correct you, Mother, Jan is not on the game, never has been, nor will she be."

"No, of course she isn't, just like all of the other dirty old bitches you've got working in this

place. Believe me, in the end, they will all pay for their whoring ways and you along with them."

With that, Monica stormed out with as much anger as she'd stormed in with. When she passed the bar area, Jan bobbed down behind the wooden front. The woman was as mad as hell, and Jan was under no illusion that Nicky's mum would knock seven bells of shit out of her if given half a chance.

As Saturdays were always the most profitable, Nicky decided to stay at the club. He'd told Janice to take the rest of the day off as she was still upset, but when the place started to quickly fill up with the evening punters, he wished he hadn't, as they were so busy and he would now have to help out on the bar, something he hated doing. That night, Mary O'Toole was the first of the girls to hook a punter. She had taken to the role of a Tom like a duck to water and now couldn't deny that she was actually starting to enjoy the sex. Her flat in Oakshott Court in Somers Town was small and very expensive, but Mary adored it. She earned enough to easily cover the rent and loved trawling the weekend markets for ornaments and soft furnishings. It was strange, but as dangerous as her chosen profession was, for the first time in her life, she felt safe. Hanging up her coat and bag in the staff room, Mary made her way over to the bar. All of the girls were given a free drink at the

start of their shift just to relax them.

"Hello Mary, you're keen love."

"I've got my eye on a nice little corner table, Boss, so I want to pull in a bit more than usual if I can."

"That's what I like to hear, so, what can I get you, sweetheart?"

"Vodka and Coke, please."

Mary had only taken a couple of sips when her first trick approached. Smiling sweetly, she placed her drink down on the bar and began a conversation with the stranger.

"Good evening, babe, you looking to do a bit of business?"

The client didn't speak and only smiled, so taking hold of his hand, she guided the well-dressed man towards the side exit and at the same time explained her terms of business. Rosie Goodson nodded her head and then noted down the leaving time as Mary and her punter left the club. The couple walked along the street to the bed and breakfast and choosing number seven, Mary led him up to the room. As soon as they got inside, she got down to business. Malcolm Gould had never used the services of a prostitute before, but after having a blazing row with his girlfriend earlier that evening, he had decided to have himself some fun. Within a few minutes, he couldn't believe how different it felt to having sex with his fiancé. Wendy was a total prude and only ever allowed him straight sex

and only then in the missionary position. By the time he entered Mary, he only had to thrust twice before he climaxed, a welcome relief to Mary as she could now get back to the club to find her next trick. Malcolm thanked her, asked if he could see her again and then left as quickly as he could. Mary took the time to use the bathroom to clean herself up, and just as she was about to leave, there was a sharp knock at the door. Thinking her punter might have returned as he'd forgotten something, she opened the door smiling.

"Can't stay away, can y.........."

She was stopped mid-sentence when she came face to face with a complete stranger, dressed from head to toe in black. Suddenly, she saw a glint of steel as a long-bladed knife was raised and plunged deep into her chest. Before she had time to complete her sentence or even scream for help, Mary's lifeless body fell to the floor with a thud. Her assailant then grabbed Mary's wrists and dragged her body further into the room so that the door could be closed. With the knife still in hand, her attacker proceeded to mutilate the victim's face to the point where it was soon unrecognisable. When the act was complete, they wiped the blade on Mary's blouse, quietly closed the door and then calmly walked out of the building.

An hour later, and when Mary hadn't returned to the club, Rosie was becoming concerned.

Walking over to the bar where Nicky was still serving, she leaned over and whispered into her boss's ear.

"It's Mary, Mr Stanton, she's been gone well over an hour, and I'm a bit worried."

"She's probably pulling a double, she said she needed to earn a bit extra. Give it a bit longer and if she still ain't back in another ten minutes, get Maxi to pop over to the B & B to check on her."

Rosie nodded, but deep in her gut, she had a bad feeling, but she didn't know why. The girls often pulled a double when a punter had shot his load too soon, and his ego felt bruised, so he wanted to have another go at getting his leg over. It was easy money as the girls earned double without having to leave the room. Maybe Nicky was right, Rosie hoped so. Fifteen minutes later, and with still no sign of the Irish girl, Rosie again left her post and walked to the main entrance, where Maxi Willmore stood chatting with Gary Smith. The club seldom had any trouble, but Nicky still liked two on the door at the weekend to cover all eventualities.

"Sorry to interrupt, Maxi, but Mr Stanton said to ask you to go down to the B & B and check on Mary as she ain't been back for well over an hour. It's probably nothing, but it would put my mind at ease."

Maxi smiled and nodded.

"Anything for you, sugar."

He liked the older woman as she reminded him of his old mum, never taking any shit and always standing her ground.

"You get back inside, sweetheart, and I'll come and see you when I have some news."

Maxi strolled along the road and nodded to a couple of the Toms as they made their way back to the club. He wasn't in any great hurry as Rosie was probably getting her knickers in a twist over nothing. Entering the long hallway, he checked the small book that acted as a register and which hung from a string on the wall. All of the girls had to sign in and out and note which room they were using. It was just another safeguard that Nicky insisted on. Seeing she was in room seven, Maxi climbed the stairs and knocked on the door. When there was no answer, Maxi tried the handle, and surprisingly, the door gave no resistance when he pressed on the wood. The sight that greeted him made Maxi take a step back, and his mouth momentarily hung open in shock. Mary had bled out and was surrounded by a pool of crimson. Her face, or what was left of it, was ashen, and her eyes stared lifelessly up at the ceiling. Maxi pulled his handkerchief out and, grabbing the doorknob, he pulled the door closed, wiped down the handle and then left the building as quickly as he could. Aware that he might have been removing evidence, he was also very streetwise. He was a black man, living a

not altogether legal lifestyle, and there was no way he was getting the blame for this. So as not to draw attention to himself, Maxi didn't run back to the club, but his strides were wide and nonetheless fast. As he approached the bar, Nicky could see the alarm on his man's face, and as Maxi moved his head towards the office, Nicky didn't ask any questions and followed behind. With the door firmly closed, Maxi just stared at his boss for several seconds, and Nicky would swear that the usual ebony-like skin had paled by several shades.

"Rosie was worried, so I went to check on Mary, and well, she's dead, Boss."

"Dead! What the fuck are you talking about?"

"She was in room seven. I knocked, but when she didn't answer, I tried the door and found her lying on the floor with blood everywhere. Well, I'm assuming it was Mary as she'd signed in for that room, but in all honesty, there wasn't much left of the poor cow's face. After that, I didn't hang about, but it looked like she'd been stabbed in the heart as well."

"Fuck me! This is all I need; Old Bill will be swarming all over the place. Go back to the main doors, Maxi, and don't say a word to anyone and that includes Rosie. I'll put in an anonymous call to the filth so they can recover the body."

Alone in his office, Nicky pulled out a pay-as-you-go burner phone from his desk and called

the emergency services. Holding his hand over the mouthpiece, he staggered his message as he told the woman operator about a body at the Bed and Breakfast. He only stayed on the line for a few seconds, and when he finished, he removed the SIM card, burned it in the ashtray on his desk and then smashed the phone into pieces. Using the internal system, he called the main bar and asked for Rosie to join him in the office. Still extremely worried about Mary, she was there in a matter of seconds.

"You want to see me, Boss?"

"Yes, Rosie, come in and close the door behind you."

Rosie had a bad feeling, and she was anxious as she apprehensively walked towards the desk.

"I'm sorry, sweetheart, but Maxi checked the B&B and found Mary's body. She's been murdered."

Tears streamed down Rosie's face.

"I knew it, I knew something was wrong. Oh, poor Mary."

"How many of the girls are still out?"

"Only Lulu and I'm expecting her back at any moment. Murdered, I can't believe it, Boss, are you sure?"

"Sure!? Of course, I'm fucking sure, but we ain't got any idea if it was her punter or not."

"Sorry, Boss, I'm just in shock."

Nicky nodded his head knowingly and then gently put his arm around Rosie's shoulder.

"When Lulu gets back, I want you to gather the other girls and tell them on my orders there's to be no more business tonight, but don't elaborate on why. They are all to go straight home, and under no circumstances are they to ply their trade outside. If any of them have a problem, tell them to take it up with me. The Old Bill will be about in a few minutes, but if they come in here, you don't tell them anything. Direct them to the office. Do I make myself clear, Rosie?"

"Yes, sure, Mr Stanton. When I've sorted the girls, would you mind if I got off home as well, only this has rocked me to the core. As Toms go, Mary had turned out to be one of the best, a real sweetie. Who on earth would want to hurt her? I mean, they all know that if a punter ever cuts up rough over a payment, then they don't get into an argument; they just walk away. I can't tell you how many times I have drummed that into them all."

"I know you did, sweetheart, but as yet we don't know what happened or why and yes, of course you can get off. As soon as things die down a bit, I'll shut up for the night as well. I think we're both in shock."

Nicky then removed another burner from his desk drawer; he seemed to be going through them at a fast rate lately. Dialling the bed and breakfast, he impatiently waited for Ahsan Abbasi to answer. Nicky kept the call short and sweet, and he didn't give his name, but on

hearing his voice, Ahsan instantly knew who the caller was.

"There's been a murder in room seven. Make sure you keep your trap shut."

With that, Nicky hung up, and when he was sure that all the girls had left, he switched on the main lights and asked the remaining customers to leave the club. When he said they would be closing early, there were a few disgruntled moans, but many who had hoped to engage the services of a Tom had already left by then. Before locking the front doors, he glanced around at the empty space, which, with the lights on, now looked seedy and sad. When he'd been alone in the office, Nicky had racked his brains trying to remember what the man Mary had gone off with looked like, but his mind was a blank. True, the club had been busy, but in all honesty, most of the punters looked so similar when you only took a glance at them. It was at times like these that Closed-circuit television would have been a blessing, but there were no cameras in the club; it was what the punters expected, as many of them were married, and if they knew they were being recorded, they wouldn't entertain the place. Still, there was a camera covering the main entrance and switching over channels on his television, Nicky began to scan the images. There was still only a minor police presence outside, and apart from an attending ambulance that would eventually

remove Mary's body, there didn't seem to be too much happening. Going into rewind, Nicky studied the images of the last three hours over and over, and he did see Mary and her punter walking along the street, but as she had used the side entrance, it was a rear view of the man, if he indeed was the culprit, as it really could have been anyone. Sighing heavily, Nicky switched off the lights and locked up the club. He would head over to Jan's flat to tell her the news; she had been quite close to Mary, so this was really going to upset her.

CHAPTER NINE

Over the next few days, things slowly started to get back to normal, but everyone was still on their guard. All the girls seemed to be nervous and somewhat reluctant when it came to punters; the only problem was that if they wanted to earn, then they had to be available. Apart from a single visit from a rather young detective named Pete Price, there were very few questions asked. Nicky had offered up the side entrance CCTV tape, and although the detective thanked him, Nicky wondered if it would even be viewed. Street workers never received the respect that they deserved, and Nicky knew that had it been the death of a member of the general public, then the Old Bill would have been out in full force covering the area like flies around shit. Sensing the atmosphere, he gathered all the girls together in the main room of the club and slowly, and with compassion, addressed them.

"Now I know you are all on edge after what happened to poor Mary, and if any of you want to call it a day, I will fully understand."

A couple of the girls looked shocked that he had even suggested such a thing, and the others slowly shook their heads.

"Then you all need to be on your guard, and I mean really be on your guard. I can only do so much when it comes down to watching out for you, well, apart from being in the room with you

when you're shagging, but I somehow don't think that would go down too well with the punters."

There were a few sniggers, but Nicky wasn't attempting to be humorous; he was trying to get over just how vulnerable they all were.

"Take extra care, all of you, and if something, no matter how small, doesn't feel right, then get the hell out of there as fast as you can."

On Saturday, the club opened as usual. Maxi was sent to patrol the Bed and breakfast. He wasn't happy about it, but knew better than to complain. He took up residence in the hallway, and thankfully, he'd been able to find himself a chair to sit on, as it was going to be a long night. The first girl to do business was Josette, and she was in and out with her punter in less than twenty minutes. Josette had a thing for Maxi, and it wasn't just because they both shared the same skin colour. As she passed him in the hall, she winked and smiled, but Maxi completely ignored her. He'd never been that interested in women or having a relationship, and even if he had, it most definitely wouldn't be with a Tom, no matter how nice or good-looking she was. The next to come in was Jojo Johnson, and as professional as ever, she didn't even make contact with Maxi. Deciding to take a cigarette break outside, he groaned when he realised he'd left the pack and his lighter back at the club. If he ran, he could make it back in just a few

minutes, and as he didn't pass any of the girls on his way, he was confident that all was well. What Maxi didn't see was Sheila and her trick as they came out of the side door; it must have only been seconds, but it was long enough for Maxi to go into the club just as Sheila came around the corner. Up in room three, she took off her coat and moved towards her client. It was Barry Sanderson's first time with a Tom, and when he couldn't rise to the occasion, he suddenly and probably due to his embarrassment, had second thoughts.

"Look, love, I ain't being funny, but I've changed my mind."

"You ain't the first who can't get it up, babe, give it a few minutes, and I'll get the little fucker to stand to attention."

"No, really, just leave it, will you?"

Shelia was about to kick off, but stopped when Barry threw her money down onto the bed. It wasn't often that she got paid for doing absolutely nothing, so why look a gift horse in the mouth?

"Guess you got off easy, sweetheart."

"Thanks, and any time you want to try again, I'm always available, Sugar."

With that, Barry pulled on his jacket and made his way down the stairs, passing what he thought was another punter as he left. Sheila made her way into the small bathroom, and with the water running, she didn't hear someone

come in and close and lock the door. Maxi arrived back, but he didn't bother checking the ledger. Ten minutes later, when Jojo came back down, she was about to sign out when she suddenly stopped. She had heard Sheila giggling quite a while earlier, but she hadn't heard any sounds for a while, and as Sheila was known to be a bit of a moaner, it was unusual.

"Sheila's been up there a while, Maxi? She came in just after me, and normally, she's the quickest out of all of us. I heard her come in, but I didn't hear her leave?"

Maxi frowned as he stood up.

"Sheila? What the fuck are you on about? I popped to get my fags, and you were the only one in here."

"Well, you obviously weren't quick enough and missed her, darling. I can assure you it was her; I'd know that dirty laugh anywhere."

Jojo tapped the ledger, and as Maxi saw the name and room number, he immediately ran up the stairs with Jojo following closely behind. Sheila Mason was forty-eight years old, which, for a Tom, well, at least one that could still pull in the punters, was getting on a bit, and she should have been well past her sell-by date. Where she differed from her peers was in the fact that she always followed a strict regime and, without exception, always would. A weekly spa, and steam treatment, facials, eight hours of sleep every night, no matter what time she finished work and no more than four punters each night. Over the years, she hadn't earned as much money as many of the other girls on the streets, but she was still able to have a nice home in Charing Cross with a good standard of living. Never having used a pimp before, Sheila had relented when it came to Nicky Stanton; he offered a certain level of safety, somewhere warm and clean to ply her trade, and if his girls didn't want to work for a few nights, then that was their decision. There was no rough stuff, and Sheila, along with most of the others, actually liked her boss, which was unusual in their line of work.

Maxi stepped back; he was afraid of opening the door, so Jojo pushed him out of the way, sighing heavily as she did so.

"Get out of the way, you pussy."

As she opened the door, the sight that greeted her was horrific, and she screamed out in terror. Whoever had killed Sheila had really done a number on her, and if it was the same culprit that had murdered Mary, then they had now accelerated their level of sadism. Sheila was lying spread-eagled on the bed, but her hands and feet were not tied. To Jojo, it looked as if her friend had been posed. Sheila's throat had been slashed, her face had again been mutilated, and her dress was ripped open to the waist, revealing what had been her breasts. The two mounds of flesh had been sliced off and now sat

on the bedside rug. Maxi pulled Jojo close and tried to console her, and it felt like an age, though really no more than seconds, before the tears began to subside.

"Come on, sweetheart, we have to get this place closed off before any of the others try to come in. I'll wait here, you go back to the club and get Mr Stanton and then tell Rosie to stop any more of the girls heading out."

A normally upright and confident woman, Jojo looked broken, and with her head down and her shoulders hunched over, she slowly nodded her head. Outside, she took off her four-inch heels and then ran as fast as her legs would carry her. At the club, Nicky was in the office, and Jojo burst through the door without knocking. Nicky was about to read her the riot act, but stopped when he saw her face.

"Oh, Mr Stanton, you need to come quickly, someone has killed Sheila. Maxi told me to come and get you; he's staying there so that no one else goes in."

"Go and tell Rosie!"

Out of his seat in seconds, Nicky reached the bed and breakfast in record time. Once inside, he locked the front door and then called out.

"Maxi!!!"

"Up here, Boss."

When he got to the room, Nicky's face grimaced at the sight before him.

"Fuck me! That poor cow, wipe the handle and

shut the door, Maxi and let's get back to the club."

Just as he'd done after finding Mary's body and doing as his boss ordered, Maxi wiped down the door handle, and the two men then quickly walked along the road in silence. They didn't notice Martin Gayle standing in a darkened restaurant, a restaurant that he had been forced to close a week earlier. Scribbling in a small notebook, Marty smiled knowingly. Whatever had happened didn't look good, and Marty hoped above hope that the house of Stanton was about to come tumbling down.

In his office, Nicky removed another burner phone from his desk drawer and called Ahsan to warn him, but also to remind him to keep his mouth shut. He then called the police and gave a short message about the murder before hanging up. Sighing heavily, Nicky then destroyed the phone and SIM card. Next, he went into the main room and instructed the girls to go home for a second time. He didn't explain about Sheila as the club was still open and there were four or five customers milling about within earshot, but he told them all to come back the day after tomorrow for a meeting. Thankfully, as there weren't too many punters in, it only took a few minutes for them to drink up and leave before he could lock up. Within thirty minutes, the road had been closed off at the Greek Street junction and where Frith Street

crossed Romilly. There were already two police cars outside the bed and breakfast, and a van soon pulled up carrying a scene of crimes team. Unlike with poor Mary, they seemed to be taking things a bit more seriously with murder number two. Martin Gayle came out of his now-closed restaurant and walked over the road to a uniformed officer standing guard on the steps.

"Can I help you, Sir?"

"I own the restaurant opposite and just wanted to offer my help regarding the local area. There aren't many folks, or at least the regulars, that I don't know or things that happen that I don't see or hear about."

"If you wouldn't mind waiting there, I'll get my senior officer."

A couple of minutes later, the constable returned with a plain-clothed officer who introduced himself as Detective Kevin Lincoln.

"Good evening, Sir, my colleague said you have a good local knowledge of the area. Do you happen to know who owns the property across the road?

"Well, when old Myrtle died, she was the previous owner; it was sold to some Asians. I've only recently met them; it's a guy named Ahsan Abbasi and his mother. They live at the rear, which you access down that small alleyway over there."

Stretching out his arm, Marty pointed across the road to a dimly lit walkway.

"That's most helpful, Sir, thank you, and should we need any further information, I know where to find you."

To Martin, the Detective appeared to be somewhat dismissive, which pissed him off, but as he returned to the restaurant, he still had a slight grin on his face. All of this commotion wouldn't help Stanton's club, as the sort of people who frequented it wouldn't hang around long, not with the street teeming with Old Bill. Following Marty's directions, Detective Lincoln, along with the uniformed officer, made their way to the rear of the property down the unlit alley. There was an old back door that hadn't seen a coat of paint in years, and as Kevin Lincoln hammered on the wooden surface, the glass pane shook, and he thought it would break if he had to knock again. It seemed to take an age before a light at last came on, and a figure slowly approached on the inside.

"Yes?"

"It's the police, madam. Could you open up?"

"Yes."

Still, nothing happened, and the two men looked at each other.

"Madam?"

"Yes."

Suddenly, the silhouette of a second figure approached.

"Who is it?"

"The police, Sir, could you open up please?"

Kevin heard hushed whispers from inside, but it was foreign, and he couldn't understand what was being said. A few seconds later, a bolt could be heard sliding, and the door opened, but only enough for the officers to see a pair of eyes staring back at them.

"I talked to the police yesterday about the murder. I don't know anything, and I can't help you, okay?"

"Please, Sir, this is important, and I need to speak to you face to face."

Ahsan slowly opened the door, but he didn't look happy and speaking sharply to the older woman, she instantly turned and scuttled back through the rear door.

"Thank you, now I'm Detective Lincoln, and this is Constable Carter. I understand you are the owner of the bed and breakfast?"

"Why do you want to know?"

The man was coming over as hostile, and it was starting to rile Kevin Lincoln. For God's sake, a woman was dead, and trying to speak to this man was like pulling teeth.

"Another woman has been murdered. Now we can do this here or back at the station, it's your choice."

Ahsan sighed heavily and, rolling his eyes in frustration, nodded his head as if to say 'here we go!'

"So, what can you tell me about your business?"

Ahsan nervously wiped the palm of his hand

across his mouth; this was all he needed, and knowing how violent Nicky Stanton could be, he had to be careful how he answered.

"The rooms are self-served with a lock box on each door. I do rent out individually, but I also block book for local businesses."

Kevin could read between the lines; no decent person would want to stay in the rundown building, so it was obviously a property used solely by Toms or, at the very least, poorly paid contractors.

"I will need you to provide a list of whom you block-book to."

Now, Ahsan was fidgeting, and Detective Lincoln had seen the same scenario many times over the years. When he didn't offer up any further information, Kevin had had enough of being messed around.

"Either you give me what I'm asking for, or you can come down to the fucking nick right now. I have an investigation to get on with, and I don't need idiots like you holding me up, or come to that, withholding information!"

"Okay, okay, but you didn't get it from me, alright? Mr Stanton, who owns Nicky's Club down the road, has seven rooms on permanent hire. Do you know who he is?"

"I do indeed."

“Then you understand my reluctance to answer your questions?”

Kevin was only too aware of who Nicky Stanton

was. There weren't many in the Met who didn't, but as yet, the man had evaded ever having his collar felt.

"Runs his Toms out of here, does he?”

Ahsan only nodded his head and then slowly closed his eyes for a second. If anyone had seen the Old Bill come down the alley, it wouldn’t be long before Stanton got wind of it.

"Thank you, Sir, that will be all for now."

As the two officers walked back down the alley, Ahsan could be heard shouting.

“Please don’t tell him it was me who told you.”

There was no reply, and when they reached the street, Kevin turned right with the constable following closely behind. After the officers banged hard on the front doors several times, Nicky couldn't be off hearing the commotion. Sighing heavily and already knowing who it was, he walked from the office to the front foyer. Opening up, he didn't speak, and as he turned and headed back towards his office, both policemen followed. Nicky sat down behind his desk and then, smiling at the visitors, held out his open palms as if to say, 'How can I help?'

"I take it you're aware of what's happened further up the Street, Mr Stanton?"

The question was rhetorical, and Nicky only nodded his head. Detective Lincoln had taken an instant dislike to Nicky on sight, and he didn't hide his tone as he spoke.

“We believe the victim was a prostitute who

operated out of this establishment. What can you tell me about her?”

"Firstly, let me correct your belief, Detective. This is a drinking and dancing venue, and I do not condone prostitution, but nor do I discourage it, as it brings in the punters. I do not allow any shenanigans on the premises, but I'm not naive; this is Soho after all, and if the Toms didn't work out of here, we would be empty. Regarding the lady in question, I have heard whispers, though how true they are, I'm not sure, that it was Sheila Mason. I know very little about the woman, only the fact that she had been a prostitute for many years and had at one time or another worked out of most of the clubs in Soho. As far as I know, she lives somewhere in Caring Cross, but that's about it really."

Kevin Lincoln was convinced the man was lying, and he also knew that at times like these, the villainous people who worked outside of the law would now all close ranks.

"That's something, I suppose. Are any of the other Toms about?"

"As I said, I do not encourage prostitution on my premises, but in answer to your question, no. I think the women are scared, and I closed this place early because when your mob flooded the street, punters and staff scattered like flies."

Detective Lincoln sagely nodded his head.

"When will you be reopening, Mr Stanton?"

"Out of respect, I will keep this place closed for a
few days, at least until the dust settles."

"Then that's when I will return. If you have any contact with your, I mean, the girls, please inform them that I will be speaking to them and I expect their compliance. Good evening, Mr Stanton."

When the officers left and the door was closed, Nicky sat back in his chair. This was bad for business, very bad, and he needed to do his own investigations before things got out of hand. He was about to take a big hit in a loss of earnings, and he couldn't let it continue, or he might as well close the place for good.

CHAPTER TEN

The night of Sheila's attack, Nicky hadn't gone to Jen's flat and instead returned to his marital home. Dodi was still up watching television, and when she heard his key in the lock, she shot up from the sofa. Glancing in the over-mantle mirror, she slowly shook her head. She looked a mess and was wearing her big furry dressing gown and slippers, something she never did in front of her husband. In the few seconds before he entered the room, she had a moment where she wondered where she had gone wrong. She was always immaculately dressed and wearing full makeup; she was a good cook, the house was kept spotless, and she never refused him sex even when she was ill or didn't feel like it. Was it the fact that she couldn't conceive, or had he just fallen out of love with her? Dodi remained standing when he entered, desperately hoping that he would beg her forgiveness and ask to come back home, but when she saw his expression, she knew that wouldn't be happening.

"Is anything wrong?"

"Did you hear about Mary?"

"Yes, I did, your mum told me, why?"

"Because the cunt, whoever he is, has now murdered Sheila."

For a few seconds, Dodi was speechless and just stared at her husband, not really able to take on

board what he had just said.

"What did the Old Bill say?"

Nicky flopped down onto the sofa and slowly shook his head.

"As usual, they're about as much use as a fucking chocolate teapot. They ain't got a fucking clue, but when I find out, and if I can get to him before the Old Bill, well, let's just say he won't ever take another fucking breath."

Dodi took a seat beside her husband and placed the flat of her hand on his knee.

“Does this mean you’re coming home?”

The look he gave her tore through her heart like a knife, and to make matters worse, he roughly pushed her hand away.

"No, it does not, and this ain't the time to talk about us when that poor cow is laying stone cold on a slab somewhere."

"There isn't anything either of us can do about that, Nicky, but don't you think you owe me an explanation? What did I do wrong? Is it because I can't give you a child? You know how hard I tried, and over the years, it's broken my heart again and again."

Pulling away, Nicky slightly moved away from her on the sofa.

"It's got nothing to do with that. If you want the truth, and it might sound cruel, but I don't love you, deep down, I don't think I ever have, well, at least not in that way, the way you want me to. You, me and Robbie were the best of mates, but

that's all it really ever was, but by the time I realised it was too late to back out. I knew on our wedding day that I was doing the wrong thing, but how could I tell you, how could I hurt you like that?"

Nicky didn't think he'd ever seen such a look of pain on anyone's face, and he immediately felt guilty, but he couldn't keep masking the truth from her; it wouldn't be fair to anyone.

“But it’s okay to break my heart now? So, why did you marry me in the first place then?”

“Like I said, I felt obligated.”

“Fucking Obligated!!!!?”

"Look, we'd been together for years, and everyone expected it, my parents, your parents. I did, do, love you, Dodi, but not in the way you want; it's like a friend and nothing more. It was always just you, me, and Robbie, like the three musketeers, and well, I didn't want to let you, or anyone else, down."

Robbie, it was a long time since she'd heard him mentioned in any detail, really not since her wedding day. Oh, his name would randomly crop up if Nicky had spoken to him on the phone, but that was about it.

"Maybe I should have married him instead of you?"

"Maybe you should have."

The words had left his mouth before he had thought about the damage they would do, and the look in his wife's eyes was murderous. In

seconds, Dodi was out of her seat and grabbing the nearest thing to hand, which happened to be an expensive Chinese vase; she hurled it in her husband's direction, but thankfully it missed. The look he gave was one of hatred, and that hurt her more than anything. Nicky stormed out of the room and, making his way upstairs, slept in the spare room. For a moment, but only that, Dodi thought about calling her mum, but since the wedding, things had been strained between them. Monica putting Linda in her place had royally upset the applecart, and when her own daughter hadn't come to her defence, to Linda Smith it was something she would never be able to forgive. In all honesty, Dodi felt closer to her mother-in-law than she ever had her mother, but from now on, seeking solace there would be difficult.

When Dodi got up the following morning, Nicky had already gone, and so were the rest of his clothes. It finally dawned on her that he wasn't coming back and that her marriage was definitely over. Sitting alone at the breakfast bar, she surveyed her surroundings and realised that as beautiful as everything was, it meant absolutely nothing without him. An hour later, when she had composed herself and gathered as much strength as she could muster, Dodi did some research to find out the best divorce solicitor that money could buy. Hayes and Tomb were situated right in the city on the

western side of Chancery Lane, and at nine on the dot she phoned them. Her appointment was scheduled for eleven that morning, but she set off at just after nine thirty to make sure she wouldn't be late. Dodi took a cab from the house to Wood Green underground station at Turnpike Lane and then boarded the Piccadilly line to Holborn. There were eight stops in total during the seventeen-minute journey, and Dodi watched all the people coming and going; most seemed like they didn't have a care in the world, though she knew that probably wasn't the case. The one thing that stuck out was the fact that no one spoke or smiled at each other. London could be a cold and lonely place if you looked hard enough. There were suited gents struggling to read their newspapers, professional-looking women chatting away as if to no one through the earpieces of their mobile phones and then there were a couple of mothers with their children. One in particular was well-dressed and was accompanied by her nanny, who was struggling to carry a baby along with several bags of shopping. The other had her baby strapped to her chest in some kind of bohemian fabric contraption that, to Dodi, didn't look that comfortable or safe, come to that. Her heart ached, and she would have gladly swapped places with either of them just to feel a child in her arms. Leaving the train, there was a further walk of around fourteen minutes, which

she didn't fancy, but she still had an hour to spare, so she decided that it would be silly to take a black cab and then have to wait around. Walking along Serle Street, which was close to Lincoln's Inn Fields, the heart of London's legal district, she passed the huge houses that commanded vast sums of money. Her area of Muswell Hill had high property prices, but this was on another level. Dodi wasn't jealous; she would have traded all that she had to have a baby and for Nicky to love her like she thought he had. Turning onto Chancery Lane, the vision that greeted her was one of suited solicitors and Barristers in their gowns, all rushing in and out of their chambers. Suddenly, she felt unnerved; this was going to be it, and this meeting was the first step in bringing her marriage to an end, something she so desperately didn't want. As Dodi stepped through the highly polished front door, she could feel the shakes start; they were so bad that she was actually beginning to feel physically sick. The feeling didn't improve when she was taken through to the office of Oswald Smeeth. Seeing the man sitting behind his desk and the room elaborately decorated with wall-to-wall, floor-to-ceiling mahogany bookcases, Dodi felt like she was in trouble. It was stupid, but she couldn't help herself. Standing up, Oswald smiled and, leaning over his desk, offered his hand.

"I'm very pleased to meet you, Mrs Stanton."

At least he came over as friendly and not the pompous prick she had been expecting.

"Please take a seat and tell me what the issue is. I know you are here to file for divorce, but I need to know the details, as there has to be a reason."

"Nicky, that's my husband, has left me."

"How long has he been gone?"

"Officially, well, since yesterday."

Dodi's eyes clouded over when she recalled the events of the previous night, and she could also see the slight glimmer of a smile on the man's lips.

"That's really not very long. Is there any possibility of reconciliation?"

"Sadly, there's not a chance."

"Well, there needs to be a continuous period of at least two years, and then we have to prove desertion, and that can only happen if he fails to return to the marital home. Do you think he might come back at some time in the future, perhaps?"

"No, he has another woman."

"Well, to turn a phrase, that's a different kettle of fish altogether."

"My husband is a wealthy man, and he would never allow me to divorce him. Nicky will be happy to carry on as things are, but I'm not."

Oswald smiled and nodded his head sagely.

"It's not up to him, my dear, and as for his wealth, a divorce begins with a fifty-fifty split, and then depending on the facts, i.e. who is to

blame and your financial needs, the amount can increase or decrease enormously. From what you've told me so far, you have a good case, but we need cold, hard proof. A Judge would not just take your word for it, or every woman on the planet wanting to end her marriage would say her husband had cheated. Now, I can suggest a private investigator, but they can be expensive."

"Well, until I'm divorced, I have no money of my own. My husband is generous, and I have several credit cards but no real hard cash."

"Then I suggest, and only if it is safe for you to do so, to gather as much proof as you can. Come back when you have more to go on, and we can talk further."

“Should I tell him I’m filing?”

"It can't do any harm, and besides, he will find out soon enough."

Dodi was feeling a lot better, and after thanking her newly appointed solicitor, she headed over to Soho. It was just before midday, and Nicky's Place, contrary to what he had told the police and his girls, was already open for business. Maxi Willmore was on door duty, but he didn't see Dodi approach until it was too late, so there was no chance to warn his boss, a mistake he knew he could be made to pay for later. As Dodi entered the main club area, the smell of stale beer hit her nostrils, and she noticed how seedy and grim the place looked in the cold light of

day. Making her way to the office, she didn't knock, and walking straight in, she saw a woman sitting on her husband's lap. They looked close and were laughing just as she and Nicky used to do. There and then, her heart shattered into a million pieces.

“What the fuck!”

"It's okay, my darling husband, I knew she was the one the first time I met her."

Janice Connolly was now red in the face with embarrassment, but she remained sitting on Nicky's lap.

"I'm sorry, Mrs Stanton, I didn't mean for it to happen, but you can't help who you fall in love with."

It was the first time love had been mentioned by Jan, and Nicky liked the sound of it.

"Give me a break, sweetheart, you ain't the first, and you won't be the last. My husband will fuck anything that moves. Didn't think I knew about the others, did you, Nicky?"

Dodi didn't give him a chance to reply as she continued with her assault.

"Do you actually believe he'd ever give up his fucking lifestyle for a piece of scrag-end when he's got fillet steak at home? You're just a little tart, who thinks she is onto a good thing, and maybe you will be for a while, but sooner or later, he will try to crawl back to me and the life he is used to. Well, Nicky, I'm here to tell you that it won't happen this time as I'm filing for

divorce."

With that, Dodi removed her iPhone and snapped several pictures of the couple. They didn't show anything serious, but at least it was a start.

"What the fuck are you doing!?"

"Gathering evidence, darling!"

With that, she marched out of the club and was able to keep her composure until she was far enough away that no one would see her tears. By the time she reached home, Nicky's car was parked out the front, and he was already inside and pacing up and down. The look on his face spoke volumes, but Dodi wasn't afraid. For the first time in her marriage, she wasn't about to try to placate him as she had done so many times over the years when he was angry. This time, she would be strong, and she was ready for anything he would try to throw at her. Hanging up her coat, Dodi headed for the kitchen, walking straight past the front room where her husband was waiting. She smiled wryly as she switched on the kettle, knowing that in a few seconds, he would come marching in to find her.

“Where the fuck do you get off coming into my club and attacking Jan?”

"Fucking attacking that bitch? I did no such thing because if I had, she would be flat on her fucking back. Regarding your club, as you put it, according to my solicitor, it's half my club. We had no prenup Nicky so theoretically, half of

everything you have is mine and by the way, I'm going to take you for as much as I can and, don't try and start syphoning it off as the judge will want all of your financial details and if he sees that you've been trying to hide money or assets it will go against you."

Oswald had warned her that her husband could try this, but he told her not to worry, as even though it might take a while, she would eventually get what she was owed.

“You fucking bitch!”

"Showing your true colours now, aren't you, Nicky?"

Now the wry smile was back on her face, and that angered him more than anything. His blood was boiling, and as he ran over to her, Dodi knew that for the first time, there might actually be physical violence in their marriage. Maybe that wouldn't be a bad thing; at least it would be more evidence.

"Lay a hand on me, and you'll be arrested and be in no doubt that I will call the Old Bill on you, my dear husband; it will also help my case no end, so you'd probably be doing me a favour."

Stopping dead in his tracks, Nicky clenched his fists and could only stare at her, a woman he really didn't know anymore.

"What happened to you, Dodi? Why are you being like this? You know the pressure I'm under, what with two of my Toms being killed."

She couldn't believe what she was hearing. Was
he delusional? Had he hit his head?

"Why am I doing this? You've wrecked my life, moved in with some old slapper and torn our marriage apart, and you have the fucking cheek to ask me why I'm doing this? As for those dead brasses, who put them to work in the first place? Just get out, Nicky, I've finally seen you for what you really are, you're nothing more than a sad little pimp! I also don't give a fuck about your whores; maybe they got what they deserved."

He momentarily studied her face. Was she the killer? Had she thought that he was with Mary or Sheila? That was ridiculous. Dodi didn't have a mean bone in her body, but then again, how she was acting now showed a completely different side to the woman he thought he knew. Turning on his heels, Nicky Stanton stormed out of the house, slamming the front door as he went. Within the hour, Dodi had made arrangements for a locksmith to call at the house later that day to change the locks. Next, she sat at the breakfast bar and began her plan of action. She wanted as much dirt on her bastard of a husband as she could get, and tomorrow, she would set the ball in motion by paying a visit to his mother and father's house.

CHAPTER ELEVEN

Dodi woke the next morning with a spring in her step, and the feeling surprised her. Heading downstairs to the kitchen, she was like a woman on a mission and, from the moment she'd first opened her eyes, had decided that nothing was going to stop her. After a quick coffee and then a leisurely shower, Dodi set off for Camden to pay her in-laws a visit at around eleven. Her relationship with Bernie had been okay before his stroke, but she didn't have much in common with him, and now that he couldn't communicate verbally, the conversation was always strained and hard going. With Monica, it was a different story; from the off, the two women had always gotten along well, but as soon as Dodi and Nicky got engaged, their closeness had become even deeper. Sadly, now and even though she loved her mother-in-law, she was taking no hostages in her quest, and besides, she knew Monica would always put her son above everything else, so after the divorce, there would be no place for Dodi in the family. They would eventually welcome that slut and treat her like a princess, just as they had treated Dodi in the beginning.

The smart double-fronted house with its white plantation shutters oozed money and class, and Dodi could feel her nerves begin as she walked up the porcelain-paved path to the high gloss

front door. She had a key but didn't feel comfortable using it now, so after knocking, Dodi waited for someone to let her in. Monica was in the middle of preparing Bernie's lunch, which was time-consuming as all his food needed to be pureed, and she sighed heavily when she heard the door and the ensuing interruption. Monica padded along the hallway in her fluffy slippers and was surprised by who she came face-to-face with when she opened up. "Oh, hello sweetheart, why on earth didn't you use your key?"

Dodi's bottom lip began to quiver, and her eyes filled with tears, but she didn't speak. It wasn't all an act, and her mother-in-law's kind tone made her realise she was going to miss being a part of all this.

"It just didn't feel right, not after what's happened."

As the tears fell onto Dodi's cheeks, Monica's brow furrowed with concern.

"It breaks my heart to see you cry. Oh, Dodi, please don't cry, darling."

Monica sighed again and rolled her eyes as she grabbed her daughter-in-law's hand.

"That son of mine can be a real shit at times. It will run its course, darling, and he'll be back in your bed before you know it. I'm sure of it, sweetheart."

"No, not now, he won't."

Monica's eyes darted from side to side. What

had her boy done now?

"Come on in, babe, and tell me what he's been up to. Bernie's having his physio, so we've got time to have a cuppa and a chat in private before he needs feeding again."

Walking along the marble-floored hall, they passed the front room door, which thankfully was closed. Monica cherished the physio time allocated to her husband as his care was twenty-four seven, and she got little to no time to herself. As selfish as it sounded, even Dodi's marital problems were a happy release from the constant nursing she was required to do. When the two women were seated in the kitchen, and when the tea had been made and poured into china cups, Monica turned to the young woman whom she looked upon as an actual daughter.

"So, what's he been up to now?"

"He's left and took all of his clothes, so I know he won't be back this time."

"Oh, love, I'm so sorry. I love my son with all of my heart, but at times I don't like him very much. So, what are you going to do?"

"I went to see a solicitor, but I can't get a divorce without a reason, and he won't willingly give me one. They won't just take my word that he's left me and is with another woman. I don't want to hurt him, Monica, but I feel humiliated, and as much as I still love him, I realise that this is the end so I have to move on with my life. He's the one who's done the damage, so why should I be

made to suffer and stay in a marriage that's in name only for the next five years?"

"So, what is it that you need, darling?"

"Well, I have a photograph of them together, but even though that bitch was sitting on his lap, it doesn't prove that they are having an affair. My solicitor told me I need concrete proof of adultery."

"Let me think about it, sweetheart, and if I can help you in any way, then I will. I love my boy, you know I do, but he has to pay for his mistakes, and it's not fair that he's getting his leg over with some slapper and you are left in limbo."

Dodi hugged her mother-in-law and, as she made her way back home, prayed that the woman would come through for her. Monica spent the rest of the day mulling things over, and the more she thought about the situation, the angrier she became. By late afternoon, she had come up with a plan, though whether it would work or not was another matter.

Reaching for her mobile, she tapped her contact list. As it was Tuesday, the club wasn't open, and when Nicky's phone rang, he was curled up on the sofa with Jan at her flat. Seeing who the caller was, he sighed heavily.

“Here we go! Hello mum.”

"Hello, son. I had a visit from Dodi today."

“Look, I ain’t getting into another row with....”

Monica cut him off before he could continue.

"That's not why I'm calling. She told me she has seen a solicitor, so I've accepted that she's moving on with her life and that you must do the same. So, I've been thinking."

"Go steady, sweetheart. I don't want you overdoing it."

Monica laughed; her son could always bring a smile to her face, but this time she was acting; the last thing she felt like doing at the moment was joking around.

"Cheeky! No, I think it's about time I met your new love and wondered if you would both like to come over for a meal and a few drinks. You know what it's like when your dad has gone to bed, and I do get a bit lonely. You could both have a good drink and stay over for the night. The spare room is made up, and I'll do you both a nice cooked breakfast before you leave. Now I know the club is closed on Tuesdays, so what say we make it tonight? It's short notice, I know, and you might have something else planned, but I've got some lovely fresh fillet steaks in the fridge."

Nicky loved his mother and was happy that they had made up after their shouting match at the club. He also loved her cooking, and her full English was legendary.

"That would be lovely, Mum, and thank you, it means a lot to me and Jan."

Just the mention of that woman's name had Monica's blood boiling, and she was glad her

son couldn't see her expression.

"Shall we say eight? It will give me time to get your dad into bed so that I can relax and spend some time with the two of you."

When Nicky ended the call, he smiled at Janice and told her all about the conversation. Jan was worried, but she knew how much Nicky's mum meant to him, so outwardly she embraced the invitation. Her anxiety was unfounded as the meal was a resounding success with wine flowing freely, though Monica limited her own intake as she had to be sober enough to carry out her plan. She made sure to be overly friendly to Janice, but inside, she was still seething. The tramp would never measure up to Dodi in any way. Dodi was smart, beautiful and classy, and this one was plain and dowdy. Her dress sense was cheap and unstylish, and for the life of her, Monica couldn't understand what her son saw in the whore. Maybe it would turn out to be just a glitch, and he was having one of those male midlife crisis things. With the meal over and Nicky more than a tad the worse for wear, Janice helped him up the stairs to bed, and the couple were snoring softly as soon as their heads hit the pillow. In the early hours of the morning, Monica silently opened the door to the spare room, and from the light in the hall, she could see the couple entwined on the bed with just a sheet covering them, though it had slipped to Jan's waist, and her bare breasts were visible,

which was a bonus. Removing her iPhone from her dressing gown pocket, Monica took several pictures and then slowly closed the bedroom door. This should be exactly what Dodi needed, but Monica would still spend the next few hours thinking deeply about whether she should forward the images to her daughter-in-law or not.

The next morning, and after having the night to sleep on it, the thought of betraying her boy weighed heavily, but her son had to learn a lesson; he couldn't just hurt people, especially people who loved him, whenever he saw fit, without paying the price. When the couple emerged, they were all over each other, and it turned Monica's stomach. The girl had no manners, another black mark on her character. After she had cooked a blow-out full fry-up, much to her son's pleasure, and when the guests had finally left, Monica called her daughter-in-law and asked her to come over to the house. Dodi didn't need asking twice, and less than an hour later, she let herself in with her key just as her mother-in-law had insisted. Monica stood at the sink, and when she heard the door close, she turned and smiled in Dodi's direction.

"Take a seat, love, and I'll make us a cuppa."

Dodi didn't know why she had been summoned; surely there was no way Monica had any news this early on. Maybe she had changed her mind about helping, and as much as it would be a hardship to Dodi, she would completely understand. Placing the mugs down onto the table, Monica took a seat beside her daughter-in-law and at the same time took Dodi's exquisitely manicured hands into her own.

"I had a couple of house guests last night. It was a bit of a last-minute invite, but it served its purpose."

Dodi's eyes opened wide, but she didn't dare to hope.

"What I'm going to show you will break your heart, my darling, but I know it's what you need to get your fair share, so you just have to be brave."

Flicking through her phone, Monica soon stopped when she found what she was looking for. Handing the mobile over to her daughter-in-law, she studied Dodi's face as the woman viewed the images and the pain, so pitiful, was evident. Wiping the tears from her eyes, Dodi gave Monica a thin smile.

"I don't know how you did this or how to thank you, but these will allow me to move on. I realise now that it's what I have to do. Up until you showed me these pictures, I still stupidly hoped deep down that he would come back to me, but I know that was just a silly pipe dream. He will go mad when he finds out, though, doesn't that worry you, Monica?"

"Not really. At the end of the day, he's my son and just as I would forgive him for anything, he would do the same for me. I love him, Dodi, you know I do, but he has to learn that he can't do this to people just to get what he wants. Bernie never brought any pain to this house. Oh, I know he cheated on me, but it was just a few flings. If it had been more serious, then I would like to think that someone would have helped me out like I'm helping you."

Monica pressed send on her phone, and seconds later, the images had been sent to Dodi's mobile, and there was no going back. At the front door, the two women hugged, and at this moment in time, Dodi still felt like part of the family, but she wondered how long it would last before she was replaced because if it came down to choosing her or Nicky, where his mother was concerned, Nicky would win hands down every time. Promising to visit soon, Dodi set off for home. She should have been over the moon with her new evidence, but all she felt was broken, like her life had been ripped apart.

The following night, Lucy Barber was rushing to get to the club as she'd been late twice before in the last month and knew it wouldn't take much for her to be given her marching orders. Nicky Stanton was a fair boss, but at the same time, he wouldn't allow anyone to take the piss. Lucy's bedsit was on Litchfield Street just off Charing Cross Road, so she was almost within spitting distance of the club and had no excuse for lateness. It was cold and mizzling with rain, and

her new Lycra mini dress offered little protection. Running wasn't an option in her four-inch stiletto heels, so she walked as quickly as she could. The traffic was heavy on Shaftesbury Avenue, and it took her a while to cross, and Lucy could feel that her hair was now wet and, in all probability, her mascara had started to run. Rosie wouldn't be pleased with her, and Lucy could hear the woman's voice in her head 'What the bleeding hell do you look like? Fucking sort yourself out, girl!' Turning right onto Greek Street and then taking a left, the club was at last in view. In all honesty and with the state of the weather, she doubted that they would be busy tonight, but that wouldn't matter to her boss. Mr Stanton ran a tight ship, and he didn't allow slacking of any kind. Due to the appalling weather,

Romilly Street was deserted, and just before she reached Drummonds Restaurant, she was suddenly pulled by her arm into a shop doorway. Thinking it was an over-eager punter, Lucy tried to smooth down her wet hair and put a smile on her face.

"If you're looking for business, sweetheart, you're out of luck, only I'm late, so come down to the club and...."

Suddenly, Lucy felt what she thought was a punch to her belly, and seconds later, her assailant quickly walked off into the night. Looking down, she could make out the dark mass as it spread across the front of her dress,

and the only thing that entered her mind was the fact that she'd only just bought the dress and now it was ruined. Kicking off her shoes and holding onto her stomach, Lucy rushed to the club and ran past Maxi Truman, who was in the middle of arguing with a drunken customer who was trying, and failing dismally, to get inside. Nicky was sitting in his office. Wednesdays were always quiet, but it was still worth opening up the club, and besides, he'd lost a packet after closing when Mary and then Sylvia had been killed. Janice was working the bar, and several of the Toms were sitting on the stools chatting as they waited for their first punters of the night. Suddenly, the double doors flew open, and Little Lucy Barber came running in. Her eyes were open wide as she clutched at her stomach, and her white micro dress was now saturated in blood. As she made it into the main area, she dropped to the floor, causing all of the other women to begin screaming. Just as Rosie Goodson, who'd been sitting at her post at the side exit, came running over, Nicky flew out of his office. The women screaming was an instant indicator that something was very wrong, but as he reached the edge of the small wooden dancefloor, he struggled to see what had happened as the girls had all crowded around Little Lucy.

"For fucks sake, you lot, move out of the way will you?!"

Nicky roughly pushed his way through just as Maxi Willmore came running from the front foyer.

"Sorry, Boss, she ran straight past me."

Nicky bent down and cradled the dying girl in his arms, but it was only a matter of seconds before Lucy let out an audible gurgling breath and the young life left her body. The women surrounding her all began to wail, and Nicky, who was now covered in blood, looked up at Maxi with pleading eyes.

"I'll call the Old Bill for you, Boss. You lot stay where you are 'cause if you scatter they will think we're involved."

Nicky gently laid down Lucy's lifeless body, and walking over to the bar, refused Jan's help as he poured himself a large, stiff shot of whisky. Heading back to the office, he flopped down in his chair, and a few minutes later, Maxi knocked and then entered.

"They're on their way, Boss. I've covered the poor little cow with a tablecloth. What the fuck is going on, I mean, it only seems to be our girls that are being targeted, and the filth don't seem to be doing much about it."

"Who was Lucy's punter?"

Maxi could only shrug his shoulders as he answered.

"She was late, so I can only guess that she must have picked a geezer up on the street, but some cunt must know something?"

"Have you checked with Rosie?"

"As far as I know, it had nothing to do with this place. Rose said the girl hadn't yet arrived for her shift and agreed with me that it could only be a pull-off on the street trick. Still don't look too good for us though."

"Are the girls still in the bar?"

"Yeah, I reminded them that you had told them to stay put."

With his nerves calmed by the whisky, Nicky walked out of the office to where the women now stood in front of the bar. A couple of them were still crying, and the others were drinking the brandies that Jan had handed out, knowing that her lover and boss wouldn't mind.

"Right! Listen and listen well, as we don't have much time. PC Plod will be here in a few minutes, and I want you all to be as friendly and helpful as you can. Obviously, you're on the game, but you do not, and I repeat, do not, work for me. Apart from that, tell the truth. I need to get to the bottom of this as soon as possible, and if the Old Bill gets there first, then so be it, so long as the cunt is taken off the street and you lot are all safe again, I don't care who catches him."

CHAPTER TWELVE

Within the hour, Soho was in uproar with car horns beeping and drivers shouting at the police. The road had been cordoned off for the entire length of Romilly Street, causing traffic issues for vehicles trying to turn off of Shaftesbury Avenue into Frith Street. Police cars seemed to be everywhere, and at least a dozen officers were positioned outside the club on the front and side entrances. Martin Gayle watched the comings and goings from the front window of his now-closed restaurant, and as he did so, he made as many notes as he could. He couldn't deny he was getting some satisfaction out of the disruption that it must be causing Nicky Stanton. Curiosity finally got the better of him, and he was desperate to find out the state of play, so donning his overcoat, he stepped out onto the street, but he hadn't got more than fifty yards before two uniformed officers approached him.

"Sorry, Sir, but you can't come down here; this is a crime scene, so the road is temporarily closed."

"It's okay, Officer, I own that restaurant over there."

Marty pointed with his finger in the direction of Drummonds, and as he looked back at the place that was once buzzing, but now somehow looked cold and sad. He felt a heavy ache in his heart."

"I don't care if you've come from Buckingham Palace; I have orders not to let anyone pass. Now you can either leave the street or go back to your premises, but you'd better decide pretty quickly."

“Can’t you just tell me what’s happened?”

The policemen looked at each other, and they both shrugged their shoulders. It couldn't do any harm, and besides, it would be common knowledge before too long.

"There has been a suspicious death, but that is all I am at liberty to share at the moment."

“What, another one?! This place is going to rack and ruin.”

With that, Marty returned to the restaurant to continue looking out of the window at the comings and goings. Sipping his freshly made coffee, he suddenly noticed movement out of the corner of his eye. Someone was loitering in the shadows, and the person seemed to be staring right back at him. He didn't recognise the stranger, but all the same, beckoned with his hand for the man to come over to the restaurant. Opening the front door, he smiled warmly.

"It's cold out tonight, and you must be bloody freezing out there. Why don't you come inside for a warm-up, and we can watch what's going on from here?"

Since finding out about his mother several days earlier, Jamie Brewer had spent every night trawling the streets of Soho. He didn't have the

first clue why, but he knew he was full of rage. Grateful for the invitation, he stepped inside the beautiful restaurant and could see by the sheets covering the furniture that it was now obviously closed.

“Is this place yours?”

"Yes, for all the good it will do me now. You know, just a couple of months ago, this restaurant was the place to be seen, and I was coining it in, but since that fucking club opened and all the shenanigans started, it's ruined me."

“Shenanigans?”

“Prostitutes.”

Jamie was surprised at the man's words, so he decided to play dumb.

“But ain’t this Soho?”

Marty stared at the stranger, trying to work out if he was taking the piss or if he was thick.

"Of course it is, but it's always been kept to certain areas, allowing other businesses to thrive. But then out of the blue, some gangster opens up, and it's a bleeding free-for-all, and my customers, some of whom had been dining here for years, well, they left in droves. I mean, when you're out for a romantic meal, who wants to see those dirty sluts plying their trade up and down the street? I'm Marty by the way, Marty Gayle."

"Pleased to meet you, Marty. I'm Jamie Brewer, and I fucking hate whores as well. As far as I'm concerned, they are nothing but scum. If you ask me, they all need wiping off the face of the earth."

The man's words shocked Marty, but he didn't comment. Jamie went on to share the story of his mother and about Wilma and the bed and breakfast.

"Blimey, you really have been pulled through the wringer, and I'm sorry to hear that, son, but I don't think they are all bad, you know."

Jamie just stared at the man as if seeing straight through him, and it unnerved Marty. A few minutes later, after accepting and downing a hot coffee, the stranger thanked Marty for his hospitality and then left. Marty was intrigued. Could the man have been the killer? Just in case, he jotted down all that Jamie had shared on one of his order pads. Now more interested than ever, he spent the rest of the evening and into the early hours glued to the window, but there wasn't much more worth reporting on.

At the club, interviews were taking place in Nicky's office, and once he'd been spoken to, he just stood around in the bar area with the others. Detective Peter Price was on night duty, and as he had attended the previous two murders along with Detective Kevin Lincoln, he had been sent with Detective Sharon Manning to get the case underway. This time, things were being looked into more carefully, as after three deaths, it now looked as if a serial killer was operating in the area, though they were under strict instructions not to mention that fact in front of the public.

When the scene of crime officers had finished, although there wasn't anything much in the way of evidence as the assault on Lucy hadn't happened where she'd died, an ambulance arrived to take the body away. By daylight, things hadn't moved on much, and Nicky and the girls were exhausted. He was also still dressed in the blood-soaked shirt, and he was desperate to get washed and changed. Finally, he knocked on the door of his own office, and it riled him when he heard the detective call out 'Enter'.

"Mr Stanton, what can I do for you?"

Nicky had taken an instant dislike to the pompous Detective as soon as they had met, but his feelings had now escalated to loathing.

"Any chance we can go now, guvnor? Only the girls are knackered. None of us has had any sleep, and there ain't anything else we can tell you."

Peter Price was new to his rank, and to say it had gone to his head was an understatement. He looked Nicky up and down and was about to deny the request, just because he could, when Detective Manning spoke, and as she was senior to her colleague regarding time served, Peter didn't argue.

"That will be fine, Mr Stanton. We might need to speak to you and your staff further along, but we have all of your addresses."

"Do you want me to leave the keys with you, but

I might add, you will be responsible for the club and stock."

"No, that's fine, I think we're done here anyway."

A few minutes later, Nicky locked up the Club, and everyone headed for their homes.

The following night, as it was one of Soho's busiest nights of the week, Nicky had decided to open the club. After what had happened, it went against the grain, but profit always had to come first, and already closing after the previous killings, he'd soon realised it didn't make any difference to what had happened if he opened or not. Arriving early, he summoned Maxi into the office and instructed his right-hand man to go through the list of women who had previously applied to work at the club but hadn't been successful. It was like a meat market, and even though he felt guilty, he needed to restock, or the punters would soon start to complain or even disappear altogether.

"We need three, but get five or six to come in, and I'll pick the best of the bunch."

Although he thought it was heartless and a little disrespectful, Maxi Willmore did as he was asked, and by ten thirty that morning, four women were sitting in the front foyer, all eyeing each other suspiciously. Street work was a competitive game, and Nicky's Club was known to be a good earner, so they all wanted jobs. The first to be called into the office were two Polish women by the names of Agata Bukoski and Lena

Kaminski. The two were friends, but where Lena spoke good English, Agata's command of the language was poor to say the least.

"I can promise you, Mr Stanton, that what my friend lacks in her vocabulary skills she more than makes up for when she's on her back. That said, Agata is very good at maths, so she won't allow anyone to rip her or you off."

Nicky held his hands together as if in prayer and touched his lips with the tips of his index fingers as he thought. Neither of the women was ugly, and if truth be told, he was getting desperate, so he decided to give them both a week's trial starting that night.

"One last thing, I don't want you encouraging men from your neck of the woods into my club. The last thing I need is a bunch of drunken fucking Polak's coming in and wrecking the place."

Nicky had experienced problems with Eastern Europeans in the past; they drank too much and were always aggressive in their manner, and he didn't want a repeat performance. The women thanked him, and as Agata opened the door to leave, Maxi was about to usher in Alina Balan. As the two Polish women passed Alina, Agata spat on the floor, and Nicky was out of his seat in seconds.

"You two, back in here now!!!"

Lena gave a look of daggers to her friend, and Agata hung her head in shame. Work was hard

to come by, and she now realised she might have ruined a good thing before it had even started.

"Now I don't know what your fucking problem is, but if you've got a beef with this woman, then the offer is off the table."

As soon as Nicky had set eyes on Alina, he knew she would be great for business. Romanian by birth, it was obvious by her skin tone that she also had gypsy blood, and the punters would love her olive skin and raven hair.

"I am sorry, Mr Stanton, please forgive my friend. For some reason, her family hates gypsies, but please do not think it is a Polish thing; on the whole, our two cultures get along very well. I will make sure that nothing else happens."

As they were about to leave, Lena looked Alina in the eyes and mouthed the word 'Sorry'. After Nicky had explained the terms, Alina Balan was also hired on the spot. She was gracious, and Nicky knew it must have taken a lot for her not to react to being spat at. Since taking over the Club, Nicky had spent more and more time away from his other businesses. He checked in from time to time, but the general running had been left in the hands of Arty Clements. Arty had worked for Bernie Stanton for almost twenty years, knew the business like the back of his hand, and there was no one Nicky trusted more, well, in this line of work anyway. Takings were brought to the club every Friday night, and the

two men would spend an hour or two going through plans and any issues that had arisen. Flicking through his contacts, he dialled Arty's number and the mobile only rang twice before it was answered.

"Hi, Mr Stanton, everything okay, nothing happened to the old man, has it?"

"No, no, nothing like that, but I need to speak to you, fancy meeting up for some lunch?"

The two agreed to meet at Milk Beach Soho, on Greek Street. Arty knew his boss liked high-end, so he was in for a good feed and had arrived several minutes early and was already consuming an expensive cocktail, as Nicky always picked up the bill. Taking a seat and ordering a drink, Nicky studied the menu and didn't start to talk about what he wanted until the food had been ordered.

“So, you’ve heard about my Toms.”

“Yeah, nasty fucking business that.”

"I've lost three girls so far, and I very much doubt that's the end of it. Don't you think it seems strange that they were all my girls?"

“What, you think it might be personal?”

"I've wracked my fucking brains, Arty, and I can't think of any other reason. The Old Bill is investigating, but getting them to solve a case is as rare as fucking rocking horse shit. I want some of the men on it; they can get answers that the filth could never get."

"Certainly, Boss, how many were you thinking

of?"

“Four or five should be enough. Get them to visit the other clubs and speak to the Toms, also see if the street workers have had any aggro.” Sharing his woes and setting a plan in motion suddenly made Nicky feel a bit better. If anyone could get info on this shit show, it would be his men.

"There's something else I need to run by you, Nicky, well, it's a bit of a problem really."

Nicky sighed. How much more aggravation could he take?

“Fire away.”

"You know the heist we've got planned over at Macey's warehouse? It seems the bloke on the inside has changed his mind. I wouldn't normally bother you, but he's a big cunt and getting him to comply would mean doing some serious damage. If he turns up at work black and blue, then the whole fucking job could be in jeopardy."

Nicky pulled a pen and a small notebook out of his pocket and handed them over.

“Give me his name and address”

With that, the food came, and all talk of business ended.

Returning to the club, Nicky summoned Maxi Willmore to the office.

"I'm going to be gone for the rest of the day, so you're in charge. I'll try and get back later, but if I don't manage it, you'll have to sort out the new

girls. Bring Rosie up to speed and tell her to go easy on them."

Returning to Jan’s flat, she was napping on the bed but woke when he entered the bedroom.

"Hi, babe, I didn't expect to see you so early in the day."

Nicky bent and kissed her forehead. He loved her so much, and that thought momentarily made him feel bad, as he had never felt that way about his wife.

“I want us to go and look at some flats, flats in better areas that are a lot safer than here.”

Since he'd moved in, Janice had given up nursing, and Nicky had taken over paying all the bills, so she wasn't really in a position to argue.

“But I like it here.”

"Babe, you ain't been in London long, and take it from me, Paddington is a shit hole. I stopped off at the agents on the way back and have picked up a few details. They said if we fancied any of them, we could view them late this afternoon. Have a butcher's while I put the kettle on."

Handing Jan five A4 sheets, he left her to it. He didn't want to scare her unnecessarily, but after the recent events, he didn't feel any woman connected to him was safe, at least until that maniac had been caught or killed, and that depended on who got to him first. He had one of his men sitting outside his parents' home, and now he had to take care of his lover. Jan instantly discounted the first property as it was

an entire house, but the other four were two-bedroomed flats. The first in Kensington looked nice, as did the next two in Chelsea, but when she looked at the monthly rent, she let out a gasp. The fourth was smaller and cheaper, but it appealed to Jan. Pimlico looked nice, and the Regency façade of the building that housed two apartments looked welcoming. When Nicky called her through to the kitchen, she handed him her choice, knowing that he would approve or he wouldn't have given her the details.

"Really, when you could have had much bigger in Kensington or Chelsea?"

"Size isn't everything, you know."

The way he raised his eyebrows made her laugh out loud.

"You're the first woman I've ever heard say that!"

"You are funny, but seriously, there's something homely about that one, so can we have a look at it?"

Nicky studied the details. It was the entire first floor of the former house, making it more secure than the ground floor.

"I'll phone the agents right away."

That afternoon, as they pulled up outside the property, Jan started to get excited. This would be their first real home that was chosen together, and she couldn't wait to start decorating. Nicky was impressed; the building had recently been renovated, and the fixtures and fittings were all

high quality, not to mention the fact that the room sizes were huge. There were two sizable bedrooms and a box room that he could use as an office, along with a front room with a fireplace and a very modern kitchen. It was nice, but what had sold it to Nicky was the state-of-the-art security system. On the main street door, there was a digital entry and a camera; further in, there was another camera. The front door to the flat was reinforced with a high-tech locking system and a spy hole. After Nicky paid six months' rent in advance, the agent assured him that he could have the paperwork done within twenty-four hours, and the keys would be available from late the following afternoon. Happy that he had made sure Jan would be safe, he gave her his credit card and five grand and told her to go and buy furniture. Her place had come fully furnished, so apart from her bed and clothes, there was very little to move. Nicky dropped her off in front of some high-end stores in Chelsea and then headed back to the club. For a while, Jan browsed the shops but couldn't believe the exorbitant prices. When she came across the large British Heart Foundation shop, she just had to go inside. Within thirty minutes, she had purchased a tan leather three-seater sofa and two tub chairs that looked brand new, a bookcase, a rug and 6 cushions, the latter actually did happen to be new. In total, she had spent a little over five hundred pounds, and that

included delivery the following afternoon. Next, she headed for Chapel Market in Islington, where she bought bedding, towels and kitchen items. By the time she had finished, Jan was worn out but far too excited to go home, so instead she headed for the club, eager to share her successful shopping buys with Nicky.

CHAPTER THIRTEEN

At Charing Cross police station, the incident room had been set up, but no one seemed to be doing very much. It was always difficult when a Tom got killed, as no one on the street wanted to talk, especially when it came to the Old Bill. A lot of the time, women working the streets who were beaten or killed didn't have any family. For those who did, the relationships were often strained, so background information was almost impossible to obtain. Chief Inspector Henry Trafford wasn't a happy man. Now that the murders had increased in number, he was getting heat from the top brass to wrap this case up as soon as possible, but as yet, they were nowhere, and he had little faith in Detective Price. Peter had only recently been promoted, and Henry knew he was still wet behind the ears. As for Detective Manning, well, she had never actually worked a murder, and in any case, she didn't seem to have the drive needed to really get her teeth into an investigation. The Chief's phone rang for the umpteenth time that day, and snatching up the handset, he barked into the receiver.

"Yes!!!"

"Sorry, Chief, but I have the editor of the Mail on the line, not to mention that a couple of the Red Tops seem to have camped out in the rear car park and are causing a nuisance to the patrol

cars coming in and out."

Henry sighed heavily. This was all he needed.

"Okay. Get someone to go out and tell them that I will give a short statement in the next few minutes."

Walking into the incident room, Chief Trafford made his way over to Peter's desk.

"For fucks sake, tell me you've got something?"

Peter slowly shook his head; he knew this case could make or break his career, and with how things were going, it seemed the latter was favourable.

"What about CCTV on Romilly Street?"

"No luck. There are a couple of cameras, but one is broken, and the other has had paint or something sprayed onto the lens."

"Well, I have to face the press, and I've got sod all to give them, so I suppose that once again I will be elaborating on absolutely nothing!"

The chief slowly walked down to the rear car park and took a deep breath before he opened the doors. As soon as he stepped through, cameras began to flash, and reporters all vied for a key position as they shouted out a barrage of questions, none of which the Chief would or could truthfully answer.

"Good morning, Ladies and gentlemen. As you are all aware, this case is in its infancy, and we are currently working on several leads. I suggest you all return to your respective offices, and as soon as there is any news, I will issue another

statement. Until then, I have nothing more to say."

Sue Davidson, a reporter for the Mirror and known for her aggressive line of questioning, boomed out words that instantly silenced everyone else.

"As it's now three murders, is there a serial killer on the loose?"

Chief Trafford took several seconds before he answered, and the crowd of press waited for his reply with bated breath.

"It's too early to say, and we still don't know if the cases are connected in any way."

"I have it on good authority that they were all prostitutes, and I thought when the number reached three victims, it automatically became classed as a serial offender?"

Henry Trafford lowered his head as he turned to go back inside.

"As I have already said, there will be further statements when we have more news. Now, if you will excuse me, I have a case to solve, and it won't happen if I'm standing out here giving a press release to all of you lot."

Walking as quickly as he could, Henry re-entered the building while Sue was still calling out that the public had a right to know and that he hadn't answered her question.

By early evening, Nicky had his men at the club. With the five men Arty had sent over and with club doormen, they totalled nine in all and were

crammed into Nicky's office like sardines. Sighing heavily and not really knowing where to start, he cleared his throat and then spoke.

"Right, for the time being, you will all be on the night shift with limited work in the day."

There was a low muttering of discontent in the room, but no one actually had the balls to say anything outright. When Nicky had taken over from his father, there had been widespread assumption that the rules would be relaxed, but it had been the exact opposite.

"I know it ain't ideal, but I'm under pressure here, and I would welcome your fucking help. Anyone who ain't prepared to step up can fuck right off here and now! I have spoken to Arty, and he is aware of the situation. I know it interferes with the firm's plans somewhat, but that can't be helped, and at the end of the day, I pay the fucking wages! I want each of you to pal up with one of my Toms. After that, keep your distance, but when they leave to service a punter, I want you to discreetly follow and make sure they're safe. The Old Bill is about, but as we all know, they're about as much use as a wet fucking fart. Off you go then."

The men all filed out and headed to the main area where the women, who had already been told about what was happening, were waiting. Jan was working the bar, and as happy as she was about the new flat, she also had a bad feeling in her gut that she couldn't shake off.

This was the first night of trading since Lucy's murder, and even though the place had been cleaned from top to bottom, she couldn't help staring at the spot on the floor where the young girl had died.

"You okay, babe? Babe?"

It took a second for his voice to register, and as she looked up, her eyes were full of tears.

"Oh, sorry, Nicky, I was just lost in thought for a moment. I can't get the vision out of my head of her just lying there. That poor, poor girl, she had her whole life ahead of her."

He hated seeing her upset, and walking to the back of the bar, Nicky took her in his arms, not bothering who saw them.

"I know, sweetheart, but there's nothing we can do about it. Why don't you go home and start packing your stuff? I'll get Maxi to drive you."

"Thanks, but I'm alright, I'd rather be here around people, and besides, it will take me all of half an hour to pack, so I might as well do it in the morning."

Nodding his head, Nicky kissed her again and then retreated to his office.

The first of the girls to hook a punter was Josette Solomon. Standing just over six feet tall in her stocking feet, she was a firm favourite with the men. Josette had quickly picked up the Soho way of talking, but the twang of her Nigerian accent was still evident and husky. Her almost black skin was silky smooth, and with lips that

were really full without a hint of filler in sight, many of the punters opted for a blow job instead of full sex. Josette was more than happy with that deal, as she could turn even more tricks by not having to wash in between clients. Alan Vincent had palled up as her minder, and when she left through the side door with a rather short and stout man, Alan followed closely behind. The bed and breakfast, much to the anger of Ahsan Abbasi, was no longer being used, and he would probably be forced to close it in the next few months as no one wanted to holiday in Soho at the moment. It was a great place to visit, a real eye-opener at times, but since news of the murders had broken, workmen and tourists on a budget now wanted to stay in the better, safer areas. With Nicky ending his contract with Abbasi, a small garage further down Romilly Street had been hired out indefinitely. Overnight, a couple of carpenters who did all of Nicky's work had been called in and had sectioned off the area into cubicles, each with a curtain to give at least some modicum of privacy. It was crude, and there were no washing facilities save for a bowl, some bottled water and a pack of wet wipes, but it would suffice until something else could be arranged or the work needed could be undertaken properly. When Josette and her punter entered the makeshift building, Alan Vincent waited at the corner of the alleyway. The act was over

quickly, and as the short, stout man exited with a smile on his face, Alan went straight in, calling out to Josette as he did so.

"You alright, sweetheart?"

The curtain opened, and Josette popped her head out.

"Fine, thanks, babe. I just need to clean myself up; that dirty old bastard hadn't emptied his sacks in weeks, it's as thick as fucking tar down there. I know it's my choice, but sometimes they make me want to fucking heave"

Her words and tone made Alan laugh. The Toms were a breed all of their own, but you couldn't be off liking them.

"Okay, as long as you're alright. Well, I need to take a piss. I'll be back in a couple of minutes to take you back to the club."

Alan walked to the rear of the garage and, releasing his penis, let out a sigh of relief as he urinated. In the cubicle, Josette was just pulling down her skirt when the curtain was pulled open. Expecting it to be Alan, she was momentarily struck dumb when she saw her attacker. As they raised a knife, the blade glinted in the light, and Josette lifted her arm in a vain attempt to protect herself, but it was hopeless. She let out a piercing scream and at the same time called out.

"Alan!!! Alan, help me, for God's sake, help meeeee!!?"

Alan Vincent didn't bother to finish urinating,

and he knew he would have piss-soaked trousers, but it didn't deter him, and with his flies still open, he ran around to the front just as Josette staggered out clutching her heavily bleeding arm. After taking off his jacket and wrapping the wound the best he could, Alan searched the sides of the building, but the attacker was nowhere to be seen. Gently, he supported her as he slowly led her back to the club, but they entered via the side door so as not to bring too much attention to the situation. Rosie knew instantly that something was wrong, as did Janice, and they both followed Josette and Alan through to the office. Nicky was out of his seat in a second and barked orders for Rosie to get the first aid kit. As soon as the makeshift dressing was removed, blood flowed like water, and the arm bone was visible. Nicky quickly replaced the jacket and told Alan to go and tell Maxi to bring the car around to the side. Together, Maxi and Alan helped Josette back through the club, out of the door and into the car. Maxi opened the passenger side, but as Josette got in, she passed out, and Maxi realised she had lost a lot more blood than they had realised. St Thomas's was the nearest accident and emergency hospital, and Maxi drove at breakneck speed. It was only a ten-minute journey, but Josette was bleeding so badly that he wasn't sure she would make it.

Back in the club, Nicky was pacing up and down

in the office. He'd tried to protect them, but it wasn't working, and he didn't know where else to turn. The door opened, but he didn't look up to see who it was.

"Babe, you have to call the police."

Suddenly, he stopped pacing and looked at Janice with a confused expression.

"Call the Old Bill? Are you mad? It was a different situation with the murders. I had no choice then, but Josette will be okay, and I don't want the plods down here again. It's fucking killing my business, babe."

His dismissive tone made her angry, and she marched over to where he stood and grabbed his wrists.

"Forget your stupid criminal rules; this isn't about you. It's about those poor women. Josette must have seen her attacker, and that bastard has to be caught. Now, as far as I'm concerned, it doesn't matter who does it as long as he's found because believe me, Nicky, if he isn't, you won't have a business left to protect for much longer."

Her words hit home, and tapping into his mobile, he called Maxi's number.

"Boss?"

"How is she?"

"Lost a lot of blood as the cunt had cut an artery, and the bone is broken. Fuck, he must have lashed out hard! They are operating on her arm as we speak."

"Good, now listen carefully. I want you to call the Old Bill, but don't mention my name. When Josette is in recovery, tell her to cooperate the best she can. I know it really goes against the grain for the girls to talk to the filth, but these are unusual times, and we need all the help we can get. We need to do anything we can to catch the cunt, and if that means breaking a few taboos, then so be it."

Nicky then called in Alan Vincent, and he wasn't pleased that the man had left Josette alone.

"Right, you cunt, explain yourself, and it had better be fucking good."

"I'm so sorry, Mr Stanton, truly I am. I waited for her punter to leave, and I was desperate for a piss. I was gone for a matter of seconds when I heard her scream, but the cunt was on their toes before I could get back. I didn't mess about, Mr Stanton, I even pissed my trousers rather than take time getting back to her. How is the poor little cow?"

"Not good, they're operating as we speak. Okay, you can get off now and keep your fucking head down, the girls will be baying for your blood."

Due to the three previous murders, the police were at the hospital within thirty minutes, though it would be a further three hours before Josette was conscious and even then, she was incoherent and not able to make much sense. Two hours later, when she was at last lucid and

could communicate, Maxi slipped in unseen through the staff tearoom which also allowed him access to the side rooms. After checking that she was okay, he passed on Nicky's orders and the story he had been told to give her. She gently squeezed his arm with her good hand.

"What about my kids? The sitter will only stay until two, and it must be getting late?"

"Don't worry about that, I've found someone to watch them, sweetheart, just you rest."

As soon as he knew she was alright, Maxi left the hospital and returned to the club. Rosie Goodson had agreed to take Josette's kids until she was back home, but for now, Maxi would collect them and take them back to the club until Rosie finished her shift.

At the hospital, Detectives Price and Manning were soon standing at Josette's bedside, and a uniformed officer was posted outside of the side room she'd been put in, albeit a little late in the day. The victim's details had been gained from the ward clerk after Maxi had booked Josette in, and Peter was grateful that they at least had a living victim this time.

"I am sorry this has happened to you, Miss Solomon. Now we have reason to believe that your attacker may have been the same person who has been assaulting other working girls in the area."

"Assaulting!? You mean fucking murdering them!"

"Possibly, but I can't confirm anything regarding an ongoing case. Did you get a good look at your attacker?"

Before Peter had finished asking his question, Sharon Manning had removed her notebook and was eagerly waiting to write down anything that might be helpful.

"You don't need to confirm anything, Sunshine, I might look as if I just stepped off of the last fucking banana boat, but I can guarantee I didn't."

Neither detective knew how to respond to the woman's racial comment, at least they thought it was racial, but given the colour of the woman's skin, they couldn't be sure, so they just looked at each other in stunned silence, not knowing how to proceed.

"As for seeing them, no, not really, the light was dim. I suppose they were around five seven or eight, definitely shorter than me, but then that ain't hard. They were dressed from head to toe in black and wore black leather gloves. They also had a full-face balaclava on, so I didn't see their face. There was a big knife, more like a machete, at least I think it was, but that's about as much as I can tell you."

"That's still helpful, and we will be back in the morning, maybe you might have remembered something else."

Just as the detectives were about to walk out of the room, Josette spoke again.

"There is one more thing, they was white. I saw their eyes, and they were like ice, the coldest blue I have ever seen."

It wasn't much, but to Peter, it was at least a lead, the first they had, and the two detectives hurried back to the station. The wipe boards in the incident room now at last had something concrete written on them. It was the early hours of the morning, and the

Chief wouldn't be in until nine, but Peter hoped that the snippet they now had, no matter how small, would appease his boss until they could find out more.

CHAPTER FOURTEEN

Nicky was up early; it was moving day, but he had something more important to deal with before he could even think about anything else. Being as quiet as he could so as not to wake Jan, he slipped out of the flat just before seven-thirty. Sitting in the car, he removed the scrap of paper Arty Clements had scribbled on and read the contents. William Davidson 15 Adler Street, Whitechapel. The previous evening, and using Jan's laptop and printer without her knowledge, Nicky had written a note. He had been careful to wear latex gloves and had pulled a sheet of paper out of the middle of an unopened ream so as not to leave any DNA evidence. Breaking the seal on a packet of envelopes and again wearing the gloves, he now placed the note inside one of them, but didn't seal it, as there was still something very important to include. The drive over to Whitechapel was relatively quick due to the hour and it being a Saturday. Nicky parked up opposite number 15 and, removing a burner from his pocket, made sure his phone was at the ready as he sat in wait. It wasn't a school day, so he didn't know how long this was all going to take, but luckily, within fifteen minutes, the front door opened, and a woman appeared with two little girls. Nicky thanked the Lord for weekend extracurricular activities as he began to snap away, and once he had reeled off ten or

eleven pictures, he started up the engine and pulled out into the street. Knowing the area well, next, he drove over to Aldgate High Street and, after parking up, made his way to Snappy Snaps. Luckily, the shop opened at eight thirty, so he was able to walk straight in. The shop had a fast turnover, and handing over the phone, he asked for the photos to be printed as soon as possible.

"No probs, babe. Take a seat over there, it shouldn't be too long."

Shayzee, the Saturday girl, chatted away on her mobile phone at the same time as serving, and she was so engrossed in her conversation that she didn't notice the customer was wearing rubber gloves. It was annoying to Nicky as he watched her continually toss her head full of braids; she never would have gotten a job in his club. The development took all of ten minutes, and after paying in cash and with the photographs in his hand, Nicky returned to his car. Once inside, he carefully opened up the packet and chose the clearest image, which he didn't mind admitting, happened to be very good. Next, he inserted it into the envelope and, with a dab of water from a bottle that he'd remembered to bring along, he secured the flap down. Scrawling on the front, he wrote the name William Davidson. Macey's Warehouse was situated close to Cannon Street underground on Allhallows Lane. The owner,

Lawrence Macey had been in the storage business for over twenty years, and although they advertised as holders of fine wines and spirits, it had been brought to the attention of Arty Clements that the company held a lot more than booze inside. Lawrence Macey had been on the fiddle for years, and stashed in a safe at the rear of the warehouse was all of his ill-got gains, five hundred thousand in used notes that couldn't be traced. It had taken a while to plan, but after a lot of investigating and discussions with Nicky Stanton, it was agreed that it was too good an opportunity to miss, so they had forged ahead. Since opening the club and meeting Jan, Nicky had distanced himself from the other businesses, but even he knew you didn't look a gift horse in the mouth. It was decided that the best point of entry would be via assistance from the security guard. Three guards worked for the company in shifts, and Arty had looked into all of the men's backgrounds. William Davidson had been the one with the most to lose. A family man with plenty of debts, it didn't take much to get him on board. He was offered a payday of ten grand, and all he had to do was open the door and turn a blind eye. It was agreed he would receive a bit of a beating so that his cover story of being overcome by four men in balaclavas was believable, but a week before the heist, and for some unknown reason, he had started to get cold feet. He wasn't sleeping, and

the more it played on his mind, the more he knew he couldn't go through with it. Phoning Arty, William explained that he had changed his mind and he was pulling out, but the haul was far too profitable to let go, and that's when Arty had told Nicky over lunch that they now had a problem.

Nicky drove towards Allhallows Lane but parked up a short distance away. About to carry out his plan, he was stopped when his private mobile began to ring. It was Jan, and he had to answer, or she would start to worry, so sighing heavily, he pressed accept.

"Hi, babe, what's up?"

"Nothing, I was just a bit surprised to find you gone when I got up. Is everything okay?"

"Yeah, sure, I just had a bit of business to sort out before the move. You packed yet?"

"Yes, and it took me all of fifteen minutes."

They both laughed, and he could tell by her tone that she was excited about the new flat.

"Can you put my stuff in a couple of black bags?. I should be back within the hour, and then we can get moving to our new little love nest."

Jan giggled, and Nicky couldn't help but smile as he ended the call. Switching off his phone so he didn't get any more interruptions, he pulled a baseball cap from the glove compartment and, with his jacket collar pulled up high around his neck, he set off for Macey's warehouse. Due to it being a Saturday, there was a limited workforce

on duty, so the front gates were locked. Nicky pushed the envelope into the post box and then rang the bell. William Davidson, known as Billy to his friends and loved ones, had been looking out of the window and saw the stranger approach. Placing his mug of tea down, he made his way outside to retrieve the envelope. When he was once more in the comfort of the security office, he was about to place the letter in the mail tray when he glanced at the name and froze. Tentatively, he opened the envelope and removed the paper and photograph. Seeing that it was an image of his wife and children made his blood run cold.

Dear Billy

You do not renege on an agreement. This morning, I had the pleasure of seeing your beautiful little family, but they will only stay that way if you change your mind and help us with our plan. If I have to contact you a second time, they will suffer. Don't think of calling the Old Bill, as they won't be able to save you. Send a text to this number to confirm everything is back on track, or suffer the consequences.

Billy puffed out his cheeks and knew he was royally fucked. Born and bred in the East End, he was only too aware of what would happen if he didn't do as he was told. It was okay to have morals, but morals only went so far; they didn't pay the bills or keep you safe, so he had no alternative but to do as he'd been told. Sending

a message to Arty's number, Billy sat back in his chair, knowing that his fate was sealed. A few minutes later, Nicky got a call from a very happy Arty Clements.

"I don't know what you did or said, but I've just had a text on one of the burners. Seems, our friend has had a change of heart."

Nicky didn't reply and, hanging up, he drove home with a smile on his face to begin his new life with Jan, and he couldn't wait.

CHAPTER FIFTEEN

That afternoon, unbeknownst to his detectives, Chief Inspector Henry Trafford had been summoned to New Scotland Yard. His ensuing appointment with Deputy Chief Superintendent Madden had him on edge and full of nerves. Henry was expecting to get hauled over the coals for something that wasn't his fault and completely out of his hands. Sitting outside the Deputy Superintendent's office, he could feel his hands begin to sweat, and when the door opened, Henry quickly wiped them on his dark trousers. Oh, how he hated putting on the uncomfortable uniform; it was itchy, and the jacket felt like it weighed a ton, but when coming to the yard, it was mandatory.

"Come on in, Inspector."

Henry did as he was asked and then took a seat when it was offered.

"I assume that you have some idea why you have been asked to the Yard?"

Henry cleared his throat and again wiped his hands on his trousers.

"I assume it's in connection with the recent murders in Soho?"

"Your assumption is correct. Now I've gone against protocol and left out the Superintendent in this meeting, as what I have to say has come from the top, and I mean the very top, Henry. The press office of the Chief Constable is being bombarded daily by the press, and it has to stop immediately. We are all now treating this as a serial crime, and under no circumstances do we

want a repeat of the Ripper Investigation, as we both know how that turned out and the length of time it took. The city relies too heavily on the tourist trade to risk a downturn in visitors, not to mention the fact that I've now got the Mayor on my case as well. Now I'm aware that you've recently had a change of team and that you've also promoted from within. I am in no way suggesting that your detectives are not capable, but they are still learning, and as time is of the essence, I am bringing in an experienced team to run this particular investigation."

Inside, Henry was seething, but he knew better than to voice that opinion, not if he hoped for further promotion in his career.

"Might I ask who the team will be?"

"I'm sure you remember Anna Draycott? She did sterling work on the snuff murders, and while there were strict orders from above when it came to charges not being brought against any one individual, Anna and her team did solve the case."

Henry recalled all that had gone on, and even though the files had been sealed, the force was a real hub of gossip, and much of what should have remained top secret had eventually filtered down through the rank and file.

"Anna has just been promoted to Chief Inspector over at Tottenham. Lou Garner has finally retired, and hers was the only name he put forward. Anna will bring her team with her, and

while she is at Charing Cross, I want you to replace her at Tottenham Station. Your men will remain on the case, as we need as many bodies on this as we can spare. I can assure you this transfer is only temporary, but we have to get results and get them fast."

Henry Trafford smiled and nodded his head in agreement, but in reality, he was angrier than he had ever been, though he didn't dare show it. They were replacing him without any discussion, and it showed that the top brass had no faith in him, which cut deeply. Deputy Chief Superintendent Madden stood up and offered his hand, a silent motion that ended the meeting, and when Henry was once again sitting in his car, he slammed both palms down onto the steering wheel several times with rage.

Early the following morning, Detective Price was hanging around waiting for the Chief to arrive, and when his boss walked in, Peter started grinning from ear to ear.

"Sir, I have some good news."

"Not out here, detective, come into my office and close the door behind you."

Henry didn't take off his coat, and walking over to his desk, he placed down a small cardboard box and began to fill it with his private items, items he didn't want that bitch looking at.

"What's going on, Sir?"

"I've been taken off the case, and I'm being forced to move over to Tottenham for the

foreseeable future. Chief Inspector Anna Draycott and her team will be taking over here."

"But, Sir, that's not fair. I'm sure if given a bit more time, we can crack this case."

Henry Trafford was just about at the end of his tether; he hadn't slept a wink last night, and the lack of sleep was beginning to take its toll. He snapped at Peter, which was unlike his usual friendly manner.

"Fair! Fucking fair! Do you think I don't know that, but what the fuck do you expect me to do when the order has come directly from Deputy Chief Superintendent Madden?"

“So does that mean I’m off the case as well?”

"No, it doesn't. As I said, DCI Draycott will be bringing her team with her, but the Super wants as many bodies on this as possible. Let me give you a piece of advice, Peter, for what it's worth. Anna Draycott is known to be one hard bitch so don't cross her. She is also very capable and has a high success rate when it comes to solving crimes, the snuff killings come to mind, and that was a fucking hard one to crack, not to mention there was a high-level cover-up, but you didn't hear that from me. Now what was it you wanted to tell me?"

Detective Price relayed all that Josette had said, but now it somehow didn't seem that important. He was told to pass on the information to Anna, and within ten minutes, Henry Trafford had left the station and was on his way to his new,

hopefully temporary position.

Anna Draycott had been informed of the secondment a day before Henry had been called to New Scotland Yard, and she was over the moon. Since all the loose ends had been tied up regarding Maggie McKay and her sick network, there hadn't been much for Anna to really get her teeth into. She'd been following the Soho murders with interest, and when the Deputy Chief Superintendent had summoned her, she already had an inkling of what it would mean. Returning to Tottenham station, Anna had called her team into her office to break the news. Since her promotion, Detective Carl Shaw had moved up to Detective Sergeant, and along with Beth Saunders, Dave Wilson and of course her trusty Sargent Steve Johnson, they were all chomping at the bit to get started. They had gone over the case to date in detail, but in all honesty, there wasn't much to go on. By the time Henry Trafford arrived, Anna had already left, and unlike Henry, her personal possessions were still in situ. As much as the clutter annoyed him, it also pleased him because if she hadn't cleared her desk, then she was expecting to return.

At Charing Cross Station, Carl, Beth and Dave entered the incident room, and all eyes were on them. Detective Price was almost hostile as Anna's team looked for somewhere to place their stuff, but there didn't seem to be anywhere available. D.S. Carl Shaw walked over to where

Peter sat with his feet up on the desk.

"Where do you want us, Pal?"

"I ain't your pal, and if you think you can come in here and take over, you can fucking think again. We were managing just fine until my Chief was ousted for some piece of skirt."

Carl didn't pull rank; he would save that for later, but there was no way he would let anyone slag Anna off without lashing out.

"Chief Inspector Draycott, ain't as you put it, 'a piece of skirt'. She's got more balls than most of this station put together. If you're going to try and badmouth her, then at least have the fucking balls to do it to her face, but a word of warning, sunshine, you won't dare do it twice, and, if you were doing just fine, then we wouldn't be here, now would we? So, just shut your fucking trap and do some work!"

With that, Carl walked over to a large, cluttered desk and, with one swipe of his forearm, cleared the contents onto the floor.

"This will do us, Beth, you take that side, and I'll sit here."

Pulling over a chair, he glared at Peter Price when he saw that the man was about to open his mouth again. Detective Dave Wilson walked to the far end of the room to a small desk that was topped with several boxes. Unlike his colleague, he gently lifted the boxes and stacked them neatly on the floor. Each desk had a landline telephone, and the new team instantly set to

work. Peter Price watched mesmerised as they dialled different sources, and the bombardment of questions began. There was so much urgency, not to mention energy, in their actions, something that hadn't occurred during his own investigation. A few minutes later, Sharon Manning walked in, and when she saw what was going on, she stopped dead in her tracks. With a flick of her head, she motioned for Peter to join her out in the hallway.

"What the fuck is going on, Pete, and who the hell are they?"

"They, Detective, are the team that's taking over the Soho murders, but don't get your knickers in a twist as we're still on the case. The Chief has been temporarily moved over to Tottenham, but their boss ain't deemed to show her face here yet."

"Her?"

"You heard me, none other than the famous Anna Draycott."

"Really? That's fantastic! I can't wait to work with her."

"What the fuck are you on about? She's only gone and got the Guvnor moved, passed over, which won't do his career any good."

"Maybe she has, but the woman's a legend, Pete, and mark my words, we can both learn a lot from her."

Peter slowly shook his head but didn't say another word as he walked back into the

incident room.

While the unrest was happening in Charing Cross, Anna and Sergeant Johnson were heading for the pathology lab at St John and St Elizabeth Hospital over on Grove End Road, North London. Mike Hanks and Anna had history, and it wasn't good, but as the senior pathologist, Mike was at the top of his field. Unfortunately for anyone who had to deal with him, he was also a very rude and abrupt man. Anna had clashed with him several times over the years, and while they didn't really like each other, she had always felt there was at least some level of mutual respect. Since the snuff murders, she hadn't had any cause to see him, and now she wasn't looking forward to the impending reunion. In the past, Mike had appeared to be dismissive of her, and it always seemed to be in front of her colleagues, which made it much worse. After taking the lift down to the bowels of the building, Steve Johnson rang the bell, and they waited for someone to let them in. Strangely, it was Mike himself, and Anna was just about to say something sarcastic, but stopped herself; it wouldn't be professional or help matters.

"Anna, how nice to see you. Sargent Johnson, not pensioned you off yet, I see."

Steve didn't reply; he loathed the man as much as his boss did and never engaged in conversation unless it was absolutely necessary.

"Hello, Mike, are you well?"

"Fine, thanks, but I'm sure you're not here to enquire about my health, so what can I do for you, Anna?"

"I'm sure you are already aware that my team has taken over the Soho inquiry. There's very little to go on, and before you ask, yes, I have read the autopsy reports in great detail, but I just wondered if there was anything at all you could add. Are the toxicology reports back yet?"

"They have just come in, but there was nothing suspicious in them. The last victim did have herpes, but in her line of work, I suppose that's to be expected. What I can tell you is that, after further tests, I can now confirm that the murder weapon was a large Bowie knife. The original was developed in Louisiana in 1826, but this knife is not the usual run-of-the-mill kind of Bowie. The one used is what is commonly called a tactical Bowie, and though razor sharp, the edge is jagged. Mike pulled an image from his drawer and handed it to Anna. The teeth on the serrated edge curled back slightly, almost like small hooks, and Anna furrowed her brow.

"That must have been agonising?"

"Just a tad, I would imagine, Chief Inspector."

Anna was somewhat taken aback; she didn't think he would know about her promotion or, at the very least, mention it, but she wasn't going to elaborate on his last sentence.

"The first victim was stabbed directly in the

chest, and the third in the abdomen, and death would have taken several minutes. With the second, it was different; she put up a fight, and as my report stated, there were numerous defensive wounds on her arms and hands. It was futile, and when her throat was slashed several times, the wounds were so deep that her larynx and oesophagus were severed. Death was due to blood loss from the carotid artery and jugular vein, and it would have occurred in a few seconds, so although the initial attack would have been terribly painful, her end would have been over far sooner than the other two victims."

“I don’t suppose you have an idea where the knife could have been purchased.”

"Sorry, but no, I don’t. If pushed, though, I would hazard a guess at somewhere abroad. These knives are generally used by hunters and campers and are perfect for close-quarter fighting, which is exactly how they were used here. Strangely, even though most of the blades are produced in Sheffield, they are most popular in the good old US of A. Whoever your killer is, he knows exactly how to use the weapon, and of course, yes, you can purchase them here, but statistically speaking, they are not a very common choice. I could be wrong, I have known to be on occasion, but I don't think so."

Anna knew he was being sarcastic, but she didn't rise to the bait.

"Thanks, Mike, at least you've given us something more to go on."

As Anna and Sergeant Johnson left the unit, they remained silent. Anna had learned her lesson from the last time she had been here, when she'd slagged off Mike Hanks to a female assistant before finding out that the woman was actually Mike's daughter.

Back at Charing Cross station, when Anna and Steve entered the incident room, they both immediately stopped in their tracks. Apart from the calls that were being made, the room was silent, and you could cut the atmosphere with a knife. Her team, along with Detective Sharon Manning, all looked up and smiled, but Peter Price continued reading his newspaper and didn't acknowledge her in any way.

"Right, you lot! We've got a bit more information from pathology, but it isn't much."

Walking over to the wipe boards, she began to write as her team, all except Peter Price, gathered around. When Anna turned, she spoke with a raised voice, and they all knew she wasn't happy.

“You!”

Peter looked up, and his face was full of fury.

“My name is Detective Price.”

"And my name is Chief Inspector Draycott, so I outrank you by a country mile. I don't know what your fucking problem is, and to be frank, I haven't got the time or the fucking inclination to find out. If you want to be a part of this team, you will get your sorry arse over here now; if you don't, then fuck off out of my incident room."

Low sniggers could be heard, but instantly stopped when Anna glared at each of them in turn. Her words had hit home with Peter Price; he didn't want to sully his career by getting a black mark from someone who was so well-liked in the force, but more than that, he would do anything to stay on this case. Standing up from his chair, Peter walked over and stood beside Sharon Manning, and when she reached down and squeezed his hand, he didn't pull away.

"Right, the murder weapon was a large Bowie knife, but not the ordinary kind. This one, which is called a tactical Bowie, has a jagged razor-sharp edge and would be more commonly found in America, as it's favoured by hunters. Now I know it's a long shot, but I want a list drawn up of all retailers within a five-mile radius of the city and then further afield if necessary. If records have been kept as they should have been, and if we're lucky, we might just find out who purchased the killer weapon. It's at least something to work on while we wait for more clues and evidence to come in. Beth, can you source a list and then divide it up so this gets done quickly?"

When the officers began their tasks, Peter Price walked over to Anna.

"I'm sorry about earlier, Ma'am."

"Apology accepted."

Peter repeated to his commanding officer what Josette Solomon had said and then retook his seat at the desk. He already hated Anna, and he had only known her for five minutes. The apology was fake, but he thought he might just have gotten away with it. What Peter didn't know was that Anna was as sharp as a pin and had read him like a book; Detective Price's card had been well and truly marked.

CHAPTER SIXTEEN

Several days later

Dodi had just got back from the offices of Hayes and Tomb, and her mood and state of mind were now far lighter than when she had set out earlier. Mr Oswald Smeeth had told her that the photograph Monica had taken, a photograph she still couldn't believe that she had in her possession, was more than enough to get her a divorce, with the added bonus that her settlement would now be highly enhanced. Over the last few days, her shock and anger had begun to subside. They say there are seven stages to grief, and the grief at losing her marriage was something she was definitely experiencing. Initially, she had gone through the first two stages of shock and denial when she found out about her husband's affair. The third was anger, moving on to bargaining when she had tried to reach a compromise with Nicky. So far, the depression had been the worst, but slowly, with the mother's little helpers that the doctor had prescribed, the emotional fog was beginning to lift a little. Dodi had decided to leave out number six, testing. She has never been much for group therapy or trying different coping methods, not even when she had lost the babies. Even though she still felt as if she was a newly made widow, Dodi knew she was onto the last stage because she now had acceptance,

but not only that, she had hope, and with that hope would come an almost endless amount of cash. Her entire married life had revolved around Nicky and his needs, but from now on, she was going to make sure that the future was all about her and what she wanted. If and it was a big if, she ever met someone and allowed a man to hold her heart in his hands again, then it would be on her terms and only her terms. Lost in thought, when the house phone rang, she nearly jumped out of her skin. Grabbing the handset, she quickly walked back over to the breakfast bar and, taking a seat, knew it would be her mother-in-law as Monica was the only one who ever used the house phone.

“Hello.”

"Hi, darling, how are you?"

"I'm not too bad, Monica thanks; it seems the more days that pass, the easier it gets. So, what can I do for you?"

There was an awkward silence on the other end of the phone, and Dodi frowned as she waited for her mother-in-law to speak. Monica coughed nervously before she continued, which was so unlike her; usually, she could be blunt, blunt to the point of rudeness.

“I had a visit today from Janice.”

"Janice? So you're on first-name terms already!"

"Please, sweetheart, don't be like that. I only called as I thought you needed to be kept in the loop. Now, you're not going to like what I'm

about to tell you, darling, and I hate to be the bearer of bad news, but...."

There was another long pause, and Dodi was quickly becoming annoyed.

"What on earth are you talking about, Monica?"

"I really don't want to hurt you, but she's pregnant, Dodi. It's early on, and she hasn't told Nicky yet, but she wanted me to know."

“Of course she fucking did!”

“Now you're upset and........”

“Upset!? I'm fucking livid!”

Dodi slammed the phone down as she felt the tears begin to well up in her eyes. That sneaky, conniving bitch was trying to get Monica on side and with the promise of a grandchild, that's exactly what would happen. She was now completely out in the cold, and it hurt, not to mention that the slut had been able to give Nicky the one thing that she had never been able to. When the phone rang again,

Dodi snatched up the receiver, expecting it to be Monica calling back.

"What! For fucks sake, what do you expect me to say?"

"I'm not sure, what would you like to say, babe. I was going to say Hello Sexy, how are you?"

A shiver ran down Dodi's spine. In the past, a dirty phone call wouldn't have bothered her, but now she lived alone, it unnerved her, and with the news she'd just received, she felt as if she was at breaking point.

"Who is this!?"

For a few seconds, there was silence, and then she heard a laugh.

"It's me, silly, Robbie."

Dodi sighed and then began to cry; she couldn't help herself.

"Oh fuck me, Dodi, what on earth is wrong, sweetheart?"

"I'm sorry, Robbie, take no notice of me. How are you? God, I haven't spoken to you since the wedding. When did you get back?"

"A while ago now, but that's not important, what's wrong, forget that, can meet up for a coffee and a catch-up?"

"I would love to, and to be honest, I could do with a friend at the moment as I don't think, no, that's wrong, I know, I can't take much more. You, free today?"

"Of course I am."

They arranged for Robbie to come over to the house later that afternoon. Dodi was intrigued as to why he had contacted her and not Nicky, but more than that, she was desperate to talk to someone. Shortly after their engagement, Robbie Evans had joined the army, but he had come back to be the couple's best man. Dodi had imagined that his friendship with her husband would decline, but that hadn't happened. Over the years, he rarely came home on leave, the wedding being one of the few times, but the two men had stayed in contact via the phone or by the odd letter, and the couple would often receive a postcard from some exotic place he was stationed in. When the call ended, and she sat in stunned silence sipping her coffee, Dodi wondered why he really wanted to see her, had he been sent by her husband, and was the visit just an ulterior motive for something else.

At two-thirty on the dot, the doorbell rang, and when she opened up, she was met by a handsome, tanned and brawny man, something Robbie definitely hadn't been the last time she'd seen him.

"Hello, soldier! I know it should be sailor, but that wouldn't have sounded right."

He laughed at her words, and suddenly she remembered back to the past when they were kids, he had always laughed at her silly little jokes, even when no one else had found them funny.

"Well, come on in then, don't stand there on parade."

Again, he laughed and, closing the door behind him, followed her into the kitchen. When the coffee was made, and they were both seated at the breakfast bar, it was Dodi who was the first to speak.

“So, how long have you been back? I must say you look really well.”

"Thank you, and just over a month, I'm actually out for good now. I can't draw on my pension until I'm sixty, as I didn't do the full twenty

years' service. I know I only had a year left to go, but I just couldn't stand it any longer. On the upside, I will still get a nice lump sum, so it will tide me over until I find something to do. That's enough about me. What was all that about this morning?"

“What do you mean?”

"Oh come on, babe, it's not normal to call someone, and they start to cry on the other end of the line."

"I take it you've been to see Nicky? Is that why you're here? Has he sent you to find out any information he could use against me in the divorce?"

"No, I haven't, and no, he didn't send me, but I did hear you two have split up. I'm not surprised, Dodi. He was never good enough for you. Was it the split that had you in tears this morning?"

His words momentarily stumped her. Robbie was Nicky's best friend, and she'd never heard him say a bad word against his mate in the past.

"Funnily enough, no, I'd just had a call from his mum telling me his whore was pregnant. I can't blame Monica for being happy; she tried not to show it in her voice, but she's been desperate for a grandchild, something I just couldn't give her, even though I tried again and again. In fact, I tried so hard that I kept losing them; that's why the news totally devastated me. You did know about the miscarriages?"

"Yeah, Nicky told me, and I'm sorry, Dodi, but kids ain't everything."

"Not to some people, but to me they are. I was slowly starting to get used to the idea that I would never be a mother, but that news just knocked me for six. He has a club now, you know."

"Yeah, I went there one night a while back, not to see that muppet but just to get a feel for the place. It was full of brasses and not good-looking ones at that. Never thought my mate would resort to being a fucking pimp! You still want him back?"

Dodi got up to make more coffee and talked as she walked.

"Not on your life! Now that he's shacked up with some piece of skirt, I wouldn't touch him with a fucking barge hole. I can't deny it almost broke me, though. I felt as if my whole world had come crashing down, and I had no control over it. This latest escalation feels like I'm breaking all over again. He knows just what this will do to me, the cruel bastard!"

"I know it almost broke you, sweetheart, and he's a complete cunt to make you go through that."

Dodi gave him a strange look as his sentence was made in the past tense. How could he have known how bad she had felt? Dismissing his words as silly, she smiled when he continued.

"I know it's a cliché, but time is a great healer,

and I'm a firm believer that what doesn't kill you makes you stronger. The things I saw in Afghanistan almost sent me over the edge, but I didn't break Dodi; I stayed strong."

"I can see that, and thank you for your kind words. On the upside, I have recently had a stroke of good news, though."

"How come?"

"Well, Monica wasn't best pleased when he left me. You know, me and her were always close, and after I told her that the divorce would be difficult without some concrete proof, she helped me out big time. You see, Nicky doesn't want a divorce; he expects me to stay in this house, married to him and put up with whatever he feels like dishing out. I don't know, maybe he's hoping to completely break me. Anyway, somehow Monica managed to get a photograph of Nicky and that tart in bed together. Her tits were on show, so no mistaking what they had been doing. The soppy sod still doesn't know, and my solicitor says I am now in for a very nice payday. I bet Monica is regretting it now, what with the baby and all, but she was so mad, and you know Monica, it doesn't bode well to cross her. Anyway, where are you staying, Robbie, at your mum's?"

"At my mum's?! Not on your life, I ain't seen the old tart for years, and I have no fucking wish to start now. She was a shit mother, and I imagine she's still on the game, that's if she can still get

anyone to shag her. I know I didn't share much about my home life when we were kids, Dodi, but that was because I was so embarrassed, can you imagine having a Brass for a mum?"

"Robbie!"

"I know, don't sound too good, does it, but imagine how I felt as a kid. Everyone at school knew and took the piss out of me, pole rotten; they only stopped when me and Nicky got friendly. For that, I will always be grateful, but I can't forgive him for what he's done to you, Dodi. I always felt that we were like the three musketeers and always would be."

"Me too. The only trouble is that people change and sadly, it's not always for the better."

Dodi took a moment to silently mull over what she was about to offer, and then, smiling, she placed her hand onto her visitor's arm.

"You know you're welcome to stay here, darling, at least until you get yourself sorted."

"I don't want to put you out, love."

"Put me out? This is a big house, and I seem to be rattling about in it, so I would love some company. You're not putting me out, nor are you helping me out; my reason for asking is purely selfish."

Robbie laughed, he didn't need asking twice, and it was agreed that he would move into the spare room the next day. Dodi hadn't felt obligated; she liked Robbie, and it would be nice to have someone else in the house again,

someone to cook and care for and talk to about the old times, the happy times that she now so longed for.

That night at the club, the atmosphere was tense as the girls were all worried after Josette's attack. If they were honest, each one of them would have chosen not to continue working until the attacker had been caught, but they couldn't be choosy, as the bills still needed to be paid. Nicky sat in his office waiting for the latest victim to pay him a visit. He hadn't gone to the hospital when Josette had first been attacked, but he had sent Maxi to tell her to assist the police however she could. When the knock came at the door, he jumped; even Nicky was on edge, and he didn't like the feeling one bit.

"Enter."

The door opened slowly, and a demure-looking Josette entered, far, far different from the normally brash, outgoing woman that they had all come to know and like.

"Hi, Mr Stanton."

Josette Solomon, even with her dark skin, looked strangely pale. Her usual trademark makeup with gold eyeshadow and bright red lipstick was missing, and she was dressed down in jeans and a jumper. Her arm was heavily bandaged, and it was protected by a sling.

"Hello, sweetheart. Come on in and take a seat. So, how are you doing?"

"Not so bad, Mr Stanton, but the quacks at the

hospital said it will be a while before I can come back to work."

Her eyes were pleading, and it was obvious she was worried about money. Josette was a good worker and one he didn't want to lose. She would be back at the club as soon as she could,

and until then, he would look after her. Opening the desk drawer, he pulled out a roll of fifties and passed them across the desk.

"Take this; it should see you through until you're back on your feet, but if you need a top-up, just come and see me."

The woman, a normally hard-hearted woman who had been one of life's punching bags and who showed little emotion, suddenly had tears in her eyes.

"Thank you, Mr Stanton, it means a lot and will stop me from worrying. The kids need feeding, and the rent needs paying, and to be honest, I didn't know what I was going to do."

"I look after my girl's sweetheart, and as I said, if you need any more, just come and see me."

Later that afternoon, and after Robbie had left, Dodi was seething as she paced the floor. With every step as she recalled Monica's news, her rage grew until she thought she was going to explode. Picking up her mobile, she dialled his number.

"Hello Dodi, how are you, sweetheart?"

“You cunt! How could you do this to me after all that I, we, went through?"

Nicky's face was full of confusion, but she couldn't see that, couldn't see how much it bothered him regarding the hurt he had caused her.

“I ain’t got the foggiest what you’re on about. I thought you had come to terms with our separation.”

"I ain't on about our separation, you bastard, I'm on about the kid you're having with that slut."

"Kid, what kid? I don't know where your mind is at, but there's definitely no kid on the horizon."

"That ain't what your fucking mother told me, seems your whore went to see her and said she was up the duff. You know the pain I went through with each baby I lost, but I continued because I was so desperate to give you a child, and this is how you repay me? You couldn't even wait until the ink was dry on the fucking divorce papers!"

"Look, sweetheart, this is the first I've heard of it, and if it's true, then I'm sorry. Let me give Mum a ring and find out what the hell is going on."

“Speak to who the fuck you like, but I know it’s true, and I think your mother might even have been gloating, the cruel bitch!”

“My mum ain’t like that, and you know that sweetheart.”

Nicky ended the call feeling full of confusion; he needed to speak to Monica as soon as possible.

Over in Pimlico, Janice was coming out of the

bathroom when there was a knock at the door. Smiling to herself, she couldn't wait for Nicky to get home to tell him her happy news. It had happened sooner than she'd hoped, but she also knew he would be over the moon and that they would both love this baby; of that she was sure. Not bothering to look into the camera as the knock was on the internal door, Janice opened up, thinking it was their ground-floor neighbour. The main entrance door was locked, so in her mind, she was safe. For a second, she was struck dumb; she didn't recognise the caller, but when she saw the knife, she was about to scream when her attacker spoke.

"Make a sound, and I'll kill you whore!"

Janice stepped backwards towards the kitchen as her attacker came in and closed the door.

"You dirty slags deserve all that you get."

Suddenly, they lunged forward, and Jan pushed out her forearm in an attempt to shield her face. The knife sliced through her blouse with ease, and blood instantly dropped onto the tiled floor. As she tried to move backwards, her foot smeared blood along the floor, and her pitiful attempt at escape was futile, as with one swift motion, her attacker plunged the knife into her stomach. It seemed to happen in slow motion, and for a second, Janice just stood there as the blood began to pour from her abdomen. Even as the life began to leave her body, she grasped at

her stomach in a desperate attempt to save her

unborn baby, but it was futile.

"My Baby, my baby!"

"Well, it's just another dirty slut that won't end up on the streets, so I guess it's a buy one, get one free kind of day."

The last thing Janice heard was her assailant slamming the street door, and then, after a heavy gasp, her life and that of her child were over.

CHAPTER SEVENTEEN

Just after nine that night, Nicky was still seated in his office and thinking about Dodi's revelation. He hadn't yet called his mother to confirm things, but knew he couldn't put it off any longer. About to dial her number, he suddenly stopped. Maybe this would be a conversation better discussed face-to-face. Telling Maxi to take over for a couple of hours, he drove the two-mile journey to Camden. Normally, it would take a good fifteen minutes, but due to the hour and with the traffic being light, he reached his old home in just under ten. The front room light was on, and by now the old man would be tucked up in bed, so at least the discussion would only be between the two of them. Wearily, Nicky walked up to the front door and let himself inside with his key. As he made his way down the hall, he coughed loudly so as not to frighten his mother, who was tucked up on the couch with a glass of wine watching one of her films on DVD. When she saw him, Monica immediately pressed pause and was out of her seat in a second with the broadest grin on her face that he had ever seen.

"Hello, son, so you know then. Ain't it the most fantastic news?"

"So it is true then. I only found out earlier, Mother, via Dodi. How the fuck could you do that to the poor little cow? I know I've put her

through the wringer lately, but what you did was nothing short of fucking cruel."

Monica just stared at her son open-mouthed as she took in what he was saying. It was very rare that they fell out, but hearing his tone, she knew this could be one of those times. What on earth had she been thinking? Had she been so caught up in the moment that she truly hadn't given a second thought to her daughter-in-law's feelings? Poor Dodi had tried again and again to conceive, but each time it had resulted in a miscarriage, and Monica was sure it had happened more times than Dodi had let on.

"I was just so happy that I didn't even think about it, son. I knew she wouldn't be pleased and that she is heartbroken by you leaving her, but this must have mortified her after all she went through trying to get pregnant. I'm so sorry, Nicky, truly I am. First thing in the morning, I'll call round and try to apologise."

Nicky nodded and kissed his mother on the forehead. She wasn't a bad woman, but she just didn't think sometimes. He was also aware of how desperate she was for a grandchild, and he couldn't stay angry with her for long. Before driving back to the club, he stopped off at the late-night shop on Tottenham Court Road and bought flowers and chocolates.

At Charring Cross police station, Anna was sitting at her desk racking her brains and still coming up with a big fat zero. There had never

before been a case that had stumped her to such a degree that she didn't have a clue how she was going to solve it. In the past, she had eventually cracked even the toughest cases and it might have taken her a while but eventually she had worked it out. This one seemed different and it was causing her a right headache. It was getting late, but since Jake's death and her return to her duties, she was never in a hurry to go home. The house now seemed cold and so quiet. She still hadn't packed up his things, as if keeping them all somehow kept him close, but she made a mental note to get on with it this coming weekend. Beth Saunders, her loyal Detective and friend, had offered to help her on numerous occasions, but Anna knew it was a task she had to carry out alone, and not until she felt completely ready, or she would end up regretting it. It was just past nine thirty, and slipping off her shoes, she began to rub at the balls of her feet. The day had been a long one, and with no further leads, to be honest, she didn't have a clue what to do next. It was now obvious that they had a serial killer on their hands, but he was clever. She was assuming it was a male, but after her last case and the shit she had gone through with Maggie McKay, honestly, it could be either sex. Due to interview Josette Solomon the following day, Anna realised that if there were no new leads, she would have to seek out the approval of the top brass to set up an undercover operation. It wasn't what she wanted, as it was dangerous to say the least, and if it went wrong, it could lead to even more shit coming down on the Met's head.

Nicky checked back in with Maxi before heading home, and when his right-hand man confirmed to him that everything was as sweet as a nut, he called it a night. He couldn't wait to see Jan and celebrate the news, and Nicky had a smile on his face for the entire journey back to Pimlico. Initially, he hadn't been best pleased when he heard about the pregnancy because of Dodi, but now, the more he thought about it, it made him realise that he was over the moon and excited. His mind was filled with images of a son, someone to take to footie on a Saturday afternoon, but mostly an heir to the empire he had expanded since taking over from his father. Parking in the street, Nicky let himself into the inner hall, climbed the stairs and made his way along the landing to where their flat was situated. When he saw the front door was slightly ajar, it didn't immediately register, and then he stopped and frowned. What on earth was Jan playing at? He'd warned her over and over again to be careful. Maybe she had gone downstairs to the neighbours, but still, he wasn't pleased and would have a stern talking to her once they had celebrated their happy news. As soon as he saw the trail of smeared blood on the tiled floor, he screamed. It looked as if she had desperately dragged herself along, and as he followed the trail, he found her lifeless body just inside the entrance to the kitchen. Nicky fell to his knees and sobbed as he cradled her head in his lap, pleading with her to wake up but knowing deep inside that it was too late. The heartbreaking sound had alerted their downstairs neighbour, and as

Steve Collins ran up the flight of stairs, he couldn't believe the sight that greeted him. Pulling out his mobile, his hands were shaking badly as he dialled the emergency services. Steve placed his hand on Nicky's shoulder in an attempt to offer some sort of comfort, but Nicky just shrugged him away. Anger was building, and getting up from the floor, Nicky ran into the front room and opened up his laptop. Pressing the camera tab, he rewound until he saw Steve Collins enter through the main door. Seconds later, and before the door had time to fully close, a second figure entered. Whoever it was must have found out about the cameras, as they were wearing a baseball cap and kept their head bowed low at all times. Even as they climbed the stairs, not once did their face come into view.

At the station, Anna heard the commotion when news came in of a murder, but didn't think anything of it. Stabbings were commonplace in the city; it was probably another gang-related incident, and she had far too much on her own

plate to get involved with another case. When a young police constable passed her room, out of curiosity, Anna called her in.

"What's the story, officer?"

“It appears a man returned home to find his partner had been stabbed to death in their home.”

"Oh my God, that's terrible."

"Yes, it is, and there's a rumour going around that he's the owner of the club that employed all those brasses who recently got attacked."

Anna Draycott was up and out of her chair in seconds, and fumbling to put her shoes back on, she called her Sergeant. Unusually, Steve Johnson had the weekend off, well, he had, but now his plans instantly changed. Anna arranged to meet him at the scene as soon as possible. Steve wasn't married, and if truth be told, he welcomed the call. He lived for his job, and working with Anna Draycott was the icing on the cake.

Outside the Pimlico flat, there were flashing lights from the ambulance and two patrol cars and the area had already been cordoned off and was being guarded by two uniformed officers. Anna ducked under the tape and, after showing her warrant card, made her way inside. The body of Janice Connolly was still in situ as the scene of crime officers were in the middle of photographing and dusting for prints, so pulling on shoe covers, Anna stepped inside the flat.

Nicky Stanton was outside, seated on the rear step of the ambulance. He was in shock, and the paramedic had wrapped a foil blanket around his shoulders. A few minutes later, Anna exited the building and made her way over to him. He looked lost and very small and not the hardened gangster she had read so much about. She smiled weakly when Nicky looked up at her with tears in his eyes.

"Mr Stanton, I am so very sorry for your loss. As you can appreciate, we will need to interview you, and in my experience, as difficult as it is, it's always better to do it as soon as possible while events are still fresh in your mind."

Just then, Sergeant Johnson arrived.

"Boss, can I have a word?"

The two officers walked into the inner hallway, and Anna quickly brought the man up to speed.

"Fuck me, it's either our serial again or that man in there has to be the unluckiest bastard on the planet, and I somehow don't think it's the latter."

"I agree, and I don't think it's the last of it either. It's too much of a coincidence, and my money is definitely on that man out there being the victim. Whoever is doing this is targeting him, and it's personal, first his working girls and now his partner."

Walking back, Anna again went over to Nicky and gently asked if he would accompany her back to the station. Like a wounded puppy, he just stood up from the step and followed her

without question.

At Charing Cross station, Nicky was led into a quiet side room, and after they both took a seat, Anna switched on the recorder. It wasn't formal, and as yet there were no charges, but Anna needed to know as much as he could or was willing to tell her.

"So, Mr Stanton, have you any idea who did this?"

Nicky slowly shook his head, and when he looked up, his eyes were almost brimming with the tears he was so desperately trying to hold back.

"Tell me about Janice. What was she like?"

Nicky sniffed loudly and gave a weak smile as if talking about her, thinking about her, made it feel, if only for a moment, as if she was still alive.

"Jan is the sweetest, kindest person you could ever meet. I found out today that she was pregnant, and I went home to celebrate with her, but I didn't get the chance. I just don't understand it. She was innocent, and if some cunt has a beef with me, that's one thing, but it had nothing to do with her."

The tears dropped onto his cheeks, and there was nothing he could do to stop them. Anna pushed a box of tissues across the table. He was starting to open up, and she didn't want him to stop.

"Can you share with me all that's happened in your life, let's say over the last six months? I

know you won't remember every detail, but anything significant that you can share may be a great help. I know about the women who work for you, and in this instance, it is of no interest to me what line of work they were in. We have three dead girls, so all I care about is catching a killer."

As Nicky mentally recalled all that had gone on, he realised he had to be totally honest with the detective if this was ever going to stop. Starting with the club and the girls, he told her about Lulu Low, Sheila Mason, Mary O'Toole, Jeanie Lovell, Jojo Johnson, Josette Solomon, the Eastern European girls and of course Jan, but he was adamant that Janice was never on the game. He explained to Anna all about Dodi, the end of their marriage and how upset she had been with him earlier in the day.

"You don't think it was her, do you? Dodi, I mean?"

Ann took a few seconds before she answered, knowing that anything said in haste could open up a whole new can of worms that she really didn't want or need at this moment in time.

"Let's not jump to conclusions. Now it's been a difficult time for you, I can see that, but is there anyone else, anyone you've had a disagreement or a cross word with lately?"

Nicky racked his brains, and then out of nowhere, he remembered Martin Gayle.

"There's that little bloke who owns the restaurant

up the road. He came to the club shortly after we opened, complaining that my girls were killing his business, but it can't be him, I mean, trade dropping is one thing, but fucking killing because of it?"

"I'm not saying he has Mr Stanton, but I know of a lot less motive to kill than that. You've given me more avenues to explore. Now, did your partner have any family?"

Suddenly, Nicky thought of Jan's dad; they hadn't met, but he had to be told.

"Her dad lives in the city with a bit of skirt he shacked up with. Initially, he rented a house here with Jan, but was led by his cock, the selfish cunt and left my Jan all alone. Anyway, I don't know his name or how to contact him."

"Leave it with me, he shouldn't be hard to trace if he was on the initial lease, and he will be required to formally identify Janice, as he is legally the next of kin. Do you have anywhere to stay tonight, as you obviously realise that you can't go back to your flat?"

"I'm good, thanks. Are we all done here?"

"For now, but I will probably need to speak to you again in the near future."

"I meant to say, there's some security camera footage on my laptop, but you can't recognise the cunt. If you want to have a look, the password is blue light."

Anna couldn't help but smile as she walked Nicky out of the building.

Outside, Nicky called Maxi Willmore and told him to get over to Charing Cross Police Station and pick him up. He didn't explain why; there would be time for that in the car. For now, he just wanted to get out of this place, as even with all of this tragedy, being in a nick still didn't sit comfortably. On the drive back to the club, Maxi listened without comment as his boss explained all that had gone on. When Nicky put his head in his hands, and when Maxi was sure Nicky had finished talking, he asked where he should drive to.

"Take me back to the club; I'll kip on the couch."

After sinking half a bottle of scotch, Nicky woke the next morning to the sound of Mandy hoovering the carpet out in the hallway. His head was pounding, and it took a few seconds for the events of last night to register. The pain hit him in waves all over again, and as the tears began to fall, a knock came at the door. Nicky quickly wiped his eyes and nose with the back of his hand.

"Yes!"

Maxi hadn't slept a wink and was at the club early to check on his boss. He wouldn't say they were bosom buddies, but he liked Nicky and had a great deal of respect for the man. Nicky had given him a chance when he was fresh out of prison, when no one else would touch him, and for that, he would be eternally grateful.

"How you feeling, Boss?"

"How the fuck do you think I'm feeling?"

Maxi didn't normally show any emotion, but Nicky's words made him frown, and it was clear by the look on his face that he was hurt. It was uncalled for, but his boss was grieving, so it was expected; he needed to lash out, and if the target was Maxi, then sobeit.

"I'm sorry, Maxi, that was out of line. I've just woken up, and it hit me all over again. For fucks sake, tell Mandy to turn that bastard hoover off, my head is killing me."

Reaching for his phone, Nicky removed a card from his pocket and dialled Chief Inspector Draycott's number. He needed to find out if Jan's dad had been located and if he could return home yet. After asking for Nicky's laptop to be brought to the station, Anna had remained in her office for the rest of the night. She was desperately trying to come up with some reason why this was all happening, but after viewing the footage over and over again, she once more hit a brick wall. Her frustration was such that she had slammed the lid of the laptop closed and then thrown her coffee cup at the wall. Now, as her phone rang, Anna felt like pulling her hair out, but instead she answered calmly.

"Hello, Mr Stanton. Yes, we found Mr Jackson, and he will be formally identifying Janice this afternoon. Regarding your property, you will be able to return to the flat later this morning. I have taken it upon myself to instruct a firm of

crime scene cleaners who should be on site as we speak. Sadly, the cost of this will have to be met by you."

It would have been comical if not so tragic, Jan had been murdered, and he had to foot the bill to clean up her blood. The only words he spoke before hanging up were 'thank you'. Nicky had never met Jan's dad, but as her next of kin, he would be in charge of the funeral, and it hurt Nicky even more that he would have no say in the send-off for his partner and the mother of his unborn child. Suddenly, he wanted to see his mum, wanted her to hug him and tell him all would be well, just as she had when he was a child.

"Maxi, bring the car around. I need to go to Camden."

When he walked into the house, Monica was just coming out of the kitchen, and when he saw her, he dropped to his knees and began to wail and pound the floor with his fists. It was a sight Monica had never seen from her son before, and it broke her heart. Running over to him, she bent down and cradled Nicky in her arms. She didn't question what had happened; there would be time enough for that when he had composed himself. It took an age, but when Nicky was at last able to speak, he broke the news that Jan was dead and there was no longer a baby. Now it was Monica's turn to weep, and mother and son remained clinging to each other on the hall

floor for a long, long time.

CHAPTER EIGHTEEN

Back at Charing Cross Police Station, Anna was leaning against one of the tables at the front of the incident room, talking to Sergeant Johnson, when the first two of her team arrived, and one look at her face told Beth and Carl that there had been a development and a major one at that.

"Morning, Guv, Sergeant Johnson."

Neither replied to the greeting, but that was nothing new. Beth and Carl both took seats close to the front of the room, and knowing the drill, they didn't ask any questions. Anna hated to repeat herself, and she would wait until everyone was in attendance before she began. Dave Wilson was the next to arrive, and Anna gave it a further five minutes, but when the Charing Cross detectives were still a no-show, much to her annoyance, she was forced to begin her debriefing. Luckily for them, she hadn't really got started when detectives Pete Price and Sharon Manning at last walked in.

"Well, good morning, and how nice it is for you to join us, Detectives!"

Sharon Manning could feel her face flush with embarrassment, but Peter Price just shrugged his shoulders as he walked across the room and noisily pulled out a chair.

"While I am in charge of a serious crime investigation, we are all on call twenty-four-seven, and when you do get time off to sleep, I

expect you back here at the crack of dawn. Understood?"

Both Pete and Sharon nodded their heads. Sharon then walked over to the free seat beside her partner at the side of the room and wished that the floor would swallow her up.

"The development since last night is as follows. The girlfriend of club owner Nicky Stanton was murdered early evening, but we're waiting to hear from the lab for a more accurate time. There is no way this is a coincidence, so obviously, and as we suspected, the man is being targeted. I want you out on the streets knocking on any properties in close proximity to the Pimlico flat. Sergeant Johnson and I will once more be visiting the pathology lab, as the autopsy should have been carried out first thing this morning. Well, what are you waiting for?"

Anna and Sergeant Johnson travelled to North London. When they entered the lab, Mike Hanks was surprised to see them again so soon.

"Chief inspector."

"Morning, Mike, we're here regarding Janice Connolly."

"I thought you would have enough on your plate, Anna, without taking on a second case?"

"Sadly, it now looks as if the two are connected. The dead woman's partner is the owner of the club where the murdered Toms worked out of. Has the autopsy been completed yet?"

"It has indeed. Come into my office, and I can

tell you my findings."

Mike Hanks was being overly polite. Anna wouldn't use the term friendly but he was definitely being polite. For a split second, a scene flashed through her brain of Mike getting his end away last night, and it momentarily made her grin.

"Is something amusing, Chief Inspector?"

"Oh no, sorry, just remembering having a laugh with my friend yesterday, funny how images just pop into your mind at the most inappropriate of times, isn't it?"

It was an out-and-out lie, but at least she got away without having to explain things, as Mike Hanks didn't question her further.

"Right! I take it you know that the victim was pregnant?"

Anna nodded her head, and the saddened frown on her brow spoke volumes.

"I just hope the killer didn't because...."

Mike Hanks looked amazed and cut the detective off mid-sentence.

“He’s a serial killer; I very much doubt he would have given two hoots even if he did know. Right, shall I continue?”

The question was rhetorical, and Anna didn't bother trying to add anything because she knew how snotty Mike could get, and this appeared to be one of those times.

"The murder weapon, which I am now, given your recent revelation, in no doubt, was the

same knife used in the other murders. It was plunged into the abdomen, but this is where things differ from the other killings. The attacker didn't pull out his weapon, but instead cut from side to side and then up and down. Almost as if he was quartering her and there was never any doubt that she would survive the attack, he made sure of that. This time it was far more vicious, and he or she is either escalating or this one was very, very, personal."

Anna momentarily closed her eyes and slowly shook her head. They were no further forward, and time was of the essence, not only before he killed again but before the top brass took the case away from her. It hadn't yet happened in her career, and she didn't think she would be able to cope with the shame if it did. They needed answers, and if Anna couldn't come up with the goods, she was under no illusion that she would be replaced. There was only one option left, something dangerous and not what she wanted to do, but means must, so thanking Mike, she told her Sergeant to drive her over to New Scotland Yard. Normally, without an appointment, she wouldn't have stood a cat in hell's chance of being seen, but these were no ordinary circumstances. Traffic was heavy, and the usual eleven-minute journey took twenty, but for once she wasn't in a hurry; for once, she wished it could take all day. Anna didn't make conversation with Steve and instead pulled out her mobile and tapped her contact list. It didn't faze Steve; he was used to her ways, and when she was thinking, she didn't like to be disturbed.

"Good morning, Sir."

"Good morning, Anna, how can I help you?"

“I’m on my way to the Yard, and I really need to see you.”

Deputy Chief Superintendent Madden knew that for the woman to come directly to him without being asked, it was urgent, and he was desperate to put this case to bed once and for all.

"I will make arrangements, and someone will meet you at the front reception area."

Due to security measures, vehicle access to the Yard was heavily restricted, and Anna instructed Sergeant Johnson to stop as close as he could. Getting out, she told Steve to drive around the block, and she would call him as soon as she was finished. Walking past the iconic sign, she shuddered. Where on earth was this all going to end? Just as she'd been advised, an upright woman dressed in a pencil skirt and a twinset was waiting at the main doors. The woman, who introduced herself as Miss Tunmore, the Super's secretary, wore her greying hair severely scraped back into a bun. The black horn-rimmed glasses did nothing to enhance her appearance, nor did they endear her to Anna, and her demeanour was unfriendly, to say the least. When Anna had removed everything from her pockets, she passed through the airport-style

security system and then, quickly gathering up her possessions, she had to almost run to keep up with the secretary. For a moment, it felt like she was back at school and following the headmistress to her office for a caning.

"Take a seat over there, and Deputy Chief Superintendent Madden will see you shortly."

With that, the woman disappeared into a side office, and after one unfriendly side glance in Anna's direction, she closed the door."

A minute or so later, the door to the Super's office opened.

"Hello Anna, nice to see you, though I do wish it were under more pleasant circumstances. Please, come in and take a seat."

When they were both in their relevant chairs, George Madden spoke.

“I see you haven’t made much progress with the Soho murders.”

"Regretfully not, Sir. Although last night we did have a breakthrough of sorts.”

Anna went on to explain about Janice Connolly and her relationship with Nicky Stanton.

“Very nasty indeed. So, where do you think it will lead, Detective?"

"As yet nowhere that's why I'm here. Reluctantly, I wanted to ask if we could put an undercover operation in place. It would be extremely dangerous, so anyone willing to take on the role would need to be made aware of that fact. It's not something I ask for lightly, but this

killer is good, Sir, and without it, I don't think we stand a cat in hell's chance of catching him, at least not in the short term."

"Let me think about it and talk it over with the Commander. I will try to get back to you later today. We have every faith in you and your team, Anna, but sadly, the general public is demanding results, and they want them quickly."

Anna Draycott thanked her superior, but as she left the Yard, a feeling of foreboding suddenly came over her like a dark cloud.

Nicky Stanton pulled up outside his parents' home in Camden, and for a few seconds, he remained seated in the car as he looked up at the house. It held so many memories, and most of them had been happy ones; now it was about to be the complete opposite. Wearily, he climbed out of the car and made his way inside. Monica Stanton had just finished feeding Bernie his breakfast and was in the kitchen cleaning up. As Nicky walked along the hallway, he stopped for a second and popped his head into the dining room.

"Alright, Dad?"

Bernie was able to muster a thin smile and nod his head a little. Continuing along, Nicky walked into the kitchen, and as Monica turned and saw his face, she frowned and then tried to smile, but didn't quite manage it.

"How are you feeling today, son?"

"Come and sit down, mum."

Under normal circumstances, Monica would have been firing questions left, right and centre, but she could see her son's pain, and it hurt her beyond measure.

"The Old Bill thinks that whoever is doing this is targeting me, and before you ask, I ain't got a fucking clue who or why. Jan's dad has been informed; the poor bastard must be in terrible shock. I haven't heard from him, and I doubt very much that I will"

"So, what about the funeral? I hope you get a say in the arrangements, you know we like to do things properly?"

Nicky could only stare at his mother; he couldn't believe what she had just said. Once again, she was putting her mouth into action before her brain had moved into second gear.

"To be honest, I don't give a fuck if he buries her at sea, nothing is going to bring her back, so whether she's buried, cremated or left on the top is the least of my fucking worries at the moment. What on earth made you say that?"

"I'm sorry, son, that was insensitive. Forgive me."

Nicky stood up, still not able to take in what his mother had just said.

"That seems to be the norm with you lately. I need to get out of here, but I just wanted you to know that's all. I'm keeping a couple of the blokes outside."

“A couple of blokes?”

“Yeah, of course. I’ve had one out there since it happened, but I want to up it.”

"What on earth for?"

"Did you not hear a fucking word of what I just said? The cunt is targeting me, he's killed Jan and my girls, so that means you, Dad and Dodi come to that, could well be in danger.”

He didn't continue the conversation or allow his mother to add any further insult to injury, and after slamming the front door, he climbed back into the car with no idea where he was going. Somehow, he ended up at the house he'd shared with Dodi in Muswell Hill. He wasn't aware that she had changed the locks, but he still didn't try to use his key; it just didn't feel right. Ringing the doorbell, he waited for her to answer, and suddenly he was filled with grief. By the time Dodi opened up, she was met with the sight of her husband with tears streaming down his face. All of the anger and the resentment instantly disappeared. Now all she could feel was the overwhelming love she still felt for the man who had wrecked her life.

"Nicky, what on earth is the matter, darling?"

He didn't know if it was her soft tone or the realisation of what a kind, caring person she really was, no matter what he had thought of her since the split. Nicky could only fall into her arms as he started to sob. Taking his hand, she led him through to the kitchen.

"Sit down and I'll put the kettle on, you know what your old mum says, 'a hot cuppa always helps'."

When the tea was made, and a liberal shot of brandy was added, Dodi placed her mug down and took hold of Nicky’s hand.

“Now what’s all this about?”

"I'm sorry to come here, Dodi, you don't need or deserve this, but I didn't know where else to go. It's Jan."

Just the mention of that bitches name and the rage began to build, but she was able to control herself.

"Why, what's wrong with her?"

“She’s dead, some cunt knifed her like a slaughtered pig, the baby’s gone too.”

"Oh, love, I'm so very sorry. No one deserves to have that done to them."

Dodi's words were genuine; she knew how much he wanted to be a dad, and that poor little baby didn't deserve to have its life ended before it had even begun, no matter who its mother was. When Nicky again started to sob, she stood up and took him in her arms, holding him as tight as she could; the tears slowly began to subside. Just then, there was a loud cough, and Nicky pulled away from the embrace and glanced over her shoulder. When he saw Robbie standing in the doorway, he couldn't believe it. Walking over, he hugged his old friend close, but the embrace wasn't returned, and Robbie's

arms hung loosely by his sides.

"What the fuck are you doing here, mate?"

Instead of a warm exchange of words and the usual banter that the two men enjoyed, Robbie was cold and distant. Making his way across the kitchen, he stood at Dodi's side.

“I’m living here now.”

Dodi just stared at him and then turned to her husband.

"Well, I wouldn't exactly say living. Robbie's left the army, so I offered him a place to stay until he gets himself sorted."

Dodi didn't know what Robbie was playing at, but she certainly didn't like it.

"Nicky's partner has been killed, well, murdered actually."

Again, she couldn't believe the behaviour of Robbie when all he did was shrug his shoulders. Nicky was stunned; he didn't know what was going on here, but he didn't like it.

"I've taken up enough of your time, Dodi. It's best if I get off now. Nice to see you again, Robbie."

Dodi followed him to the front door, and as he opened it, she tenderly touched his cheek.

"I'm sorry about that, Nicky. If you need me, need to talk, night or day, just come round or pick up the phone. No matter what's happened between us, I will always love you and always have your back."

Nicky could only nod his head and give her a

thin smile. Back inside, she turned on Robbie with vengeance.

"Where the fuck do you get off treating him like that?! This is my house, Robbie Evans, and you would do well to fucking remember that!"

“I can't believe you would even let him in here after how he treated you with those filthy whores. Coming around here and crying like a fucking baby about some slut who has died.”

"Robbie! The woman was pregnant, and that poor baby didn't ask to be conceived. Yes, Nicky hurt me, broke my heart in fact, but love doesn't die overnight, and I can't bear to see him in pain. Now I'm going upstairs to get dressed, and I would appreciate you not being here when I come back down."

“You mean you're throwing me out?”

"Not exactly, but I need some time on my own."

With that, Dodi walked into the hall towards the stairs. Alone in the kitchen, Robbie started to get agitated. Maybe he'd gone too far; he knew he was obsessive and a manipulator, but he also knew that he could never change, so he made a conscious decision to hold his thoughts and feelings inside for the time being, anything rather than lose her friendship.

CHAPTER NINETEEN

That afternoon, as Anna was sitting in her office contemplating the case and realising that she might never solve it, her thoughts were suddenly broken when the phone began to ring. Unless it was from the internal switchboard, her team doing research or a call from the top brass, it hardly ever rang as mobiles were mostly used nowadays. Praying it was the latter, she picked up the receiver and placed it to her ear.

"Hello, Chief Inspector Anna Draycott speaking."

"Hello Anna, Deputy Chief Superintendent Madden. I've thought about your suggestion, and although I'm reluctant, I realise you have hit a brick wall. Detective Cherry Graham will be with you tomorrow morning. She's been on secondment to Manchester's CID drug department for the past six months, so there will be little chance of her being recognised. Now I know you have vast knowledge and a lot of experience in serious crime, Anna, but Cherry can teach you so much more regarding undercover operations, and I would advise you to take on board anything she has to offer."

"Understood and thank you, Sir. Hopefully, we can now get out of second gear and catch the bastard before he strikes again."

She wasn't speaking out of turn; they all referred to serious criminals with expletives. With that,

the call ended, and Anna sat back in her chair with folded arms and a grin on her face. Deciding to try and get some sleep as the next few days were going to be busy, she headed home to the house on Royal Crescent in Holland Park. It had been their dream house, but ever since Jake's death, she had hated spending any time here. Now, with the hope that the case would progress, it didn't seem so bad. Opening a bottle of red, she took a seat in the front room, but as she looked around, the sadness and emptiness of her grief once again hit her, so placing her glass down onto the coffee table, she screwed on the bottle top. Drinking didn't bode well when you were feeling low; past experience had taught her that. Deciding to turn in and after taking a couple of zolpidem that she had left over from the last prescription the doctor had given her after Jake died, Anna climbed into bed fully clothed and within a few minutes had fallen into the deepest sleep she'd had in over four years.

The following morning, Anna woke early and, yawning, stretched her arms up to the ceiling. Her head felt a bit groggy, and sniffing her armpit, she knew she had to take a shower, but all in all, she felt a lot happier about things. Nothing lasts forever, and somehow she would solve this case; it might take longer than she would have liked, but solve it she would. Reaching the station by seven thirty, she was

confident that the newest member of her team wouldn't have arrived yet, but she was wrong. Walking into the incident room, she momentarily stopped when her eyes fell on a pretty blonde woman sitting at one of the desks. Short and petite, Cherry Graham wasn't at all what Anna had been expecting.

"Cherry, I mean Detective Graham?"

Cherry was instantly on her feet.

"Yes, Ma'am. I thought I'd get in before everyone else just to familiarise myself with the station and, of course, the wipe boards and info you've already gathered."

"Please, no need to stand up, I ain't the Queen. So, what do you think?"

"Well, if I'm being honest, and please don't take this the wrong way, but there doesn't seem to be very much of anything regarding evidence."

Anna placed her bag and jacket onto one of the desks and walked to the front of the room.

"That's exactly why you are here; we've hit a massive brick wall. I'm glad you did get in early; it makes life a lot easier not having to come up with a story about you to my team. For the time being, I would like to keep your work on a need-to-know basis only. We inherited part of this station's team, and as yet, I'm not sure who I can or can't trust. With the best will in the world, you can't stop tongues wagging. Now, we need to be quick, as I don't want you to be seen by the rest of the squad. And as you so

rightly said, we don't have much, that's why I requested you or at least an undercover officer. So, tell me a bit about yourself, Cherry, or do you prefer to be addressed under your rank?"

The woman smiled warmly, and Anna had a feeling they were going to get along well.

"Cherry is fine, Ma'am. Well, I joined the force ten years ago as a plod and worked my way up to detective within four years. It didn't take long to get on the serious crime team, as I had a knack for undercover work, and as you are aware, females willing to risk, well, I can't sugarcoat it, willing to risk their lives, are thin on the ground. I'm single with no dependents, and my parents are both dead, so I have no ties or people to worry about me. I don't resemble what a criminal would expect an undercover detective to look like, so that also helps. For the Met, that makes me disposable, and that's why I'm always assigned to dangerous high-profile cases, but that suits me fine, and my pay reflects the risks I take. I love the buzz of the job and the adrenaline that a dangerous situation gives me. That said. I don't take unnecessary risks; I don't want you thinking I go into a situation gung-ho."

"If you did, you wouldn't have come so highly recommended. Now, as you can see, we have very little to go on; actually, we have sod all really. Nicky Stanton is a local club owner, but I might add, has his fingers in far more pies than that. He's the son of Bernie Stanton, a well-

respected, well, within the criminal fraternity that is, villain. Stanton senior had been able to keep under the radar for a long time, but a couple of years back, Bernie had a massive stroke. His only son took over the various businesses and expanded into all sorts of things his father, who was an old-school villain, would never have entertained. Nicky is clever and, as yet, hasn't had his collar felt, not that the relevant departments haven't tried. I'm of the opinion, though I have no proof, that he has bent coppers on his payroll. He has been somewhat helpful, but I still don't want him to know about you being undercover. His girls wouldn't accept you, and the added fact that you might be able to gain some Intel for future charges would put him on his guard. Your main priority has to be luring out the maniac who has so far murdered four women and disfigured another. I have a gut feeling that he or she, though the latter is doubtful, will not stop until we catch them. The most important thing is for you to get yourself installed into the club. Working the street outside won't cut it as our killer only targets brasses who work directly for Nicky Stanton."

"When do you want me to start?"

"Yesterday!"

Cherry laughed. She liked her new boss, which would make working together all the more enjoyable. Anna opened her bag and removed a mobile phone.

"Here's a burner, you need to call in once a day, let's say seven each night, and that is non-negotiable, no matter what you are doing. By the number, I will know it's you, so even if you say something trivial or can't talk at all, I will still know you are okay. I, along with the Super, are the only people presently aware of your position, so we need to know daily that you are safe. If, for some unexpected reason, you do have contact with another officer, be mindful of who you talk to; there are too many loose lips at this station, and we can't risk word getting out. A bedsit has been rented for you on Bridle Lane, number ten, room three, and you had better put your name on the bell, as you know all Toms let punters know where they live. Your digs are rough, but it's what's expected of someone in your newfound profession. What will your cover story be?"

"Well, I'm originally from Bristol. Though that now feels like a lifetime ago, I'm still able to slip back into the old accent. So this is what I've come up with, I've been working the streets since I was fourteen, but after getting into a spot of bother with a couple of pimps, I decided it was time for a change, and the bright lights of London started calling."

Anna pursed her lips and slowly nodded her head.

"Sounds plausible. Well, I suppose that's it until I hear anything further from you, but remember

you must call in every day."

“Understood.”

Anna almost forgot, and pulling a manila envelope from her purse, she handed it over to the detective.

"There's two grand in there, as they will expect you to hand over any money you get from punters. Obviously, we don't expect you to actually earn it, but try and make it last a while, you know what it's like attempting to get any funds from the big boys, and I don't want to ask for more unless it's absolutely necessary. Good luck, Cherry."

"Thanks, Boss."

Less than ten minutes later, the team began to filter in, and Anna realised just how close she had cut her earlier meeting. They were a nosy bunch at the best of times and would definitely have asked questions.

Cherry Graham returned home to transform herself, and when she re-emerged, she was almost unrecognisable. Wearing a skirt so short it could be at best described as a belt, her blonde hair was piled high on her head in a messy do that screamed she hadn't taken too much care with her appearance. Even though her makeup was thickly applied, she was still attractive, hopefully attractive enough that she would be hired by this Nicky bloke. With a case in one hand and a rolled-up duvet under her arm, Cherry made her way to the bedsit. Bridle Lane

was narrow with buildings on both sides, and she imagined it would feel oppressive, not to mention dangerous, in the small hours. The street door was directly on the pavement, and when she entered the building, she grimaced at the state of the communal hallway. Someone had chained an old bicycle to the wall, the stair carpet was threadbare, and there was a strange smell that she couldn't quite identify. Her room wasn't any better and stank heavily of damp and cigarette smoke. Some of the ancient wallpaper was badly peeling, and the carpet was slightly sticky underfoot. There was a small kitchenette in the corner that contained a stained and very blackened cooker, a sink and a fridge, but little else and the bathroom was shared, very rundown and located at the end of the hall. Placing her small suitcase onto the floor, she decided not to unpack except for a pair of clean sheets she had allowed herself, and she was so pleased that she had.

At eleven that morning, Cherry Graham tottered into Nicky's Place on her four-inch platform mules, which with their clear Perspex uppers would have been better suited to a pole dancer. As usual, and even though the place was not yet open, Maxi Wilmore was guarding the front door, and when Cherry approached, he was off the stool he was sitting on in seconds.

"Good morning, sugar, your guvnor about by any chance?"

Maxi furrowed his brow as he looked her up and down.

"Who wants to know?"

"No need to be unfriendly, sugar, I'm just a working girl trying to make a living and wondered if there is any work going?"

As she talked, Cherry continually chewed on a piece of bubble gum, and when she finished her sentence, she blew a huge bubble for effect. The sight did nothing to endear the woman to Maxi; in fact, if he'd been paying for it, she would have been the last one he'd pick.

"Stay here."

Maxi disappeared into the club and, knocking on the office door, waited to be invited inside. Since Jan's death, his boss had been like a bear with a sore head; it was understandable to Maxi, but he didn't want to be the one to antagonise Nicky any further.

"What?"

The single word was instruction enough for Maxi to enter. Walking over to where Nicky sat behind his desk, it was easy to see that his boss's eyes were red from crying, though he knew better than to comment.

"Bit of skirt out the front, Boss, says she's in the market for work."

"Looking?"

"Not bad, I suppose, but not my cup of tea. Want me to tell her to sling her hook?"

"No, bring her in. We're short on Toms as you

well know, so I can't afford to be too choosy at the moment."

When Cherry walked into the office, she was still chewing and blowing bubbles. Not waiting for an invite, she plonked herself down onto the chair opposite Nicky's desk and, with one swift movement, moved her leg so that it hung over the arm of the chair. Her position left nothing to the imagination, and the V of her bright red knickers was clearly visible. If she was trying to shock him, it didn't work. Over the years, Nicky had been in the company of hundreds of girls. Even when he was a small kid and went to work for his father, the brasses in the area would all make a fuss of him, but he found this one funny and let out a short laugh.

"I hear you're in the market for work. Do you know what we do here?"

Cherry giggled as she continually stared at the man.

"Look at me, guvnor, what do you think I do for a living?"

"So how come I haven't seen you in the area before? I know most of the street girls, and you ain't one of them."

"Because I only got here last week, so I'm fresh meat, so to speak."

"I doubt that very much."

"Cheeky sod!"

His comment didn't offend her; she had heard far worse in the past. Cherry then removed the

gum and looked around for a bin. When Nicky handed over his wastepaper basket, she pressed the offending pink gloop onto the side of the plastic liner. Nicky very much doubted this was the girl's first rodeo, but he continued to explain how things worked and how payment was made.

"I'm short of Toms at the moment, so you will be expected to service a minimum of three punters a night, though most of my girls far exceed that number. Now, are you aware of the problems we've been having over the last couple of weeks?"

"Can't be off it, but I can take care of myself, and your terms sound good enough."

"A strong wind would blow you over, sweetheart, so don't get cocky. Okay, I'll give you a try. Be here at seven tonight, and we'll see how it goes."

When Cherry Graham left the club, she could have jumped for joy, and would have if not for her high heels. She was also very relieved knowing that a lot of the pimps, because that's exactly what Nicky Stanton was, often liked to try out their girls themselves. It had happened to her on a couple of occasions in the past, but thankfully, she had been able to push the incidents to the back of her mind. It went with the position, and if you weren't prepared to throw yourself into the job one hundred per cent, then you had no business being an

undercover copper. When she got back to the bedsit, she called Anna and explained all that had happened. Although pleased with how things were moving along, Anna knew that the detective needed to be seen with Nicky to lure the killer in, but she hadn't got the first clue how Cherry was going to manage that. She needn't have worried, the detective was on the same page, and she was also very good at her job and already had a plan B in mind should it be necessary. Back inside the club, Maxi again knocked on the office door.

"Enter!"

"How did it go, Boss? Told you she was a bit rough, a right leery cow if you ask me."

"She probably is, but I only care about how much she brings in, and some of the punters like a skirt that's a bit on the wild side. She starts tonight, so look out for her, and when she gets here, show her over to Rosie."

At seven on the dot, Cherry Graham walked into Nicky's Club, and she had a swagger in her step. Experience had taught her that if she didn't act tough, she would get eaten alive by the other women who worked the streets. They were a rough breed, had to be, or they wouldn't have lasted five minutes. Maxi greeted her, but it wasn't friendly, and after walking her over to where Rosie Goodson sat with her ledger, he introduced the two women and then left them to it. Rosie didn't work the street any longer, but

had previously been on the game for over thirty years and knew all the angles if the Toms tried to pull a fast one. To Rosie, the job Nicky had given her was like winning the pools, and she guarded it with her life.

"You log out every time you get a punter and log in again when you return, no exceptions. Mr Stanton insists on this for safety reasons; forget one time, and you're out the door. Understood?"

"Understood, babe."

Cherry smiled and nodded before giving the woman her details. Everyone's address and next of kin had to be logged in case of emergencies, and thinking on her feet, Cherry gave Anna's cell phone number. When everything had been completed, she made her way to the toilets and called her Boss.

"All okay?"

"Fine at the moment, but they wanted a next of kin, and the only person I could think of was you. You're now Barbara Graham, my aunt."

Cherry laughed, and Anna smiled to herself. She'd never been anyone's aunty before, and come to that, she wasn't old enough for this scenario. Cherry must have been closer in age for them to have been more like sisters, or at least that's what she told herself.

"Bloody cheek! Listen, stay safe and no heroics."

"Will do."

With that, the call ended, and Cherry walked back into the bar, ready to start the first shift in

her new line of work.

CHAPTER TWENTY

Robbie had stayed away from Dodi for a couple of days, but now, in the hope that she had calmed down, he let himself into the house and made his way to the kitchen. Sitting with her back to him, Robbie softly cleared his throat so as not to frighten her. Dodi wasn't mad at him any longer; she was just very sad, and turning, she smiled warmly.

"Hi."

"Hello sweetheart, you okay?"

"I suppose so, just feeling a little down today, that's all. I had a letter from the solicitors saying that Nicky hadn't contested the divorce and had signed the papers, so that's it, I suppose. Within a few months, I shall be a single woman again. I didn't expect that to ever happen, especially not in my thirties."

Robbie walked over to the breakfast bar and, taking a seat beside her, took hold of her hand.

"Well, that's a good thing, isn't it? You'll be free of that prick once and for all."

"I wish you wouldn't call him names. I'm the only one allowed to do that, and besides, you're supposed to be his best friend. I just realised that when you get divorced, it makes you feel invisible. I'm new to it and am feeling the effects already, and I can tell you it hurts deeply."

"He was my best mate, but not anymore, not since he cheated on you. Invisible, what on

earth do you mean by invisible, Dodi?"

As she began to speak, a lone tear dropped onto her cheek, and it broke his heart to see her in so much pain. Nicky Stanton had a fucking lot to answer for.

"When I got married, it was like two became one, but now I'm alone, no one sees me. We had a large group of friends that we used to go out with socially, but none of them want to know me now. It almost feels like they see me as some kind of threat to their husbands, but I would never try to take another woman's man; I know to my cost the pain it causes. Then there's the family side of things. I love my dad, but you know, I didn't really ever get on with my mum, and Monica and Bernie kind of took over from my parents. I love them both dearly, but that's now all gone, I mean, it was on the cards as soon as divorce was mentioned, and even though Janice is dead, Nicky will soon find someone else, and I'll be out on my ear again. I didn't think emotional pain could hurt so much, Robbie, really, I didn't."

"Then they are the fucking losers, babe. You are the most beautiful, kindest person I have ever known, and if they can't see that, then they don't deserve you. As for your friends, they were never your friends in the first place, not if they can turn their backs so easily. One day you'll be happy again and in a relationship where you are loved and cherished."

With his last words spoken, Robbie leaned forward and kissed her on the lips. Dodi pulled away so sharply that the stool moved backwards a couple of inches and its legs made a scraping sound on the floor tiles.

"What the hell are you doing? What did you think that now I'm alone, I am easy prey or something? Thought you could come around here and get a quick leg over?"

"No, no, not at all. After all these fucking years, I don't know how you could even think such a thing. You must know how I feel about you, Dodi, how I've always felt? For God's sake, you were the reason I joined the army in the first place."

“Me? What on earth did I have to do with it?”

Robbie got to his feet and walked over to the sink as he spoke. He couldn't bear for her to see the hurt in his eyes, and placing her mug into the bowl, he remained looking out of the window as he continued.

"I joined up because I couldn't bear to see you with him. I've loved you from the first moment I set eyes on you all those years ago in school, but you never gave me a second thought, you only ever had eyes for that nasty, cruel, cunt, the one who's now broken your heart. The pain I felt whenever I saw him kiss you, and the images I had of you on your wedding night, knowing what he was doing, and so desperately wishing it had been me. I just hoped that maybe now

you would see me, see me for the one who adores you from afar and always has. I took a chance and kissed you, and I was wrong, but it's easier to ask for forgiveness than for permission and get rejected on the spot. I'm sorry, Dodi, really I am, but I can't help how I feel, and God only knows I've tried to stop, why do you think I have stayed away for all of these years?"

Dodi couldn't believe what she was hearing. Never had she thought of Robbie Evans in that way. Getting off the stool, she took a step backwards. For some reason, she suddenly felt very uneasy.

"I'm sorry too, Robbie, but I don't and will never have those kinds of feelings for you. Nicky was, is and always will be the love of my life, no matter how many other women he has. I don't want anyone else, a man, I mean, in my life ever again unless it's my husband. Our marriage might be over in the eyes of the law, but where God is concerned, we are still and will remain to be, husband and wife."

Robbie's eyes narrowed, and walking over to her, he pinned her up against the wall, and as he tried to kiss her again, his hands were everywhere. When he tried to lift up her dress, Dodi bit down hard on his lower lip, making him instantly pull away in pain.

"Why, you bitch!"

It did the trick, and as soon as he released her, Dodi ran into the hallway and was about to run up the stairs when she heard him behind her, but rather than attack her further, as he stormed past, he roughly pushed her down onto the stair treads.

"You'll be sorry for this, you cunt!"

Not daring to get up, but on hearing the front door slam, Dodi looked down at her hands and could see she was trembling badly. Running to the door, she locked it and then, remembering he still had a key, she slid the top and bottom bolts over. Taking a seat at the bottom of the stairs, she suddenly burst into tears. What on earth had just happened? Had she encouraged him in any way? No, she hadn't; all she had done was try to be a friend to him and give him a roof over his head, but Robbie Evans had taken advantage of her kindness. It was a good thirty minutes before she composed herself enough to make the call, and when he answered, and she heard his voice, she began to sob all over again.

"Dodi? Dodi, what on earth is the matter, babe?"

"Help me, Nicky, I need you. He's just assaulted me!"

Nicky Stanton didn't wait to be asked twice, and, grabbing his car keys, he ran from the building. His wife had never been the clingy, needy type, so if she was asking for his help, she really meant it. Reaching Muswell Hill in record time, he banged as hard as he could on the front door, but it wasn't until he called out that Dodi answered; she'd been so frightened that it was

Robbie coming back again. Opening up, she fell into her husband's arms and howled; it was genuine, and he could feel her whole body shaking. Lifting her face to meet his gaze, he gently wiped away the tears and then led her through to the front room.

"Now take your time and tell me exactly what's happened, babe."

By the time she had finished explaining all that Robbie had said and done, Nicky was raging, but he hid it well, so as not to upset her further. Even though he had fallen out of love with her romantically, Nicky would still always love her if that made any sense, and to see her hurting, especially at the hands of another man, almost drove him crazy. Sitting beside her on the sofa, Dodi nuzzled into his neck; his smell was warm and safe, and she didn't want him to ever leave again. Looking up into those beautiful brown eyes, eyes that she had instantly fallen for all those years ago, she tilted her head and kissed him. Nicky responded, and moments later, they were tearing each other's clothes off. As he entered her, Dodi let out a gasp of bliss. He still had the ability to turn her on, and as she clawed at his back, she couldn't get enough of him. Clenching his buttocks in her hands, she pulled him deeper and deeper inside of her, and with each thrust, it felt as if electricity was surging through her body. Within a couple of minutes, they had both climaxed, but stayed in the same

position as they panted, waiting for their heart rates to return to normal. Finally, Nicky rolled back over on the sofa, allowing her freedom to get up. Dodi pulled on his shirt just as she always used to, and after a quick visit to the toilet to clean herself up, she made her way to the kitchen and flicked on the kettle. She turned when she heard him padding along the hall, and as he stood in the doorway in just his jeans, she couldn't take her eyes off his well-toned torso. It was like seeing him for the first time all over again. Maybe that's what the problem had been, they had gotten too used to each other and didn't see what they had together. She smiled, her long, black, curly hair was all messy, but Nicky didn't think he'd ever seen her look more beautiful.

"Tea?"

"No, I think I need to get off. Dodi, look, I......"

Walking over, she placed her index finger on his lips, smiled and slowly shook her head.

"Don't say it, Nicky, please. I love you and always will, and whatever that just was, don't take it away from me, at least not yet. Give me a minute to get dressed, and then you can have your shirt back."

Slowly, he nodded. He realised she was aware that whatever she had felt, it wasn't the same for him, and nothing had changed. The passion that had come from Nicky was a desperate attempt to heal his grief, a need to feel close to someone

and at that moment, that someone could have been anyone. For Dodi, it was all about the love she had for him, and guilt engulfed him. How could he do that to her?

"Please don't think that I expect anything from you, Nicky, but I thank you all the same from the bottom of my heart."

Leaving the kitchen, she was only gone for a few moments before she returned dressed and carrying his neatly folded shirt.

“Did you give him a key?”

Dodi, feeling stupid now, bit down on her bottom lip as she slowly nodded her head. Nicky sighed heavily and then, picking up his phone, called Charlie Fox. Foxy had been on the Stanton's payroll for years. A locksmith by trade, he had also been a very adept safe cracker, and in the early days Bernie had often used him. Things had changed when the world went digital, and now Foxy had returned to making his living as a locksmith. It didn't pay anywhere near what safe cracking did, but he was free to choose his own hours, not to mention he was free from the worry of the Old Bill hauling him in whenever a robbery had occurred.

“I need a couple of locks at my house changed like yesterday.”

There was no more to the conversation, and ending the call, Nicky smiled.

"Think I will have that cuppa after all, sweetheart."

Within twenty minutes, there was a knock on the front door. Nicky went to answer; he wasn't about to take any chances by letting his wife go. Standing on the front porch was a short, strange-looking man. Foxy was portly and balding, but that wasn't what made him stand out; it was his eyes. One looked slightly down, and the other looked slightly upwards. Nicky wanted to laugh, not at Foxy but when he remembered what his old dad used to say when referring to the locksmith 'one in the pot and one up the chimney'.

"Hello Foxy, my old son, how are you?"

"All good thanks, Mr Stanton, how's Bernie keeping?"

"Oh, you know, about the same. Now I need the lock on this door and the one at the back to be changed as soon as possible."

"Not a problem. How about if I fit a couple of deadlocks as well, just to be on the safe side?"

Foxy didn't ask why the urgency; he knew only too well that when Nicky said 'as soon as possible', he wanted the job done there and then, so there must be a real threat of danger. Within the hour, Charlie had completed the work on the wooden front and rear doors and, walking into the kitchen, handed Dodi two new sets of keys.

"There you go, Mrs Stanton; with the deadbolts on that door, it ain't going anywhere, nor will it let anyone get in, but you are still vulnerable because of the glass."

As soon as the words had left his mouth and he saw the look of fear on her face, Foxy knew he shouldn't have said them.

"Well, thanks a bunch, you cunt! What the fuck did you say that for? Now you can go and get a couple of sheets of reinforced steel mesh cut."

Nodding his head, Charlie Fox almost ran from the house. The Stanton's were known for their level of violence, and he didn't want to be on the receiving end. Nicky stayed until the work was at last finished, and he was satisfied that Robbie couldn't get back in. The windows were triple-glazed, so she would be relatively safe where they were concerned. It was now mid-afternoon, and he needed to get going, so after seeing Foxy out, he walked back to where Dodi stood.

"I need to get back to the club, sweetheart. You're going to be okay, I know the metal on the glass looks a bit gross, but it's only in the short term, I promise."

Tenderly, she touched the side of his face and smiled.

"Thank you, Nicky, for everything. I know you will always be there for me, just as I will for you."

"Ring me if you need me for anything, and I do mean anything."

"I will."

Standing on the doorstep, she watched Nicky get into his car and then going back inside the house, Dodi locked and bolted the door.

Wearily, she climbed the stairs and, turning on the shower, stepped into the steaming hot rainfall. Suddenly, she let out a howl like that of a wounded animal, but she wasn't physically hurt; it was pure raw emotion. Legally, she had known that her marriage was over when she'd received the court papers, but now, after what had just happened with Nicky, the look in his eyes telling her he didn't feel the same somehow cut far deeper, and she knew that no matter what, her marriage in every sense of the word had ended. She must have stayed under the water for several minutes, almost as if she was in a trance and only came to when she heard the front doorbell ringing. Switching off the shower, Dodi grabbed a couple of towels and wrapped one on her head like a turban and the other, a bath sheet, around her body. Tip-toeing over to the window, she was able to peer through the blinds without being seen, and she breathed a sigh of relief when she saw it was Marion from next door. For a second, she feared it might be Robbie and inwardly hoped it would be Nicky. Not bothering to go down and answer, she dried her hair, dressed in a tracksuit and then lay on the bed just staring up at the ceiling. She must have lain there for hours because it was starting to get dark when she finally stood up from the bed. Making her way downstairs, she suddenly felt hungry but really couldn't be bothered to cook, so pulling a massive bag of tortilla chips

and a bottle of wine from the cupboard, she headed to the front room. Maybe a binge night with a good movie would make her feel better; she really hoped so because she didn't know how much longer she could cope with this heartache.

CHAPTER TWENTY-ONE

Cherry's first and second nights as a prostitute had passed without any hassle. The few fictitious punters she'd made up had all paid the bare minimum, but it had at least kept Rosie happy. Each time Cherry had logged out with the woman, she had made up the ruse that she had agreed to meet the men outside as they had either gone ahead of her, just gone to the toilet or were finishing off their drinks. Rosie wasn't happy about it, but after using the story twice, Rosie only sighed and nodded her head. After the fictitious fourth punter on her second shift, and having been loitering about for most of the night in the cold, Cherry called it a day and headed back to the bedsit. Sleep wasn't on the cards, as unlike in the daytime, the small road was busy with tourists passing through on foot, and they weren't the quietest after having been on the drink for most of the evening, and then there were the street brasses carrying out blowjobs in the doorways opposite. With the continual sound of sirens and car horns, Cherry pulled the pillow over her face and groaned. It had been less than forty-eight, but it felt like weeks, and she would be happy when this assignment was over. She must have eventually drifted off because when she woke and looked at her phone, it was almost ten hours later. Slowly swinging her legs over the side of the bed,

Cherry let out a loud yawn. She really wasn't relishing another night of walking the streets to kill time. Her feet were still aching from last night, and she now had a newfound respect for the women who trod the pavements night after night to make a living. Hopefully, if she could soon put her plan into action, it wouldn't be for too much longer and besides, after handing over the fake takings to the woman named Rosie, she was down almost eight hundred already. After going out for breakfast, Cherry returned to her room to kill some time. Taking a shower in the grim bathroom, she then climbed back into bed to catch up on her sleep. At six thirty that evening, and feeling rejuvenated, she was up again, dressed and now wearing her thick trademark makeup. Cherry was ready to become a common street Brass again and visualised some scenarios to get herself into character. Her shift again went without event, but she knew to get a result, she would need to step things up a pace; it would be risky, but it had to be worth a chance. After another night of broken sleep, she pulled herself from the bed. Glancing around at the disgusting room she was living in made her shudder. Her pay from the force was good, but was it that good? Sometimes she did wonder. Cherry was tired and not just from a lack of sleep; she was emotionally tired as well, and she made up her mind that when this was all over, she would

take some leave and go on holiday somewhere quiet and hot. Counting out her funds to pay punters, she had already spent a large wedge, and she was only two shifts in. At this rate, the money Anna had given her would run out in the next couple of days. At exactly ten to seven and just before setting off, she dialled Anna's mobile to check in.

"Evening all!"

Anna laughed. The woman was a real character, and her manner was out of the ordinary for an undercover officer.

"Hi Cherry, I assume all is well?"

"It's okay, but nothing's happening. I have a plan, and I need to put it into action, but it's risky, and I'll need your approval."

"Go on."

"Well, if what you suspect is true, that whoever is targeting these women does so because of Nicky Stanton, then we need to show some contact with him. I mean, I could just wait it out, but the chances of him actually targeting me and not one of the other brasses are pretty slim, not to mention the fact that the cash is running out fast. I tell you, these women earn well. I can see why they do what they do, mind you, some of the punters are gross, but that's another story."

"So what do you have in mind?"

"I need to get Stanton out on the street, embrace him for some reason and hope to fuck that the killer is watching."

Anna took a few moments to mull over the suggestion.

"You still there, Guv?"

"Yes, sorry, I was thinking. It's a bit of a long shot, but what other option do we have?"

"Careful there with the thinking, you don't want to strain yourself."

Anna laughed. Normally, she would have shut down an officer who was trying to be smart, but she liked this one, liked her a lot in fact.

"Don't go to the club tonight, phone in sick. No one wants to shag an ill Tom. There's something I want to look into before I give you the go-ahead, not to mention it will make the cash stretch a bit further."

With that, they both hung up, and Cherry then phoned the club. Putting on her best blocked-up nose voice, she called in sick. Changing her clothes and after taking her makeup off, she scraped back her hair, and in all honesty, if anyone from the club saw her, there was no way they would recognise her. Heading up west, Cherry went for a nice meal at Sherlock Holmes on Northumberland Street. It was a detective-themed pub and restaurant, but that wasn't the reason she went there; they served the most delicious fish and chips and right at this moment, she needed to get away from all that was seedy. Just after eleven, Cherry finally climbed into bed, hoping that she could get to sleep before the lane got too busy, but sadly, she wasn't in luck.

After her earlier chat with Cherry, Anna had left it a couple of hours before she and Sergeant Johnson headed over to Soho. The night had closed in, and the street lamps were on, casting gloomy shadows everywhere. Anna held Steve's arm, and to anyone passing by, they were just another couple out for the evening.

"So, where are we going, Guv?"

"I want to pay a visit to that closed restaurant. A couple of plods said the owner was asking a lot of questions and paying too much interest for my liking."

"You think he will be there?"

"If he's as nosy as I think he is, then yes."

Approaching Drummonds, they could see there were no lights on inside, and for a moment Anna thought they would have to come back in the morning, but then she saw the Venetian blind move and knew someone was there. Knocking on the street door, she heard footsteps approach from inside.

"I'm sorry, but we are shut!"

"Could you open up, please? Sir, it's the police."

The door was open in seconds, and Marty was ushering his visitors inside.

"Please do come in. I'm sorry about my initial rudeness, but you can't be too careful, especially after what's been happening of late."

"I completely understand, Sir. Now, this is Sergeant Johnson, and I am Chief Inspector

Draycott."

"Martin Gayle. Very nice to meet you both. Please take a seat."

As Marty switched on a couple of the table lamps, Anna glanced around and could tell the place had at one time been a pretty classy place.

"So, Drummonds is now closed, Mr Gayle?"

"Sadly, yes and please call me Marty. The business was going downhill fast since that knocking shop opened up down the street, but now with the murders, well, it just isn't worth opening the doors. I've had to let all of the staff go, which was most upsetting. Do you know my father started this restaurant in the early sixties? It is, was, one of the longest-running successful restaurants in the area until that horrible man brought his prostitutes in."

"So you don't like Mr Stanton then?"

Marty's eyes narrowed; he wasn't daft and could see where this was leading.

"In all honesty, I don't know him. Oh, I paid him a visit and asked him to stop his girls plying their trade, and he had his gorilla throw me out, so if I had to answer truthfully, then no, I don't like him."

"We believe someone is targeting the women who work only for Mr Stanton. Do you know anything about that?"

Marty was immediately on his feet and walking towards the door in readiness to ask them to leave.

"If you are insinuating I have had something to do with any of this, then you are totally off the mark. Now, if you don't mind, I would prefer it if you left my premises."

Anna realised she hadn't handled the situation very well and needed to backtrack if she was to get Martin Gayle to continue talking.

"No, no, not at all, Marty, but we have to follow up every avenue. Now, a couple of the beat officers informed me that you were interested in what was going on outside."

"That doesn't mean I'm a killer!"

"No, of course it doesn't, but as you have shown interest and I noticed when we arrived that you were watching the street, I just wondered if you had seen anything. It might be small and not mean anything to you, but you'd be surprised how many cases have been solved with just the smallest snippet of information?"

Now Marty was interested and, walking back over to the table, took a seat.

"As it happens, I might just have something for you. A couple of nights ago, I was watching the goings on outside, not much else to do now that I've lost this place, and I saw a man standing over the road. He seemed to be hiding, and anyway, it was cold, so I beckoned for him to come inside and get warm."

Marty went behind the bar to retrieve the order pad that he had used to make notes on.

"Ah, here it is. He said his name was Jamie

Brewer and he was from Leicester and was staying at a bed and breakfast over in Islington. He didn't say which one, only that it was run by a woman named Wilma. He also said that he hated prostitutes, and was actually very angry when he said it."

"Description?"

"About five nine, slim build, mousy brown hair, but other than that a bit nondescript really. Sorry, I can't be of more help."

"That's fine, Mr Gayle, you've been very helpful."

Anna thanked the man again as they left, and Marty now felt important, and his chest swelled. Out on the street, Steve was grinning as he looked at his boss; she could get blood out of a stone when she was on the ball.

"What next, Guv?"

"Back to the station, I want to track down this man. It shouldn't be too hard; I mean, there can't be that many women named Wilma who run a guest house in the Angel. First thing tomorrow, we'll call at the address, and then I want to pay the wife of Nicky Stanton a visit."

Just, as Anna predicted, it turned out easy to locate the property and the woman named Wilma Claxton. Deciding to get some rest as she had an idea that tomorrow was going to turn out to be a busy day, Anna and Sergeant Johnson called it a night.

The next morning, and several hours before

Chief Inspector Draycott would call, Dodi decided to visit her parents and see if she could build a few bridges. As she travelled over to Somers Town, all of the old memories came flooding back. Dodi hadn't been to the flat in Levita House for several years, and it now looked more run-down than she remembered. Kids no longer played in the communal square, and the lines of washing that she remembered from her childhood no longer hung from the long lines spanning the yard area. Rubbish was piled high on top of the bins, and she swore she saw a rat run over the concrete. Parking up her Range Rover Evoke, Dodi wondered what condition it would be in when she returned, but at this minute in time, all she cared about was seeing her family. Climbing the stairwell to the first floor, she walked along the open-air landing and wrinkled her nose at the smell of urine. Back in the day, each woman of the household would scrub the front area of their flat, and then the only smell would be that of disinfectant. Number ten was situated at the end of the landing and, as such, was slightly larger than the rest but only by a few feet. Dodi didn't feel comfortable just walking in, so, knocking on the glass pane, she waited for someone to answer. When he heard the knock, Wally Smith had been engrossed in his Racing Post but knew better than to even look in his wife's direction. Linda was fixated on homes under the hammer, and

God forbid anyone who interrupted her viewing. When he opened up, Wally gasped, and then his face broke into a broad grin.

"Well, bless my soul, girl, ain't you a sight for sore eyes."

"Hello, Dad. I hope you don't mind me just popping round, only I've missed you so much."

Wally stepped forward and, without warning, hugged his daughter tightly to him.

"Not at all silly, and I've missed you too, Dodi. The place was never the same after you left, but I've kept an eye on you and all that you've been doing."

Dodi looked at her dad with a quizzical expression, which made him smile.

"Cabbies talk, sweetheart, and they love nothing more than telling each other what's been going on, especially in Soho. I know all about Nicky's club and the goings on there, but I never had him down as a pimp, though."

"Dad! He isn't a pimp, the girls all work for themselves, and at least he offers them a bit of safety. So, how's mum?"

Wally only rolled his eyes upwards. His life with Linda had been hard, and if given half the chance, and if he hadn't had the kids, he would have been on his toes years ago. By the time Dodi got married, he felt he was too old to start again, so now his life was one of a henpecked drudge.

"Come on in then, go in the front room and I'll

put the kettle on, and we can have a good long catch up over a nice cuppa."

Dodi followed her dad inside, and as he continued down to the kitchen, she turned into the room that hadn't seemed to change in a decade. The wallpaper and carpet were exactly the same as the worn-out sofa and mismatched armchairs. Linda glanced up for a second, and on seeing her daughter, her mouth hung open in shock. Dodi wanted to laugh, but instead, she only smiled.

"Hello, Mum. How are you?"

"Well, look what the fucking cats dragged in."

"Nice to see you too, Mum."

Just then, Wally came in with three mugs of tea, and he made sure to hand Linda hers first.

"Well, ain't this nice. So Dodi, how's Nicky keeping?"

Dodi took a seat on the old sofa and nursed her mug. There was a big chip on the rim, which was putting her off, but she knew better than to say anything, as her mum would blow a fuse.

"He's okay, Dad, but we're actually in the middle of getting a divorce. He met someone else, but we're still friends. That's life, I suppose."

"To tell the truth, I had heard a whisper, sweetheart."

"Well, you never shared it with me, Wally?"

Finally, something more important had drawn Linda from her programme, but her husband ignored her remark.

"He must be bloody mad to let you go. How are you coping?"

"To be honest, it's broken me, Dad, but there's nothing I can do about it."

"You should have given him a kid. I was always saying to your dad that a Stanton man wouldn't stay around if he didn't have to. I bet Bernie would have left that old cow years ago if she hadn't got up the duff with Nicky."

"Linda!"

"Pardon me for speaking the bleeding truth."

Dodi was staring down at her drink, and when she looked up, she had tears in her eyes. Wally instantly noticed, but if Linda did, she didn't comment, nor did she offer any sympathy to her youngest daughter.

"I tried, Mum, really I did, and I actually conceived a few times, but I lost them all. The last was only a couple of months ago, and it tore me to pieces."

Wally was heartbroken for his girl, and taking a seat beside her, he placed his arm around Dodi's shoulder.

"I'm so sorry, sweetheart, truly I am."

"Oh, for fucks sake, Wally, leave her alone, she's a grown woman for God's sake!"

Dodi put her cup onto the side table and stood up. Nothing had changed, and she wasn't going to put herself through all of this again. She must have been out of her mind to think the rift with her mother could ever be healed.

"And where do you think you're going? I bet that bitch Monica don't want to know you now, does she? It's probably the only reason you've shown your sorry face here today, I'm right, ain't I?"

Dodi slowly shook her head and walked to the front door with Wally following behind in hot pursuit. Linda was calling him to get back into the front room, but for once, he ignored her, even though he was well aware there would be hell to pay when Dodi had left, and they were once again alone.

"Take care, sweetheart and don't be a stranger. I know you won't want to come back here, where that old bitch is, but maybe we could meet up for a drink and a coffee? I would love to see you regularly for a catch-up, darling. It's broken my heart not having any contact, and I would love to see at least one of my daughters, and I don't give a flying fuck what your mother thinks."

“I would love that to Dad. Do you not hear from Emily at all?"

"Not a word. She got out while she could and has done well for herself by all accounts, married a banker, or so I was told."

“You sure they said banker?”

Wally let out a little giggle as Dodi hugged her father and shrugged her shoulders.

"You know what they say, Dad? You can't pick your family, though I would always pick you, just not that old cow."

Wally laughed again, kissed his daughter warmly on the cheek and then watched as she walked away. Her shoulders were slightly hunched over, and her step was noticeably slow; that bastard had a lot to answer for, that was for sure. Linda could rant and rave as much as she liked, but for once, he felt good, and it was the first in a very long time that he had a smile on his face. It pained him terribly that his baby looked so sad, but he was adamant that he would put a smile back on her face as soon as he could.

“Wally!!!”

"Coming, Linda, my love."

CHAPTER TWENTY-TWO

As she left Somers Town, Dodi let out a sigh; it felt as if the dark cloud hanging above her head had finally lifted a little. Acceptance was a great healer; she was glad that she had reconnected with her dad, but now she knew a relationship with her mother would never happen. Dodi was in no rush to get home, so she decided that an early lunch was in order. The Gatehouse on North Road had nice food, so she stopped and went inside. An hour later, and with a full belly, it was finally time to set off again. It was only a ten-minute journey, and as she pulled up outside the house in Muswell Hill, Dodi noticed a man and a woman standing on her doorstep. She wasn't in the mood and had planned on having a nice nap, so she really hoped they weren't from the Bible-bashing brigade again. Getting out of the car, she walked up the path, and her tone was short and not overly friendly.

"Can I help you?"

"Mrs Diana Stanton?"

"Yes, for a while longer at least, and you are?"

"I'm Chief Inspector Draycott, and this is Sergeant Johnson. I wonder if we could come inside and have a chat?"

"There's nothing wrong, is there? Nicky's okay isn't he?"

"Yes, I can assure you there's nothing to worry about regarding Mr Stanton."

Dodie opened the door and made her way down the hall to the front room. As Anna followed, she couldn't help but notice the newly installed steel panels on the door. Dodi offered tea, which was accepted, and when they were all seated in the front room, Anna spoke.

"Mrs Stanton, I'm sure you are aware of the recent murders in Soho, particularly in close proximity to your husband's club?"

Dodi only nodded her head and wondered where this was going.

"Are you also aware that all of the victims worked for your husband and that Janice Connolly, the last victim, was your husband's partner?"

Dodi couldn't believe what she was hearing, and her brow furrowed deeply as she looked in Anna's direction.

"Of course I bloody am, but I hope you don't think I had anything to do with any of that?"

"No, no, of course not. May I ask a question?"

Dodi nodded but still looked confused.

"Why has your door had newly installed steel grates over the glass?"

"Someone scared me, but I don't want to talk about it. Nicky had some security added to make me feel safer, but I really don't think there was any need. Now, if you haven't got anything else to say, I suggest you get on your way as I have things I need to get on with."

Dodi stood up and walked into the hall towards

the front door. It silently told Anna and her sergeant that she wanted them both to leave. When they were back in the car, Steve turned to his boss.

"Well, we didn't get much from that, Ma'am."

"I didn't expect to, I just wanted to see her reaction."

"And?"

"I'm not sure yet."

"So, where to now, Ma'am?"

"I think we need to pay Mr Stanton another visit; after what I've just heard, it tells me he hasn't been completely honest with us."

As it was still early in the day, Nicky was taking a break at the flat before he went to the club. He liked his new home even though it was where Jan and his baby had died; in a strange way, it kind of made him feel close to them. Just about to drift off on the sofa, Nicky was disturbed when the street doorbell rang. Rubbing his bleary eyes, he looked into the monitor and sighed heavily when he saw who was at the door. Pressing the release button, he walked into the inner hall just as Anna and Sergeant Johnson approached, and he opened up before they had time to knock.

"Mr Stanton."

"Inspector, what can I do for you?"

Nicky didn't invite them inside, and instead, he walked back into the front room. Anna looked at Steve, shrugged her shoulders and then went

in. Taking a seat on the sofa without being invited, she turned to face Nicky.

"We have just paid a visit to your soon-to-be ex-wife."

"What the fuck for? Dodi ain't got anything to do with all of this."

"I will be the judge of that, and maybe she hasn't, but it seems there were some recent events you didn't bother to tell us about. Namely, Mrs Stanton, being scared by someone, and you arranging for extra security at her home."

Nicky stood up and walked over to the fireplace. He was rattled, and Anna could see he was hiding something.

"That is a separate issue and none of your business, Chief Inspector."

Now Anna was the one to get rattled. This case was turning into a nightmare, and having information withheld wouldn't help anyone.

"Do you want this man caught or are you happy for your girls to keep on being attacked and killed?"

"That's a stupid fucking question, of course I do, and just to remind you, they are not my girls. Look, an old pal of mine turned up out of the blue and showed an interest in Dodi, which wasn't returned. He didn't hurt her, but he scared her, and the locks and steel grills, though unnecessary, were only installed to make her feel safe and nothing more."

"If that's the case, you have no need to hide

anything. If I feel it's irrelevant, then I won't follow it up, but at the moment, I need to know every little detail. So, Mr Stanton, are you going to explain the events that led to the upgraded security measures at Muswell Hill?"

Running his hand through his hair, Nicky studied the woman for a few seconds. She was like a fucking dog with a bone, and it pissed him off; he wasn't used to having to answer to anyone, least of all a woman.

"Me, Dodi, and Robbie Evans grew up together. Just after we got engaged, Robbie joined the army, and apart from our wedding, he ain't been home much since. We kept in contact by phone and the odd letter, and then, suddenly and unbeknownst to me, he turned up out of the blue. Me and Rob were best friends, and I mean, were! When he scared my wife, even though me and Dodi are getting divorced, he ceased to be a part of my life. As far as I know, he only tried to kiss her, but when she pulled away, he grabbed her, and she got frightened. That's about as much as I can tell you, and before you ask, I ain't got any fucking idea where he is now."

"Parents?"

Nicky began to laugh, which Anna found strange until he explained why.

"Rob never knew who his old man was. There was speculation on the manor about some old lag locked up in Pentonville, but it was never proven. His old lady was on the game, maybe

she still is, for all I know. They lived in Walker House in Somers Town, but I can't remember the number, and she might have moved on by now. Now, if that's all, I need to get some kip before the club opens tonight."

Anna was now intrigued and didn't need to be asked to leave. Back in the car, she phoned through to the station and got the Evans's address.

"Steve, let's get over to Somers Town."

Walker House was a mirror image of Lavita House, where Dodi had been raised, and not only regarding its building style. The rubbish was piled up in the communal yard, and the stairwell smelled strongly of urine. The Evans flat was on the second floor and situated about halfway along the landing. Steve knocked on the door, and a few seconds later, repeated the action, only this time much harder. A faint huffing and puffing sound could be heard as someone slowly approached the door.

“Hold your bleeding horses, I’m on me way. Christ, anyone would think the place was on fire.”

Rita Evans was just past her fifty-fourth birthday, but her lifestyle had long since caught up with her, and with the excessive weight she was carrying, she could now easily pass for a woman nearing seventy. Getting pregnant with Robbie at fifteen, Rita had been thrown out of the family home by her parents for bringing

shame to their door, and after a few months in care with her baby, she had finally been given the flat in Walker House. Rita hadn't wanted Robbie, and it was often bandied about, though not confirmed, that she only got pregnant so she could get a council flat. Not virtuous and with few morals, Rita Evans had liked the boys from an early age. There had been so many of them that she didn't even know who Robbie's father was. Her nickname at school had been ankles, as that's where her knickers were more often than not, but she didn't mind; she found it amusing. By the time she turned eighteen, she was sick to death of struggling to make the measly amount she received from the state stretch from one week to the next. Robbie had just had his second birthday, and as he was such a quiet child, Rita decided to take a chance, and one Saturday night, after getting herself dolled up to the nines and settling Robbie into his cot, she set off for Kings Cross. To begin with, it was difficult as most of the local street Toms worked out of the same area and fiercely guarded their patch. However, after several days, Rita Evans was eventually accepted as a regular. Due to her young age, she earned well, but instead of a nice home and good food on the table, the money went on fags and booze. Life continued that way for the next sixteen years until Robbie turned eighteen and joined the army. Mother and son didn't like each other much, and Rita never shared with him how she made a living, but it was common knowledge, and the shame he felt was immense.

"Yeah?"

"Mrs Evans?"

"It's Ms and who wants to know, cause if you're gonna try and convert me or you're hawking your wares, you can sling your bleeding hook right now."

Anna had seen the same scenario many times over the years and knew that Rita was going to be uncooperative, so pulling out her warrant card, she held it in front of the woman.

"Oh fuck me! I ain't done anything, look at me, I couldn't pull a punter if me snatch was covered in gold."

"It's not about you, Ms Evans. Look, can we come inside instead of airing your linen in public?"

Anna was careful not to say dirty linen; she didn't want to rile the woman any more than she already was. Rita Evans puffed out her cheeks. This was all she needed, and the whispers that Rita had a visit from the Old Bill would have already begun to circulate in the block, which never went down too well, especially with the crack dealers who lived on the floor above her.

"Oh, I suppose so if you must."

Anna and Steve Johnson walked in, and Steve closed the door. He had already realised that this was going to be a dead end, but he knew

better than to voice his opinion without being asked for it. When Anna got the bit between her teeth, there was no stopping her, so it was best to just go along for the ride and remain silent.

Entering the front room, it was dire; the plain walls, once magnolia in colour, were now heavily discoloured with yellow nicotine. The only furniture was an old, dilapidated and stained armchair, a coffee table and a seventies' smoked glass dining table with three odd chairs. What was a surprise was the forty-eight-inch smart television that sat in the corner. Rita had obviously got her priorities right! Flopping down into the armchair, Rita placed a cigarette into her mouth.

"So, what can I do for you? And I'll warn you both in advance, I ain't no grass."

"Ms Evans, we're interested in the whereabouts of your son Robbie."

The look of surprise was instant on Rita's face as she slowly shook her head.

"You're flogging a dead horse, love, at least where that nasty little cunt is concerned. I ain't seen him in years, nor do I want to. He never cared about me and ran off as soon as he reached eighteen. I mean, how can a son do that to his old mum?"

Anna didn't reply, but she silently answered the question in her head, 'Very easily, as it happens'.

"Well, thank you for your help, and if we need any more information, we know where to find

you. Don't bother getting up, we can see ourselves out."

Rita had no intention of getting up and had already switched on the television and turned the volume up before the door was closed. Anna and Steve left the flat and made their way back down the stairs. As they reached the car, three or four teenagers on bikes were loitering about, and Steve knew if they had been any longer, there would have been damage done to the car.

"Hi, Mister, want your motor watching?"

Steve gave a look of contempt, but didn't reply as he got into the car and, at the same time, called Beth Saunders. Anna waited impatiently until he hung up before continuing.

"Can you imagine living with that? I feel sorry for the bloke, and I haven't even met him yet. So, what do you think?"

"Well, I don't want to speak out of turn, Ma'am, but you have asked, and to be truthful, I think you're way off the mark. As far as we know, this Robbie bloke has only just left the army, and from what Nicky Stanton told us, was too wrapped up with Dodi Stanton to worry about anything else. Back to the station?"

Anna only nodded as she was deep in thought about what her Sergeant had just said. Seeing them enter the incident room, Beth Saunders came straight over and handed Anna a piece of paper. Peter Price, who was sitting opposite Sharon Manning, was all ears. For the last few

days, he had felt as if they had all been twiddling their thumbs.

"What am I looking at, Beth?"

"After Sergeant Johnson called in, I emailed the Ministry of Defence and explained the situation, and they were really helpful and sent this straight over. This is the last picture taken of Corporal Robert Evans. As far as they could tell me, it's less than two years old, but he's been out of the army for a while now, and they couldn't give me a forwarding address."

Anna was over the moon, and when she gave a broad grin, Beth felt chuffed with herself. The guv didn't give praise lightly, but when she smiled at something you'd done, it was praise enough. Detective Price bit down hard on his bottom lip. Why hadn't he thought of that? His partner, Sharon, had been watching him; she'd become concerned lately as he was behaving out of character.

"What's up, Pete?"

"This fucking place gets on my tits at times. You know something, I think they are leaving us out of things on purpose."

"Don't be daft, of course they ain't. They're just better at the job than us, that's all, but we'll get there in time."

Peter didn't like what his partner was saying; as far as he was concerned, he was at the top of his game. No, it was that bitch Draycott and her fucking supposedly hot-shot team. Anna

glanced over, and she knew by the look on his face what he was thinking, but she didn't have time to babysit or nurse his bruised ego. As far as Anna was concerned, if an officer couldn't handle the heat, then they had no business being on her team or in her incident room.

"Beth, get this circulated. I want this bastard caught."

Steve Johnson frowned. He knew Anna was good at her job, damn good in fact, but she had so little to go on.

"Are you sure, Ma'am? I mean, that's a bloody big jump, not to mention we have no proof."

Anna gave her sergeant a sideways glance, and he knew not to press the issue any further.

“Trust me on this. I might be wrong, but what if I’m not Steve?”

Back in the privacy of her office, Anna called Cherry.

"Hi, Boss, how's it going?"

"Not so well, we have a lead, but it's weak at best. You said you had a plan?"

"I'm going to somehow, and don't ask me how, as I don't yet know, get Stanton outside. I plan on clinging onto him like a limpet, and hopefully, the killer will see me."

“When?”

"Tomorrow night, if you give me the go-ahead."

"Okay, I'll get some more plain clothes on the street, but for God's sake, be careful, Cherry."

"I will, and as soon as we have a result, should I

say hopefully have a result, I'll call you."

With the call over, Anna sat back in her chair and placed her hands on the top of her head. This was dangerous, and she wasn't happy in the least. At the end of the day, it was Cherry's call, but Anna had also given it the green light. If anything happened, it would be her career on the line, but more than that, she was worried about the young officer's safety.

CHAPTER TWENTY-THREE

Anna Draycott had, to such a degree, convinced herself that Robbie Evans was the killer that instead of going to see Jamie Brewer herself, she sent Detectives Beth Saunders and Carl Shaw. Peter Price was raging: he felt that the Chief Inspector was leaving him and Sharon out on purpose, and if Anna was being truthful, the detective was probably right. He showed an air of arrogance that she didn't like, and as he was partnered with Sharon Manning, she was being pushed out as well.

"Tread lightly, Carl, we have no real reason to pay him a visit other than the fact that this Brewer bloke was on Romilly Street, and I don't trust a word that little man at the restaurant said. If you ask me, he's out for a bit of glory."

"Understood, Guv, you ready to leave Beth?"

The Detectives drove over to Duncan Street and pulled up outside the bed and breakfast; Beth removed a card stating that they were police on duty and placed it on the dashboard. This area of Islington was notorious for traffic wardens, and she didn't want to have to go back to the station and explain to Anna why they had got a parking ticket yet again. The house was in a row of terraces, not overly big and in all honesty, apart from the neon light in the window showing 'Vacancies', you wouldn't know it was a business. Knocking on the door, they waited to

be let in, and when Wilma Claxton opened up, she was all smiles in the hope that the couple were possible guests. When Beth showed her warrant card, the smile instantly disappeared.

"Mrs Wilma Claxton?"

"That's right, how can I help you, Officer?"

"Actually, it's Detective Saunders, and this is Detective Sergeant Shaw. Would it be possible to come in for a few minutes, as we have some questions regarding a man who has recently been staying with you?"

Wilma opened the door further so that the visitors could enter.

"Follow me through to the kitchen, please, as I would rather none of my guests know I have the police here."

The door was open when they passed the first room in the hallway, and it was clearly the guest's lounge. The next door had the word 'private' written on a small plastic sign, and Beth guessed this was Wilma's room. Walking into the kitchen, Wilma closed the door so that they couldn't be overheard. With the exterior design of the house and expecting a galley kitchen, Beth was surprised at the size of the room. A large scrubbed pine table took centre stage with an armchair in the corner facing a small television perched on a dresser.

"This is very cosy, Mrs Claxton."

"Thank you, I have my bedroom, but I spend most of my time in here. I have six letting

rooms, and that's including the loft conversion, so as you can imagine, space is at a premium. Now, how can I help you?"

"I believe you have or had a guest by the name of Jamie Brewer?"

"That's correct, lovely boy as well."

"Is he here at the moment?"

Wilma didn't like betraying a confidence, but she felt it was only fair if it would help poor Jamie in any way.

"No, he left a few days ago. After he saw his mother, he got a little angry, but he's calmed down now."

"What do you mean by angry, Mrs Claxton?"

Wilma motioned with her hand for them to take a seat at the table.

"It's not really my business, but as you're here and are the police, I suppose it's okay. He was adopted, and after his parents died, he wanted to find his real mother, who's in a home over on Dame Street. Really sad circumstances, but that's another story and definitely not mine to tell. Needless to say, he was angry with the street Toms, but he's over that now and has gone back to Leicester to start his life again. I'll miss him, but I'm glad really, this shit city ain't a good place for a nice young man to be spending his time in."

"Do you have a forwarding address?"

Standing up, Wilma pushed her chair back underneath the table; she had finished speaking

and wanted the visitors to leave. If they wanted to see Jamie badly enough, then they would have to work hard to find his location.

"No, I'm sorry, I don't."

Beth and Carl thanked the woman for her help and then returned to the station to bring Anna up to speed. It wasn't much, but Beth was sure they should follow it up; just the mention of Jamie's hatred of Toms had alarm bells ringing in her head. At the station, Anna was in her office, and when Beth and Carl entered, she listened intently to what they had to say.

"It's a lead and an interesting one at that, but hold off for now. If this Brewer bloke has gone back to Leicester, then the threat is reduced. Hopefully, I have something going down tomorrow, and I will need you both on board. I can't go into the exact details yet, but be ready to move on my say-so. For now, go home and get some rest, as I feel the next twenty-four hours will feel like a month."

Anna then called Cherry and arranged a meeting for the following afternoon.

Up bright and early, she drove over to Nicky Stanton's home. He was still in bed when she rang the bell, and he was reluctant to answer. Since Jan's death, he hadn't been sleeping much, and last night was the first decent sleep he'd had. It was sod's law that someone would disturb him, but after what had happened, he knew he had to respond. Padding through to the hall, he looked at the camera on the street door and tutted when he saw Anna Draycott's face looking up at the small screen. Buzzing the door open, Nicky quickly pulled on his trousers and grabbed a shirt just as she knocked on his door.

"Good afternoon, Inspector. This is becoming a regular occurrence; people will begin to talk. Well, come on in then."

Leaving her standing in the doorway, Nicky went to the kitchen and switched on the coffee machine.

"You'll have to excuse me, but I've only just woken up, and I can't function without a coffee. Want one?"

Anna nodded to be polite; she needed him on her side, so she didn't want to come across as standoffish by declining.

"Go take a seat in the front room, and I'll bring them through."

Doing as she was asked, Anna took a seat on the sofa and glanced around as she waited. The place was furnished nicely, but nothing like the home he had shared with his soon-to-be ex-wife. Picking up a picture frame from the coffee table, she studied the images of Nicky and Janice. They looked so happy, just as she and Jake had been, and for a second, images of her late husband flooded her mind. As Nicky entered, he coughed, bringing Anna back to the here and now and making her put the frame down onto

the table.

"Nice picture."

"Thanks, it's the only one I have of her. Here you go."

Nicky handed Anna her drink and then took a seat beside her.

"So, what can I do for you, Detective Inspector Draycott?"

Anna hesitated for a moment before she spoke.

"I want to set up a sting tonight or at least attempt one. Now there's no guarantee that it will work, but I have to try anything I can before that monster strikes again, and I am under no illusion that he won't. To pull it off, I need your cooperation."

"This sounds intriguing. Tell me more, Detective."

She knew he was flirting with her, and as Nicky gave a short laugh as he spoke, it riled Anna that he could find anything about the situation remotely amusing.

"This is no joking matter, Mr Stanton; you above all else should know that."

Her words hit home, and suddenly, he was overcome with guilt.

"I'm sorry, and I don't find it funny in any way, shape or form. It's just the way I am. So, what have you got planned?"

"There will be a woman outside your club tonight at around nine. She will become distressed, and when she calls for help, I want

you to come outside and embrace her. I know you usually have a man on the door, but just before nine, I want him to go inside. As you are the one being targeted, it needs to be you that the killer will hopefully see. Lead the woman inside and take her to your office, that's all I want you to do. The killer may not be in the vicinity, and it might all be a waste of time, but we have to try. So, are you in agreement?"

“Of course I am, anything to catch the cunt that butchered my Jan.”

Anna quickly drank her coffee, thanked Nicky for his help, and, after reiterating her instructions, returned to the station to drop off her car. There would be fewer questions from her team if she told them she had some private business to attend to and would be back later. Entering the underground, she took the northern line to Temple and then finished the short journey on foot to link up with Cherry. Arranging to meet at a small coffee house on Fleet Street, Anna had chosen the area as it was unlikely anyone from the club or station would be in the vicinity. When she walked in and scanned the tables, she didn't immediately see Cherry. It wasn't until she saw a bangle-covered arm in the air, waving at her, that she did a double-take. No wonder the young woman was good at her job;

Anna hardly recognised her. Cherry Graham looked the epitome of a prostitute, and Anna could only gasp. Taking a

seat opposite Cherry, she studied the woman for a few seconds before she spoke. The usually neat and tidy blonde hair was messy and piled high on the top of Cherry's head. Large, garish earrings swung whenever she moved her head, and the bright blue eyeshadow and crimson lipstick were almost comical. High boots and tight leggings were topped off with a gold puffer jacket, and the numerous bangles on Cherry's arm continually jangled every time she reached for her coffee. Anna also noticed the look of contempt her friend was receiving from the staff and other customers, and it made her realise how judgmental people were at times, and she had to include herself in that, but none of it seemed to bother Cherry.

"My, you scrub up...., well, I don't know how to complete that sentence. Doesn't it bother you looking like that and all the nasty glances people are giving you?"

"And good afternoon to you as well, Guvnor. The answer to your question is no, if I didn't look this way and have people looking down their noses at me, then I wouldn't be doing my job properly, now would I?"

"Sorry, I should have said hello first, it's just you really have shocked me, but in a good way."

Anna beckoned for the waitress to come over, and after ordering a cup of tea, she leaned in close so that they couldn't be overheard.

"I've arranged for plain clothes to be on the street

tonight, and Nicky Stanton, although he doesn't know it's you, has agreed to take part. It might all turn out to be a waste of time, but it's worth a shot, and we can't then be accused of not trying. At nine o'clock, you need to be at the front of the club and cry out for help. Stanton will then come running out and embrace you before taking you back inside. Your cover will be blown, but we can't carry on in the hope that the killer will randomly pick you to attack."

Cherry had a broad grin on her face; she loved it when chances were taken, and she could already feel the adrenaline rushing through her veins.

"I will have officers follow you for the rest of the evening and then back to the bedsit, as that's when you will be at your most vulnerable. I don't want you taking any unnecessary chances, Cherry."

"I won't, I promise, so I suppose it's fingers crossed until tonight then. I'd better get back and get ready."

“You mean to tell me you’re not ready with how you’re dressed now?”

"Oh no, I have to get sexy, Ma'am. I take it the coffee is on you?"

Cherry stood up and, not waiting for Anna to reply, swaggered out of the café, calling out as she went.

“See ya all later, bitches!”

Anna scanned the small area and couldn’t help but try and fail dismally, to stifle a giggle as she

looked at all of the middle-class faces, some with their mouths open in shock. About to return to the station, Anna's mobile burst into life and, glancing at the screen, she slowly closed her eyes. She had hoped to get the Supers' permission for tonight via the phone, but now she had been summoned to the Yard, and she wondered if this would be the end of her involvement in the Soho case. From Fleet Street, it was less than a mile, so hailing a cab, she was soon on her way. Fred Maynard, the cabbie, a middle-aged man who voluntarily informed her that he hailed from Bermondsey, asked question after question. The main one was what she was going to Scotland Yard for. Anna smiled in a friendly manner as she told him it was top secret, and if she told him, she would have to kill him. The reply had Fred even more interested, but no matter how hard he tried, by the time he pulled up close to the destination, he was no further forward in getting an answer. Passing through the rigorous security, Anna was again met by the upright woman dressed in a skirt and twinset. Miss Tunmore, the Super's secretary, was no more friendly than she had been on Anna's last visit and without a word being spoken, Anna followed the woman up to the Super's office and took a seat outside without being asked. A couple of minutes later, the door opened.

"Come on in, Anna and take a seat."

Her palms were sweating far worse than they had on her initial visit, and she nervously wiped her right hand onto her skirt before the Super even tried to shake it.

"So, how much further forward are we? I've got the basic reports, but they are never in minute detail, as you well know. I suppose it gives the station involved a bit of a get-out clause."

Anna explained that there were two possible suspects and that they were, with his permission, hoping to put a trap into place that night to lure out the killer.

"That's risky, Chief Inspector. If anything goes wrong, it will be your neck on the block."

She knew by his referring to her by her rank rather than her name, as he'd done a few moments earlier, that he wouldn't take any prisoners, and her career could be over.

"I'm only too aware of that, Sir, but all traps are dangerous. I have taken extra measures, and there will be plenty of plainclothes officers on the street to keep an eye on Cherry. If we don't do this, then I haven't got a clue how to proceed, as we still have nothing concrete to go on."

“And, the two suspects?”

"As I said, Sir, they are possible suspects, but we have no real evidence, to be honest, not even enough to warrant pulling them in for questioning."

Deputy Chief Superintendent Madden tapped his bottom lip with his index finger for a few seconds before he spoke again, which made Anna even more nervous.

"Alright, you have the green light, but I say that with grave reservation. I'm not happy about it Chief Inspector, but I understand your team is between a rock and a hard place. I'm under pressure from above, but I don't want to remove you from the case as I feel you're the best suited, but just tread carefully, and for your sake, I hope to God that nothing goes wrong. To be on the safe side, have a couple of armed officers in attendance as well."

When she reached outside, Anna breathed a sigh of relief, but there was still an awful feeling of foreboding. Deciding to walk to the nearest underground station to clear her head and get the plan firmly fixed in her mind, she set off along the embankment.

CHAPTER TWENTY-FOUR

Anna returned to the station at Charing Cross and called all of the team into the incident room, and as usual, Peter and Sharon were the last to enter, much to Anna's annoyance. This time, she let things slide; they had both been on their game today, and Peter wasn't harbouring any further ill will about being reprimanded, or at least none that she had noticed. There was a lot of chatter and low murmuring, and she waited for the room to fall silent before she began.

"As some of you are now aware, there will be a trap set this evening. What I haven't as yet been able to share with you all is the fact that an undercover officer has been working at the club."

Peter Price was seething and whispered under his breath, though still audible to the majority in the room, Anna included.

“That’s bang out of fucking order!”

It was a step too far, and this time Anna couldn't let the remark go.

“I beg your pardon!”

Her tone was loud and stern, and Sergeant Johnson could only bow his head and roll his eyes upwards as if to say, 'Here we go. '

"I said, it's bang out of order, Ma'am. I mean, if you're keeping us all in the dark, how are we supposed to solve this crime, Ma’aaaam?”

His use of the word Ma'am was elongated and

said with sarcasm, which everyone noticed. Anna had never been spoken to so disrespectfully in front of her team before, and she was having none of it.

"Detective Price, I have let your previous lateness go as we need to be on the ball, especially today, but that fucking remark was a step too far! Your work is shoddy at best, and the reason my team and I are here is because you are inadequate at your job. I allowed you to stay on this team, though God above knows why, possibly in the hope that you would redeem yourself. For your information, there was nothing to be gained by any of you knowing about the undercover operation, and a bloody lot to lose for the officer involved should word have got out. You know something, I do not have the time or the inclination for this. Clear your desk."

"You can't do that!"

"Oh, believe me, I can, and whether you have a job on the force at the end of all this will be up to me as well, and at the moment, that is looking highly unlikely. Get out of my incident room, now!!!"

Peter's face was scarlet with rage, not to mention embarrassment, as he stormed out of the room, slamming the door closed as he went.

At eight forty-five that night, the black transit van was parked up in the car park of St Anne's churchyard on Dean Street. At eight-fifty-five,

Anna gave the order, and everyone disembarked. Beth and Carl were dressed for an evening out and would pose as a couple. Sergeant Johnson wore a long beige mac and was supposed to be a punter, but Anna wanted to laugh when she saw him, as he resembled a flasher more than anything. Anna was dressed down in jeans and a bomber jacket and was carrying a bucket of roses; it was a regular sight as the flower sellers often frequented the restaurants and clubs in the area. There were also two armed officers situated on the upper floor of the building opposite Nicky's place, but Anna was still feeling uneasy. At nine on the dot, Cherry Graham walked towards the club. Maxi Wilmore was nowhere to be seen, and Anna sighed with relief. When Cherry was almost at the door, she feigned slipping on the curb, and as she fell to the ground with her legs in the air, she screamed out in agony. Within a few seconds, Nicky was on the street and helping Cherry to her feet. Embracing him, she wrapped her arms around his neck and kissed him on the cheek as he helped her into the club and down the hallway to his office.

"Oh my Knight in shining armour, thank you, babe."

Nicky Stanton didn't speak until the office door was firmly closed.

"Well fuck me, girl, I never would have taken you for Old Bill."

Cherry laughed and then smiled at her former boss.

"That's because I'm good at my job, Mr Stanton."

"Too bloody good! So what happens next?"

"In a few minutes, I will hobble out of here and head home. Hopefully, the killer will follow me, but it's a long stretch and probably won't happen. Thanks for taking part in all of this anyway."

Nicky only nodded as the mouthy girl he had so readily accepted as a brass left the office. Laughing under his breath, he was stopped when one of his burner mobiles began to ring. He immediately answered, but obviously there was no called id.

"Hello?"

"Hi, Boss. Everything went off as sweet as a nut, but we ain't done a final count yet. By the size of the haul, I'm estimating well over half a mill."

"So, what's the state of play regarding our helpful friend?"

"He was totally believed, and that greedy cunt Macey can't call the Old Bill as he'd hidden all of the cash from the tax man."

Arty Clements had been careful not to mention any of the firm by name. The victim's name or location didn't matter much. In their game, it was second nature to use aliases if it was necessary, as you never knew who was listening, but that wasn't needed today. The firm relied heavily on burners, and Nicky often joked he

should have shares in one of the suppliers, but still, he never took anything for granted, as the Old Bill had high-end technology which was getting better by the day.

"Good job, I'll call over in the morning."

With that, Nicky hung up, and he was now beaming from ear to ear. Maybe things were starting to pick up, and if they caught the cunt that'd been hurting his girls, it would be the icing on the cake. Out on the street, all eyes were on Cherry and limping along the pavement, she slowly made her way home. It had been timed to perfection with Steve Johnson walking ahead of her by a hundred yards. Beth Saunders and Carl Shaw followed behind, but at a safe enough distance that they wouldn't be connected, and Anna was a few feet behind them. The armed officers had been told to stand down; she hadn't actually thought they were necessary, but Chief Superintendent Madden had insisted, and you didn't say no to him if you knew what was good for you. It had been highly unlikely that a shoot-out would happen, and they had only been in situ in case the killer had taken a pot shot in front of the club and put Cherry in danger. From the past attacks, it wasn't his MO, but she supposed all bases had to be covered. Reaching the bedsit on Bridle Lane, Cherry went inside, and when Anna saw her enter, she decided it was safe to go back to Romilly Street. Sergeant Johnson continued

along until he was out of sight, and Beth and Carl did the same. Within a few minutes, they had all rejoined Anna back at the van.

"So, Guv, how do you think it went?"

Anna puffed out her cheeks and slowly shook her head.

"I haven't got the foggiest, Beth. Only time will tell, but at least Cherry's safe for now. Let's call it a night and resume tomorrow bright and early."

In her bedsit, Cherry lay on the bed and wondered if she'd done enough. Either way, this particular job would be over in the next day or so. Until she was told otherwise, she would continue with the ruse of being a brass, but she had an idea that Chief Inspector Draycott would soon be contacted by the men on high and told to stand down. The adrenaline had left her body, and she now felt exhausted. Removing her makeup, she crawled into bed and, for the first time since she'd been here, Cherry instantly dropped off to sleep; even the usual noise from outside didn't disturb her.

The following day, Anna was the first to arrive at the station, so she decided to check in with Cherry. As it was all out in the open now, there was no need for secrecy, but she still preferred to talk to the woman privately. The phone rang several times before it was answered, and for a few seconds, Anna could feel the concern as it rose from the pit of her stomach. Finally, Cherry

picked up, and Anna breathed a sigh of relief.

"Thank the Lord, you had me worried for a minute, Cherry."

"Sorry, Guv, I slept like a baby and have only just woken up. So, what's the state of play?"

"I have a meeting with the Super later today, so go back to the club tonight, and I'll be in contact first thing tomorrow. I expect him to end the undercover soon, but then I imagine you already know that. Do you have any money left in the kitty, although I don't think Nicky Stanton will expect you to be with any punters?"

They both laughed, and after Anna ended the call, Cherry lay back on the bed and drifted off to sleep again.

At just after five, Anna had her meeting with Deputy Chief Superintendent Madden, and it went exactly as she had thought. He wasn't best pleased that, as yet, the operation had proven fruitless, and there was still a serial killer on the loose.

"I must say, it all seems to have been a waste of time, not to mention money, Chief Inspector, and it won't go down well with the Chief Constable, and as I gave the go-ahead, it will be down to me to deliver the results."

His tone pissed Anna off, and as such, she spoke out of turn, regretting it immediately.

"And what the hell do you expect me to do, magic the culprit out of thin air?"

"I beg your pardon. Don't forget your rank,

Inspector!"

Slowly closing her eyes for a second, Anna knew she had stepped over the line big style. Remarks like the one she'd just made would be an invisible black mark on her record, but a remark all the same when it came to promotion.

"Forgive me, Sir; it's just that I'm at my wits' end with this case. No matter what we do, we just seem to hit a brick wall at every turn. The undercover operative will work her last shift tonight, and then, to be honest, I don't know what to do next."

It was a rhetorical question, but the Super answered all the same.

"Apology accepted, and the only advice I can offer is good old-fashioned police work. Start at the beginning. I know your record, Inspector Draycott, and if you can't solve this case, then no one can. Admittedly, it's taking far longer than I had initially hoped, but you will get there, just keep chipping away at it, and if the Chief Constable isn't happy with that, then he should get off his arse and do some real police work for once."

Anna let out a giggle; the mood was now relaxed, and she knew her record would thankfully remain unblemished.

That night, Cherry set off for Romilly Street. Approaching the club, she sighed heavily. She hated not getting closure on a case, but she was also relieved at not having to play this role

anymore. In the past, she had acted as a prostitute on several occasions, but there was something about this case that just didn't feel right. It was a little before eight thirty when she walked into the bar, and the place was packed. The other girls all welcomed her and enquired how her ankle was, so she was confident that Nicky Stanton hadn't blown her cover.

"Is the Boss in Rosie?"

"Yeah, babe, he's in the office."

Cherry knocked on the door and waited until she heard his voice call out, 'Enter.' To say Nicky was shocked to see her was an understatement.

“Didn’t think I’d set eyes on you again?”

Cherry smiled; even though she was undercover, she had come to like the man. He was good to his girls, something very unusual in the world of vice.

"My last night in Soho, so I'm just having a mooch about, but no punters."

Now it was Nicky’s turn to laugh.

"Did you really do it?"

"Of course I didn't, but you never knew that, did you?"

"You got me there, love. So, was there any joy from last night's little drama show?"

"Not as yet, but it was a long shot hoping the killer would be watching, but we had to try something."

"Are things really that dire? I mean, you must

have something to go on by now. I fucking hate the thought that my Jan died and no one will ever be brought to book over it."

He felt a bit bad saying what he had just said, as even his men hadn't been able to find anything out. Cherry took a seat on the opposite side of the desk, and when he offered her a whiskey, she nodded her head.

"Thanks. That won't happen, Nicky, I can assure you of that. One way or another, we will get him, and it's definitely when and not if. Whoever is doing this is one smart operator, but my boss is like a dog with a bone and will never let it drop until she finds them. Not only that, but this city needs to feel safe, and while he's still on the loose, no woman is safe anywhere. Eventually, all criminals slip up, and you would do well to remember that, Nicky."

“I don’t know what you mean, Cherry!”

They both laughed, and after finishing her drink, Cherry called it a night. After saying her goodbyes to the girls, she set off to spend the last night in her squalid accommodation. Bridle Lane had several people milling about, a brass was giving a blow job in one of the doorways opposite, and a drunk was taking a piss in another. A group of rowdy youngsters were cutting through the lane on their way to Brewer Street, and Cherry smiled to herself. She couldn't remember feeling that young and carefree, and for a moment it bothered her. She

wasn't old by any means, but was she putting too much effort and time into her career? The only problem was that she couldn't afford not to; if she did, then her life would be in constant danger, well, at least more than it was already. Climbing the stairs, she let herself into number three. Locking the door behind her, she then tried the handle again just for good measure. As she turned, Cherry didn't immediately see him standing in the corner, but by the time she did, it was too late to open the door and get out. The blade glistened in the dim light from the open curtains, and for the first time during this entire job, she felt scared. She took a sharp intake of breath as the man took a step forward. Cherry couldn't see his face clearly, but she still knew deep down that he was the killer.

"Thought you could draw me out last night, did you? I've been on this bleeding planet a lot longer than you, you stupid slag. I was behind all those fucking idiots as they followed you home."

"But I'm not a prostitute, and you only kill prostitutes."

"I did, but for you, I'm going to make an exception, and besides, you've seen my face now, sweetheart, so it's too late."

Cherry knew that if she had any chance of survival, she had to keep him talking. Walking over to the bed, she sat down, and in seconds, he was standing in front of her.

“Can I ask you why you have been doing this? What did those poor women ever do to you?”

"They are disgusting, dirty whores and have been the cause of a lot of hurt for someone I love very much, and I will continue wiping them off the face of the earth for as long as I can."

Cherry was trying to think fast, anything to stop him from killing her, but she was running out of things to say and more importantly, she was running out of time.

"A lot of those women don't have a choice or were put on the streets when they were so young that they have never been able to get off."

"Shut the fuck up, I've had enough of your shit, you're as bad as them."

With one swift move, the blade slashed through Cherry Graham's neck, and blood spurted out. She couldn't speak, and with eyes bulging wide open in terror, there was just the sound of gurgling. Her attacker hadn't finished; he wanted to send a message to the police that he wouldn't stop, and he didn't care who got in his way. Arranging Cherry's body so that it was spread-eagled on the bed, he ripped open her clothes and then plunged the blade into her chest over and over again until his frenzy slowly died down. Rubbing his hand in her blood, he then daubed the wall. The words read 'All whores and anyone who saves them will go to hell!' After removing his gloves and washing his hands in the sink, the killer then let himself out

of the bedsit and after checking the street was relatively clear, he pulled up the collar of his coat and slowly walked down the lane, unnoticed by anyone.

The next morning, Anna was back in the office by seven, but delayed calling Detective Graham in case Cherry was having a lie-in. Walking into the incident room, she couldn't be off noticing that it was unusually quiet. The team were all there, and she'd seen the same scenario in the McKay case when they had continually hit a brick wall. Walking to the front of the room, she coughed loudly.

"I know you are all feeling a bit dejected that we haven't had a result, but that's the nature of this job, and you all know that. As the Super told me yesterday, we have to start at the beginning and do some good old police work; it's the only way we are going to find this fucking maniac. Sergeant Johnson, you're with me, Beth and Carl, as usual, you'll be together. Sharon, now that you're on your own, you can team up with Dave. Decide between yourselves who's doing what, start with the brasses and then go on to the club. It's unlikely, but see if Nicky Stanton has remembered anything else. Talk to that restaurant owner again, and if you have no joy, the two of you take a trip to Leicester and speak to Jamie Brewer. I shall be paying Dodi Stanton another visit, and then I'll get Detective Graham in to tell you all that she knows, and any

hunches she might have. Her experience working with the Toms might give you all a better insight. Oh, and Beth, get that photograph of Robbie Evans out to all of the beat Bobbies; someone must know where he is. Come on then, you lot, roust yourselves."

Her pep talk seemed to have done them all the world of good, as within seconds the incident room was once again a hive of activity.

CHAPTER TWENTY-FIVE

Dodi was saying goodbye to her father at the front door, and she sighed heavily when she saw Anna and Sergeant Johnson pull up. She really didn't want to deal with anyone today.

"What's the matter, sweetheart?"

"Oh, nothing, Dad, it's just the police again. I don't know how many times I have to tell them that I don't know anything about what's been happening to Nicky's girls, but they still keep coming around. Anyway, you get off and send my love to mum even though she doesn't want it."

Wally Smith laughed as he leaned in to kiss his daughter on the cheek. Since she had called at the flat, the two had made a pact to meet up at least once a week, and he enjoyed visiting his daughter at her home.

"Will do, sweetheart, and tell the filth to sling their bleeding hooks."

Dodi was a good girl and had been through so much recently, things she didn't deserve. Anyone giving her more stress pissed Wally off big time. Anna eyed the portly man with spectacles as she walked up the path. Dressed in jeans and a Harrington jacket, he was pretty nondescript. Wally touched the peak of his cap as they passed each other, Anna smiled. She wouldn't have given him a second thought until he was about to get into his car and called out.

"I would think you'd have better fucking things to do than to keep harassing my daughter."

With how the case was going, or not going in her case, Anna had just about had enough and walked back down to the pavement. She peered into the passenger side of the car just as Wally got into the driver's seat and opened the electric window.

"We are doing everything we can, Mr?"

Wally didn't offer his surname; he, like most of his generation, had little time for the police. Anna was scanning the interior of the car when she was suddenly stopped by the man's next sentence.

"Well, it's a fucking liberty, and my girl should be left alone, all you're doing is fucking causing her more aggro, and it's bang out of order."

"Sir? If we have to come back here a hundred times, then we will."

Wally still didn't offer his name and only sneered at her before closing the window and driving off at speed.

"I'm sorry about my dad, Officer. He's a cabbie, and you know what they are like, a law unto themselves most of the time. He always thinks he can say whatever he wants, to whomever he wants, without any consequences. He really doesn't mean any malice; he just cares about me, that's all. Please, come in, and I'll make some tea."

When they were seated in the front room and

after Dodi had placed down the steaming hot mugs, Anna once again asked her to go over the events of the last few weeks.

"Really? As I told you before, my marriage came to a sudden and upsetting end. I'm sorry that the woman my husband was having an affair with has died, but it has nothing to do with me. I've only seen Nicky a few times since then, and he doesn't want to talk about it. I suppose one reason might be because he hurt me so badly, and even mentioning her name gets my blood boiling."

"Don't you find that a bit strange? I mean, his girlfriend was murdered, and he doesn't mention it?"

Dodi couldn't believe what she was hearing or how insensitive the woman was being.

"Did you not just hear what I said? No, I don't, my husband might have fallen out of love with me, but he still cares, and to talk to me about his other woman would be cruel, even you must see that, Inspector?"

Anna immediately realised that she had spoken out of turn, and after apologising, she stood up and motioned with her eyes to Steve Johnson that it was time they left. Dodi glanced down at the mugs on the coffee table that remained untouched.

"I'll see you both out, and I really hope you don't need to come back as there is absolutely nothing more I can tell you."

Back in the car, Sergeant Johnson turned to face Anna.

"Well, you royally fucked up there, Guv, if you don't mind me saying."

"Well, I do mind; now drive me over to Bridle Lane, I need to see Cherry."

The Lane was narrow, so Steve Johnson stopped the car and switched on the hazard lights. Anna told him to wait as she would only be a minute. Climbing the stairs to number three, she knocked and waited for her newfound friend to answer. Knocking again, Anna started to get agitated when there was no answer. Cherry hadn't said she was going out. Removing her phone, she pressed call, and when she heard the woman's phone ring on the other side of the door, she suddenly felt sick. Running down the stairs, she screamed at Steve and then ran back into the hall. When Sergeant Johnson reached her, he could see that her face was as white as a sheet.

"What's wrong, Guv?"

"It's Cherry, I knocked, but there was no answer. I called her phone, and it's ringing from inside. There's no way she would go out without it. Are you up to breaking down the door?"

Steve Johnson was in his mid-fifties and took her words personally as if she thought he was past it. Not bothering to answer her, he ran up the stairs with Anna following, and a second later, he kicked out with all of his might. Like the rest

of the house, the door and its lock were old and in poor condition, so they gave way without much effort. Strangely, Anna allowed her sergeant to go in first, and as he glanced around the room, he stopped dead in his tracks. As soon as he saw the carnage, he walked back onto the landing and turned towards Anna, who was impatiently waiting for an update. Steve's face was ashen as he vigorously shook his head.

"Don't go in there."

"Why? What the fuck has happened?"

"She's dead, boss, we need to call it in."

"I want to see her, Steve!"

He grabbed his boss's arms and stared directly into her eyes.

"I know, but you can't risk contaminating the scene. Now come on, Guv, we have to do this by the book, you know that."

Still holding on to one of her arms, they walked back down the stairs, and when they stepped out into the fresh air, Anna suddenly vomited into the gutter. Thankfully, she hadn't yet seen the state of Cherry; her reaction was purely down to the fact that the woman was dead. Wiping her mouth with the back of her hand, Anna told Steve to make the call. He was worried about her, and while they waited, he tried to make conversation about anything that came to mind, but Anna wasn't interested.

"What did she look like?"

"Honestly, Guv, I didn't see much, but what I

did glimpse didn't look good. I'm confident it was our killer, let's just hope that the scene of crimes team can get something this time."

Anna was on tenterhooks for the next hour as the investigators carried out a thorough examination of the bedsit. Due to its size, it didn't take too long and when Anna was at last informed that a pair of rolled-up latex gloves had been found down the side of the fridge, she hoped beyond hope that they belonged to the killer and they would at least be able to extract some DNA. Cherry's attacker had placed the gloves down when he washed his hands, and they were so close to the edge of the fridge that he hadn't noticed when they had rolled off. It was obvious that getting any prints would be nigh on impossible, but when they finally did catch him, then any DNA could seal his fate.

"Well, that's something, I suppose. We should get back to the station, Steve, so that I can file my report. I have no doubt I'll be called to the Yard tomorrow and hauled over the coals, so I want everything to be done properly."

Phoning the Lab, Anna was able to speak directly to Mike Hanks, who, when informed that he was about to receive the body of an officer, offered his condolences.

"I don't want to put any pressure on you, Mike, but when do you think you can carry out the autopsy?"

"It's one of our own, so as soon as Detective

Graham arrives here, I will begin. Come and see me tomorrow morning, and hopefully, I will have some news for you by then."

Anna thanked him. Mike was normally an arsehole, but not this time and for that she was grateful. The guilt was beginning to consume her, and knowing that her career was on the line, though second to losing Cherry, was still playing heavily on her mind. At Charing Cross station, the two officers entered a very sombre incident room. Her team all hung their heads as she entered, knowing how personally their boss would be taking the loss. Anna told Steve Johnson to call it a day once he had written up his own report. She would stay for as long as it took to write hers and then check his, but Anna didn't confide in her sergeant that she just didn't want to go home. In the solitude of her office, she closed the door and finally allowed herself to break down. The tears came thick and fast, and Anna had to place her hand over her mouth so that no one in the hallway would hear her cry out. An hour later, she had completed her statement of events, and after checking her sergeants, she walked over to the sofa and took a seat. She had only planned to take a five-minute break, but didn't wake until six the next morning. Rushing back to the house, Anna showered, changed her clothes and was back at the station a little before eight. When she walked in, Steve Johnson was already in the

incident room, and he smiled when she entered.

"Morning, Guv, did you manage to get any shut-eye?"

"Strangely, yes, but I need to speak to you before the others arrive. We need to get to the lab before the Super calls me to the Yard, as I'm under no illusion that a suspension is on the cards."

Sergeant Johnson went to speak, but was silenced when Anna held up her palm.

"Please just listen, we haven't got much time. Now, when the suspension comes, I want you to guide Beth, as she will be the one to temporarily take over. I trust her totally, but she still lacks confidence. I know Carl and Dave are more senior, and both have more years under their belts, but Beth has a more sensitive side, and as we are dealing with females both dead and alive, I think she will be better suited to the role. Right, let's get on our way, shall we?"

It was a rhetorical question, something Anna often did, and he knew her so well by now that he didn't even attempt a reply. The four-mile journey over to St John's Wood took almost forty minutes due to the commuter traffic, but there was no other option, and to say Anna was frustrated by the time they arrived was an understatement. Steve had seen his boss like this many times over the years and just hoped she wasn't about to kick off at Mike Hanks when they got inside. Making their way down to the

basement, and after Steve had rang the bell, he could see Anna out of the corner of his eye, and she was slightly moving from one foot to the other, desperate to get inside. One of Mike's assistants opened up, but he'd seen the officers before, so he didn't ask for any identification. Leading them through to Mike's office, the assistant knocked on the door and then walked off. A few seconds later, Mike could be heard calling out 'Enter!' Steve tried to stifle a sigh as Anna walked in, but luckily, Mike Hanks wasn't alone, so Steve knew she would be on her guard and hopefully behave without getting Mike's back up.

"Hi Anna, and before you ask, yes, I have already carried out the post-mortem. Let me introduce you to Roger McCormack. Roger, this is Chief Inspector Anna Draycott."

Roger and Anna nodded towards each other, but no words were spoken.

"Now I know how personal this one is to you and your team, Anna. Come to that, it is personal to all of us, so getting as much information as possible is paramount. Roger and I were at Oxford together, and he's one of the leading figures in criminal psychology. Roger, over to you."

"Thanks, Mike. Now, I've looked at all of the previous reports, Inspector, and the attack on this latest victim differs from the others."

Anna was intrigued and also grateful for the

extra help.

"How so?"

"Well, this one was very personal, and if, as you suspect, the others were regarding a vendetta against a certain man, this one wasn't. It might have been in the beginning, but the way the victim was posed and from the photographs of the writing on the wall, this is a payback crime targeting the police."

Anna had yet to see the Scene of Crimes report, so she was in the dark about what he was talking about. She gave Steve a look that said, 'Writing, what writing?' Mike Hanks was looking smug, and it galled her as she knew he was aware that she didn't have a clue what Roger McCormack was talking about. Smiling, Mike then began to discuss his findings.

"I'm sorry for what I'm about to reveal, as this will be upsetting, Inspector. The victim's throat was slashed, but not so deeply as to cause immediate death; it would have taken several seconds. She was then stabbed over and over again in a definite frenzy."

Roger McCormack waited for Mike to finish his sentence and then took over the conversation. "Mike stopped counting at twenty wounds as they began to merge into one another. The one thing I can tell you, Anna, if I may call you Anna? It is the same person, though his viciousness has now escalated. Mike has confirmed that the cuts are a perfect match to the

other victims, and once again, it was the same commando Bowie knife that was used."

Anna was still thinking about how poor Cherry was killed and how much she must have suffered. Thanking Mike and his friend, she walked from the room with Steve following close behind, and she couldn't hide the tears as they rolled down her cheeks.

"Take me back to the station; I need to see that report as soon as possible."

The incident room was still quiet when Anna and Steve walked in, but Beth approached her boss as soon as she saw them. The team had been privy to the report, and Beth handed over a copy.

"It makes for difficult reading, Guv."

Anna only nodded her head and then retreated to her office alone. Seated behind her desk, she opened up the manila folder and began to read. By the time she finished and after studying the scene and the post-mortem photographs, the tears were again falling thick and fast. Poor Cherry had really suffered, and the images Anna studied were horrific. Blowing her nose, she sniffed hard just as her mobile rang.

"Chief Inspector Anna Draycott, speaking."

Anna already knew it was a call from New Scotland Yard, but she wasn't about to crumble on the phone.

"Good morning, Inspector. This is Deputy Chief Superintendent Madden's secretary."

Anna had a vision of the stern woman grinning on the other end of the line, but that actually wasn't the case.

"Deputy Chief Superintendent Madden would like you to attend a meeting, so I'm calling to schedule. When is it good for you?"

“I don’t mind, whatever suits.”

What the woman said next surprised Anna, but she didn't comment.

"There is time today, but I can delay it until tomorrow if that would help you, as I imagine there are things you would like to get put into place."

Reading between the lines, Anna knew it was going to be bad news, but why would this woman even want to help her? After agreeing to a ten o'clock slot the following morning, Anna thanked the secretary and then phoned through to the incident room and asked for Steve and Beth to come to her office. When the door was closed, she offered them both a seat.

"I've been called to the Yard tomorrow, and I expect a suspension at best and the end of my career at worst. Whatever happens, Beth, you will be standing in, and I want you to rely heavily on Steve. I have every confidence in you, but Sergeant Johnson is experienced and one of my oldest colleagues, not to mention a friend. I doubt you will have any problems with the rest of the team, but if you do, then refer them to Steve; he will handle it for you."

Beth was shocked and could only nod her head.

“Steve, could you drive me tomorrow?”

"Certainly, Ma'am."

"Best if you collect me from the house, there's no point in going from here, and to be honest, I don't think I could face everyone. Right, now that's all sorted, I'm leaving for the day. I have a lot of things to get sorted out, and there isn't much more I can do here. Thank you both for all of your help, and it's been an honour working with you."

Anna didn't wait around for a response because she knew if Beth started to cry, which she undoubtedly would, then Anna would also break down, and that was something she would never allow any of her team to be witness to. Quickly exiting the station, she climbed into her car and set off for home. It was strange how the most stupid things entered a person's head, and as she drove along, she laughed when it crossed her mind that she would have to hand back her car, as it belonged to the force. Jake had always wanted her to have her own, but she had argued it was a waste of money; now he was probably going to get his wish.

CHAPTER TWENTY-SIX

By the time Steve Johnson tapped on the front door, Anna was already dressed and seated at the breakfast bar in the kitchen. Nursing her second cup of coffee, she sighed heavily when she heard the sound. Her sleep had been almost non-existent, and after tossing and turning for most of the night, she finally gave in and got up. Her stomach was churning at the thought of no longer having a job, as without it, she had nothing to live for. Opening the door, she smiled weakly and beckoned for Steve to step inside.

"Ready?"

"Ready as I'll ever be, I suppose."

"Ma'am, I just wanted to say...."

Anna held up her hand to stop him.

"Don't Steve, please, I'm gutted at what I know is about to happen, and if you start being overly nice to me, I know I won't make the meeting, that or I will go in with red eyes, and I will not give those bastards the satisfaction of seeing me like that. I've tried so hard with this case, but it was a non-starter from the off, and now they just want someone to carry the can and are making me the scapegoat. I know Beth is leading in the interim, but I feel sorry for whoever takes over next. I'm confident that it won't be Beth; the top brass won't allow it as she's too inexperienced. Come on then, let's get going"

The journey would take just over twenty minutes, and to begin with, it was carried out in silence, but just as they passed the Royal Albert Hall, everything changed when Anna suddenly shouted out.

"Fuck, fuck, fuck!!!!!"

She then slammed both of her open palms down hard onto the front of the glove box.

"I don't fucking believe it, how could I have been so blind!"

It was so sudden that Steve jammed on the brakes, which almost caused an accident. Car horns began beeping, and cabbies were giving rude hand gestures as they passed the car, but nothing could get Steve to continue as he just stared wide-eyed at his boss.

"What on earth is wrong, Ma'am?"

Anna held up her hand to silence him as she closed her eyes and bit down hard on her bottom lip, something she always did when she was deep in thought. It was several seconds before she opened them again, and then she stared directly into her sergeant's eyes.

"Why in God's name didn't it register that's not like me?"

"I'm not sure I know what you mean, Guv, actually, I know I don't."

"I mean, I think I know who it is and when I tell you, it will sound ridiculous."

Steve had worked with Inspector Draycott long enough to know that she didn't take anything

she saw as gospel nor believed everything she heard; come to that, she always had to be completely certain before she even voiced any real opinion. For an outburst such as this, she was sure, of that he had no doubt.

"An image just flashed in my mind. I don't know what made it happen, but I'm fucking grateful it did. You remember the last time we went to see Dodi Stanton, and her father was coming out of the house, and he was rude to us?"

"Yes, but what's that..."

Anna again held up her hand to cut him off; it was becoming a regular occurrence and one that was starting to irritate him a bit.

"When I went over to his car, and he was giving me all that verbal, I was pissed off and wasn't really concentrating on the job in hand. My head was all over the place with this case, and I haven't really slept much in the last couple of weeks."

“Ma'am?”

“Well, now I'm convinced I saw a knife on the floor of the passenger side foot well."

"Was it a Bowie?"

"I'm not sure. I mean, who drives around with a knife in the front of their car? I can't believe I was so preoccupied with what was being said to me that I completely took my eye off the ball."

Steve Johnson puffed out his cheeks; he didn't know how to reply to that.

"It could be innocent, I suppose."

"Really, you think so? I doubt that, and I have a gut feeling about this, albeit a little late in the day. Look, I have to get to this meeting, and I'm sure that when I get out of it, I will no longer be in charge of the case, but right at this moment I still am, so I want you to listen to exactly what I am about to say, well, drive then, or you'll make me late!"

Reaching New Scotland Yard, Anna took a moment to thank her sergeant for all his past help, both professionally and privately.

"It's been an honour, Ma'am."

"Likewise, Steve, now get back to base and start the ball rolling."

Sitting outside the Super's office, Anna could feel the nerves start, and standing up, she walked back and forth along the thickly carpeted corridor. Oddly, Miss Tunmore, the Super's secretary, wasn't on the scene; unbeknownst to Anna, she loathed these meetings. A lifelong staunch supporter of the police force, she hated it when an officer's career was brought to an end through no fault of their own. When the Super opened the door and invited Anna into his office, she swallowed hard and walked inside. She was surprised that there wasn't anyone else there; usually under these circumstances, there were at least two other high-ranking officers in attendance.

"Please, take a seat, Chief Inspector."

Anna only nodded her head as she did as she was asked.

"Well, what a complete royal fuck up this has turned out to be. I warned you, Anna, you can't say I didn't."

"I know you did, Sir, and I am heartbroken about what has happened to Detective Graham, but I swear we took every safety measure imaginable. As you insisted, we even had armed officers hidden at the scene. There was no way I or any of my team could have foreseen that the killer would follow Detective Graham and then go to her address the following day. That said, I have something to inform you of. It will probably make little difference to the outcome of this meeting, but I had a very strong, well, I feel it's strong, lead this morning."

"Proceed."

Anna went on to explain all about the knife, and as she spoke, she monitored the Supers' face for any expression that his faith in her might have been restored somewhat.

"And you actually think this ageing man could be responsible?"

"For me, Sir, it's too much of a coincidence for it not to be, and where murder is concerned, coincidence rarely comes into play. The man is very protective of his daughter. I experienced that first-hand, and Dodi Stanton is definitely a wronged woman. You refer to him as ageing, Sir, but I wouldn't put him at more than sixty, so

he's still agile enough to commit these crimes. It was pure luck that I remembered. My head has been all over the place, and I'm heartfelt sorry that I didn't recall what I saw sooner, if I had then..."

"No point in going down that road, Anna. Hindsight is a wonderful thing, but it's no use to anyone. You have carried out your duties to the letter and have nothing to reproach yourself over. Detective Graham was an exemplary officer and well aware of the risk she was taking. Well, there will still have to be an internal investigation into Detective Graham's death, that's completely out of my hands. That said, and I will probably live to regret this, Anna, but I'm giving you a reprieve. I just hope to God you can finally get to the end of this case."

Anna couldn't believe her luck and, thanking the Super and not waiting to be excused, she almost ran from the building.

Back at Charing Cross station, Steve Johnson was in Anna's office and had already filed the request for warrants to search Wally Smith's address and also his car. When Beth walked in, she was a little surprised to see him there.

"What are you up to, Sergeant?"

Steve proceeded to share all that Anna had told him to do.

“So, how far have you got?”

"I've applied for the warrants; hopefully, they will be granted, and then we can get moving. As

much as I have confidence in you, Beth, it won't be the same without the guvnor, though."

“What won’t?”

They both turned sharply at the voice and couldn’t believe who was standing in the doorway.

“It seems that lady luck was shining on me today after all. Although the I.P.C. investigation is still ongoing regarding Cherry, for now, I've been permitted to continue with the case. Well, let's get to work. I want to be ready when those warrants come through."

At Lavita House, Wally and Linda were sitting in the front room, tucking into their lunch. The boiled ham sandwiches that Wally had made were going down a treat, and as he noisily slurped at his tea, his wife gave him a look of disgust, but he knew better than to speak when Bargain Hunt was on. The look only lasted for a few seconds as Linda rarely took her eyes away from the screen, and if one of the teams purchased something she didn't like or agree with, she would shout at the television, calling them all the names under the sun. Today, she was really enjoying her viewing as Eric Knowles was presenting, and secretly, she had a crush on the expert. Suddenly, there was a loud banging on the front door, and Wally sighed heavily. Placing his lunch onto the sofa, he got to his feet and slowly made his way along the hallway. Seeing the uniforms through the net curtain that

covered the glass, he hoped it wasn't bad news as he opened the door.

"Officers?"

"Mr Walter Smith?"

Wally nodded, and as he did so, Anna stepped forward and thrust two sheets of paper into his chest.

"I am Chief Inspector Anna Draycott, Mr Smith, and we have warrants to search this property, along with the interior of your car."

"My car, or my cab?"

Anna now felt stupid as she hadn't given his taxi a second thought, even though Dodi Stanton had already told her that her father was a cabbie. It momentarily crossed her mind that she was losing it and maybe it was time to take early retirement, but the thought was only fleeting.

"Your car. Officers, please begin."

Wally was escorted back inside and asked to take a seat in the front room as several men swarmed the tiny flat and began to open cupboards and drawers.

"What, the fuck!?"

Finally, Linda had broken her trance with the television, and she couldn't believe what she was witnessing.

"Mrs Smith, we are searching your property in connection with an ongoing case."

"Wally! What the fuck have you done?"

Linda was cut short when two officers appeared from the bedrooms and shook their heads; next,

a woman officer emerged from the kitchen and did the same. Anna began to panic. Had she got it so wrong? Those searching the front room were also coming up with a big fat zero, and Anna was about to apologise to the couple when Beth and Sergeant Johnson appeared, and Steve was holding up an evidence bag containing a large Bowie knife.

"Mr Walter Smith, I am arresting you on suspicion of murder. Anything you say may be taken down and used in evidence against you."

Linda began to scream as Wally was placed into handcuffs, and Anna heard him sigh, almost as if he was relieved that it was over. Back at the station, the knife was immediately sent over to the lab, and Wally was put into a cell while he awaited an interview.

Three hours later, just after Dodi had got back from the supermarket, the house phone rang several times, stopped and then began to ring again. Glancing at the telephone, she furrowed her brow. For a second, she considered not answering, but only a handful of people had the number, so it might be something important.

"Hello?"

"It's your mother."

"Hi Mum, what's up?"

"It's your dad; he's been arrested for murder."

For a few seconds, although it felt like hours, there was only silence; Dodi couldn't believe what she was hearing.

"Are you there? Did you hear what I said?"

"Yes, yes, sorry, of course, I heard you; you've shocked me, that's all."

"You're fucking shocked, how the hell do you think I feel?"

"Where did they take him?"

"Some snooty bitch said Charing Cross, whatever am I going to do without him? He does all the shopping and most of the cooking and..."

Dodi cut her mother off mid-sentence, as per usual; Linda was only thinking about herself.

"I'll go and see what I can find out and then ring you back, okay."

Dodi didn't wait for a reply as she hung up and then called Nicky. After speaking earlier to Arty about their successful haul, his tone was upbeat when his phone rang again, but that was until he heard what she had to say. After explaining what she'd been told by her mum, he drove straight over to the house to collect her.

At the Lab, Mike Hanks had rushed the knife through testing and within a few hours, just after the interview with Wally Smith had begun, it would be confirmed that the blade and hilt contained the blood of Cherry Graham. By the time Dodi and Nicky entered the station and asked to see Wally, they were informed that Mr Smith was currently being interviewed and they would have to take a seat, as it might be some time before Chief Inspector Draycott, who was

in charge of the case, would be free to speak to them. Dodi told Nicky to go, as there was no point in them both being stuck there for hours, but Nicky wouldn't hear of it. In the interview room, Anna took a seat opposite Wally. Detective Saunders sat beside her, and both of them couldn't wait to get started, but Anna was under no illusion that Wally would be very forthcoming, not after his hostile manner outside Dodi Stanton's house. Even so, she was a little puzzled as to why he had refused any legal representation, but that was his prerogative. Switching on the recorder as a backup to the cameras that were situated in the corners of the room, Anna gave her name and rank, along with those of Beth.

"So, Mr Smith, I am sure you are aware of the violent incidents that have taken place in Soho over the last few weeks?"

Wally only nodded his head to indicate his acknowledgement.

"Could you please be vocal for the recording?"

"Yes."

"What can you tell us about the murders of the three prostitutes, the attack on a fourth and the murder of a member of the general public and also an undercover police officer?"

Wally was tired, and to be honest, he knew they had him bang to rights. By pleading guilty, he would spare his daughter the pain of a court case, so he was willing to get things off his chest

once and for all. His next sentence shocked Anna to the core.

“I did it; I killed all those filthy bitches.”

“And, what about Detective Cherry Graham? She wasn’t a prostitute?”

"Maybe she wasn't, but she was trying to catch me, and I don't like people playing fucking tricks, so she had to go. The black bitch was lucky, and if you hadn't caught me, she would have got hers in the end."

A few minutes later, Carl Shaw tapped on the door and beckoned through the small pane of toughened glass for Anna to come out into the corridor.

“Interview suspended at five ten pm.”

Anna wasn't happy at being disturbed, and it showed on her face and in the tone of her voice as she pulled the door closed behind her.

"What is it, Carl?!"

"Sorry, Ma'am, but the Lab results have just come in. Cherry's blood, along with that of two of the other girls, was found on the weapon."

Anna thanked her detective, but she already had a confession, so returning to the room, she retook her seat.

"Why, Mr Smith, why did you murder them?"

Wally leaned back in his chair and sighed.

"Have you got kids, Chief Inspector?"

Anna slowly shook her head.

“Then you wouldn’t understand.”

“Humour me, I want to try.”

"I’ve had a shitty life, and that’s not an attempt at an excuse, as much of it was my own fault. I didn't have the balls to change things, so I only have myself to blame. My wife is a prize bitch who treats me, has always treated me like a fucking doormat. I thought it was easier to go along with everything she said and wanted, in the hope of getting some peace, but it never worked out that way. I have two daughters, Emily and Diane. Emily is a carbon copy of her mother, but my Dodi is and always has been a complete Angel. I adore her, Detective and always have, even if I didn't stick up for her much when she was a kid. Don't get me wrong, my Diane ain't perfect, but you know something? I even adore her imperfections. Growing up, my wife bullied Dodi mercilessly, and I never stepped up and stopped it, so you see what I've been doing is the least that I can do for her. Those whores hurt her badly, and I wasn't going to allow anyone to hurt my baby ever again. Years ago, when she got in with that cunt Stanton, she seemed so happy, and to begin with, I liked him. He gave her everything money could buy, a nice house, car, jewellery, anything her heart desired, but it turned out that my girl can't have kids of her own, and it isn't through the lack of trying, I can tell you. She's lost so many babies, and with each loss, I knew she must have died a little more inside."

"That's all very interesting, Mr Smith, but...."

Wally slammed both of his fists down onto the table.

"I ain't finished yet, so just let me fucking get it off me chest, alright!"

The uniformed officer who had been standing in the corner stepped forward and only stopped when Anna held up her hand.

"It's okay, officer."

"If you really want to know why, do me the fucking courtesy of listening to what I have to say."

"I apologise, please continue."

"Well, they've been married for just over five years, and my girl loves her husband more now than she did on the day, but I came to realise that cunt didn't feel the same about her. He started shagging about pretty much straight away, probably was even before they got married, and it's been with the whores and sluts who work for him, before that, probably any tart who would open her legs. That selfish cunt could have taken any nasty diseases home to my girl, but he didn't give a shit; it might even have been the reason she lost her babies. You know I'm a cabbie, well, they gossip like fucking fish wives, and I had to hear all about what Nicky Stanton was up to through my workmates, can you imagine what that feels like? I was ashamed, but more than that, I was devastated for my girl."

"I can't imagine."

"No, you can't!"

Anna had heard many stories over the years of why people had committed murder, and even though she didn't show it, she had no sympathy for Wally Smith; he was a cold-blooded killer, no matter what his reason or self-justification. After he had been formally charged, Wally was placed into a holding cell, and when she'd been informed that Nicky and Diane Stanton were at the front desk, Anna asked Beth to take them into the side room for some privacy. When Anna entered the room, it was evident that Dodi was a bag of nerves, and Nicky Stanton looked completely bewildered.

"Mr and Mrs Stanton, obviously, I can't share much information with you other than to say that your father, Mr Walter Smith, has, at this moment, been charged with five counts of murder and one count of attempted murder. He will be brought before the courts tomorrow morning, and I am in no doubt that he will then be remanded."

"Can I see him?"

"I'm sorry, but no. Once he has been processed and is on remand, then you may apply for a visiting order. I am very sorry for you, Diane; this must all be a terrible shock."

Dodi didn't reply, and as she ran from the room in tears, Nicky followed closely behind her.

CHAPTER TWENTY-SEVEN

A month after Wally's arrest and just a few weeks before sentencing, Dodi finally got to visit her father. Nicky had driven her over to Belmarsh prison, but she asked him to wait for her in the car. In all honesty, he felt relieved as these places gave him a bad feeling, and as he sailed close to the wind where the law was concerned, he hoped he would never have to set foot inside one. Going through the extensive security checks, Dodi at last got to the visiting area, and after buying some chocolate and two cups of tea, she took a seat to wait for her dad. Glancing around the room, she saw all types of visitors, old ladies who were visiting their sons or maybe even their husbands. There were children running about and babies being held by their worn-out and tired-looking mothers. Thinking about the ensuing years, she puffed out her cheeks as all sorts of images now flashed through her mind when she imagined Wally, gaunt and thin or even worse, badly beaten. Finally, the metal door at the rear of the room opened, and inmates began to file in. Straining her neck, Dodi did a double-take when she saw her dad walk in. Wally Smith looked better than he had in years, and as he approached, he was grinning from ear to ear.

"Hello there, sweetheart! You're a sight for sore eyes; I can tell you."

Dodi smiled, but at the same time, tears dropped down onto her cheeks.

"Hi Dad, I can't believe how well you look."

Wally pulled out a chair and sat down. Without asking, he opened one of the bars of chocolate and slurped on his tea, a noise that always sent Linda into a rage and now made him grin whenever he did it.

"That's because I'm loving life, sweetheart. So, what do you want to know?"

Dodi's brow furrowed at the question.

"I don't understand what you mean, Dad?"

"Well, you've come all this way, and while it's a real treat to see you, you must have some questions for your old dad?"

Dodi pushed herself back into her seat as she studied the man in front of her, a man she didn't really know after knowing him all of her life, if that made any sense.

"Fair enough. Yes, I do want to ask you, but it's only one question, Dad. Why?"

Wally's smile disappeared, and his gaze was serious as he stared into his daughter's beautiful eyes. Eyes that had, and probably were, still going through so much pain, pain she didn't deserve.

"When you were growing up, you were such a sweet little thing, and that cow Linda, she's divorcing me by the way, that cow was wicked to you, and I never stopped it, never stood up to her, and for that, I'm heartfelt sorry, darling.

After you got married and I didn't see you, I learned all about what you were up to and, more importantly, what your cunt of a husband was up to, from the other cabbies on the rank. I don't mind telling you that it fucking gutted me when I heard about your babies and the whores Stanton was shagging behind your back. You know something, sweetheart? In all the years I've been married to your bitch of a mother, I never cheated once."

“Was that out of loyalty or lack of an opportunity?”

“I'm a cabbie, babe, there was more fucking opportunity than you could ever imagine.”

Dodi didn't comment, but she was still shocked at her dad's language. It was the first time in her entire life that he had ever sworn in front of her, but it now seemed to flow so naturally.

"The more I thought about it, the more the rage grew inside me until I thought I was going to bloody explode. I thought it would only be the one, and then I couldn't stop myself, especially with the one he was shacked up with, that bitch really got my goat."

"But she was pregnant, Dad!"

"Yes, with his bastard when it should have been you having the baby, my grandchild."

"That baby was innocent."

"Casualty of war, I'm afraid. I'm sorry about it now, but there ain't anything I can do."

"And the policewoman? What did she do to

you?"

"She tried to trap me, and I couldn't have that love. As much as I knew what I was doing was wrong, I still didn't want to get caught, but strangely it's turned out for the best."

"So now you're going to spend the rest of your life in prison. Was it worth it, Dad?"

Wally screwed up his mouth and sagely rubbed at the bottom of his chin as he thought.

"It sounds ridiculous, but I love it in here, Dodi. I ain't no spring chicken and my time is running out. In here, I get three good meals a day, and I can buy chocolate and sweets without that old cow giving me aggravation. I get to read my paper in peace, my pad mate, that's the bloke who shares my cell, is nice and the best thing of all, I don't ever have to look at your mother's miserable, fucking ugly mug again, so yes, it was worth it."

Wally began to laugh, and Dodi wondered if he had maybe developed dementia or was even going insane. Whatever it was, he couldn't be in his right mind, or he wouldn't have done all of those terrible things.

"What does your solicitor say? Could they go for diminished responsibility?"

"I ain't got any legal representation, and before you start, I don't want any. Look, love, I'm guilty pure and simple, and I ain't going to try getting off with it no matter what you think. I knew very well what I was doing. Don't you get

it? I'm happy to be here, and I don't want to get off. That would never happen, but for argument's sake, let's say it did. What life would I have, where would I go at my age? I'm too long in the tooth to be starting over again. I should have left her years ago, but I was a coward, so now this is as good as it gets, and in all honesty, it ain't too bad, sweetheart."

Dodi began to cry, and it broke his heart to see his baby hurting.

"Please don't, sweetheart. Look, you get off now; there ain't anything you can do for me. Once I get settled and have been sentenced, it would be nice if you'd visit me now and again."

"Of course, I will, Dad, I love you. Are the other prisoners okay with you, or do they give you a hard time?"

"The complete opposite, being a serial killer ups your kudos in a place like this. You going to see your mum?"

Dodi didn't answer and instead just smiled as she kissed his cheek and then walked away. Back in the car, she cried in Nicky's arms. She shared a lot of what her father had said, especially about him, and the look of pain on his face was evident. He felt guilty for all those lost lives that had been taken and guilty for how he had treated his wife. He was to blame for all of this; he couldn't deny it. Oh, he didn't strike the blows, but if he had just kept his cock in his pants and been loyal to Dodi, then none of this

would ever have happened.

"Come on, babe, I'll take you home, or would you like to pop in to see your mum?"

The look she gave him was one of shock, but then she laughed.

"Not a chance, but thanks for asking."

A month later, it was the day of sentencing. The courtroom was filled to capacity, but Linda Smith was nowhere to be seen. The atmosphere was strained as the gallery appeared to be split into two factions. There were the Toms, dressed to the nines in their best finery and all baying for Wally Smith's blood, and then there was Dodi and Nicky sitting alone and away from the others. Nicky felt uncomfortable as he knew he should have been supporting his girls, but Dodi needed him today more than she ever had; he just hoped his Toms realised that and would make allowances. When Wally was brought up to the dock from the holding cell, he held his head up high. He didn't try to stare out the Toms and instead focused his gaze on his baby girl. He was shocked that she was with Stanton, but maybe he had turned over a new leaf; even a leopard could change its spots, couldn't it? As Dodi looked in his direction, Wally winked. He knew better than to smile, as it would have looked like he was trying to rub salt into the wounds of the Toms. When the judge entered, everyone got to their feet, and it was going to go against Wally even more as it was a woman

sitting in judgment. As circuit judge, the Right Honourable Hermione Cavers-Bateson entered the room, a pin would have been heard if dropped. Hermione was known for her dislike of men, and none more so than those who took the lives of women. When everyone was asked to take a seat, Wally did as he was told, but he was then poked in the side by a court guard who informed him that the invite didn't include the accused and that he had to stand.

"Walter Reginald Smith, you have been brought before this court for the heinous crime of murder. It has been noted that you have given a plea of guilty, and as such, that will be taken into consideration. Nonetheless, for the murder of five innocent women and the attempted murder of another, the punishment must be severe and send out a clear message to others. I hereby sentence you to a term of no less than thirty-five years before you will be eligible for parole. Officer, take him down."

The gallery was instantly in uproar as the women all cheered and clapped, but it was Dodi's solitary scream that seemed to be heard above all the other noise. Nicky didn't try to calm her and instead, placing his arm around her shoulder, he led her out to the car via the side door of the court. It was such a high-profile case that it wasn't rocket science to know the media would be in a frenzy to get any information they could from the murderer's

daughter. In the car, Nicky told Dodi to duck down until they were out of sight. Pulling away, he glanced in the rear-view mirror and knew he had been correct in his assumption regarding the press; there were hordes of them on the front steps, all vying for the best position.

"It's okay now, babe, no one's following us. You want to go straight home?"

Her reply shocked him, but nodding and without comment, he drove over to Somers Town. Dodi knocked and waited for the door to be answered, which seemed to take an age as Linda was in the middle of watching one of her programmes. About to call out for Wally to go and see who it was, she glanced around the room at the dirty cups and dishes piled up on the coffee table, and it suddenly hit her how much her husband had done around the house. Sighing heavily, she hauled herself out of the armchair and made her way along the hall. When she opened the door, she didn't speak and only raised her eyebrows, then turned and went back into the front room. Dodi slowly shook her head. Nothing had changed; it never would.

"I thought you might be in court today?"

"And why on earth would you think that? Your father has brought shame on this family; I can't even show my face on the street without some bastard making a sarky remark."

"He needed you to be there, Mum."

Linda slammed her open palm down onto the

arm of the chair as she glared in her daughter's direction.

"I don't give a flying fuck what he wanted or needed, what about me?"

"You selfish old bitch, it's always got to be about you, mum hasn't it?"

"Oh, just get out! As far as I'm concerned, I'm a widow now, and Wally can rot in hell for all I care."

Dodi turned on her heels and stormed out. When she got back into the car, she broke down in a flood of tears as she told Nicky all that her mother had said.

"I'm not one to say I told you so, but babe, in all honesty, did you expect anything different?"

"Probably not, but we all live in hope. Will you take me home, Nicky? I'm not feeling so good."

When they reached Muswell Hill, Dodi kissed Nicky on the cheek and thanked him for today and all of his support, but deep down, she knew nothing had altered in their relationship, and it still cut like a knife. Over the next couple of months, she visited her dad once a fortnight, and slowly they got to know one another all over again. Wally really did look happy, and he was always so pleased to see her. Father and daughter laughed on the visits without any sarcastic interruption from Linda, and Dodi soon realised it was the first time in her entire life that she was able to talk openly and honestly to her dad without her mother poking her nose in.

Wally shared his life story, the one she didn't know about. He told her of his hobbies, likes and dislikes, things she never knew and as much as it saddened her, it also filled her heart with joy that they were getting to find out so much about each other that they had never known.

Six months later, in the early hours of the morning, Dodi woke up in excruciating pain. The bed was soaked through, and she was in a blind panic. Reaching for her mobile, she phoned the only person able to help her. Just as he picked up his phone, a new wave of pain shot through her body and as she screamed out, she dropped her phone onto the floor. Nicky was there in less than fifteen minutes, and in that time, Dodi had at least been able to get herself dressed. When she heard him race up the stairs, she smiled. Apart from cheating on her with other women, he had never let her down.

"Hi, sweetheart, what on earth is going on?"

"It's time, my waters broke a while ago, and I woke up in agony."

It was like he had blue flashing lights on his car as he flew along the roads. The traffic was light due to the hour, and luckily, he didn't see any patrol cars. Screeching to a halt outside the accident and emergency department of the Whittington Hospital on Magdala Avenue, Nicky blasted the car horn several times. The birth was smooth, and just four hours later,

Nicky held his son for the first time. He had never known a feeling like it before, and tears of joy and regret dropped down onto his cheeks. Their last hook-up, which had happened after their split, and when he was mourning Jan, had resulted in the most beautiful gift in the world. Now he wondered if he had ever really been in love with Jan, or if it had just been infatuation. Dodi was home from the hospital two days later, and she made it clear to Nicky that she didn't want any visitors for the time being. Monica's name wasn't mentioned, but it was clear she meant his mother.

"The first person apart from us to meet our baby will be my dad. I've got a visit booked for the end of the week."

Nicky was so in awe of his child that he didn't want to do anything to upset Dodi and nodded his head even though he knew it would upset his mum.

"Whatever, you say, sweetheart. I'll take you if you like?"

Friday morning at ten o'clock, Nicky walked up to the front door and lightly tapped, mindful that Nicky Junior might be sleeping. When Dodi answered, she had the baby strapped to her chest in a kind of wrap. Her skin and hair looked great, and he didn't think he'd ever seen a more beautiful sight before. The security at the prison was as strict as usual, but the staff were very gentle with the baby, and for that, Dodi was

grateful. When Wally entered, he almost ran over, and as soon as he saw them, he began to sob. Dodi removed baby Nicky and placed him into his grandfather's arms just as Wally pulled a small grey furry elephant from his trouser pocket.

"Oh my Lord, he's so tiny. Look at his little fingers. Oh, Dodi, he's wrapped them around my thumb, bless him. He likes it, I made it myself, you know, in one of the craft classes."

"It's lovely, Dad, and I'll make sure he treasures it always."

The next few minutes were spent walking around the room as Wally proudly showed off his grandson to the other inmates and guards.

"So, how are you, love? Been to see the witch yet?"

"I'm good, and in answer to your question, no, I haven't, nor do I intend to. She didn't treat me well as a child, so there's no way she's getting her claws into my son."

"So, what about his father?"

For his daughter's sake, Wally had stopped calling Nicky a cunt, and now that the baby had arrived, it wouldn't have been right.

"Nicky looks after us, and he's in love with his boy, but that's as far as it goes, Dad. When the man you love breaks all of your trust, then there just isn't any going back, I'm afraid."

The visit seemed to fly by, and as Wally was led away, she promised they would both be back in

two weeks. She wished she could visit every week, but as fortnightly was all they were allowed, it would have to do. Back in the car, Nicky asked after his former father-in-law and was pleased to see Dodi looking so happy. When they reached the house, he switched off the engine and, turning in his seat, looked at them both. The baby was now snuggled in his wrap and sleeping, so he felt it was a perfect time to say what he had on his mind.

"Can we have a chat, Dodi?"

She knew what was coming, but she wasn't dreading it; in fact, she would be glad to get it over and done with. Nodding her head for him to continue, she smiled.

"I know I hurt you, and so much has happened, but is there any way we could try again, sweetheart?"

Dodi took a few moments before she spoke. It wasn't that she didn't know what to say; nothing could be further from the truth, but she wanted her words to be calm and, above all else, kind. Her tone was soft, and there wasn't the slightest hint of anger.

"You didn't just hurt me, Nicky, you broke me. I felt as if my heart had been ripped out, especially when I found out that Jan was pregnant. I love you, Nicky, always have, and I always will. You gave me my miracle baby, and for that, I will be eternally grateful, but in answer to your question, it's no. I think in time I

will be able to forgive you, but I will never be able to forget. Love and trust go hand in hand, and when the trust has gone, there isn't anything left to build on. You smashed our foundations, Nicky, and that's the saddest thing of all. That said, you are his daddy, and I wouldn't ever do anything to stop you from having a relationship with him, but sadly, there will always be this invisible wall between the two of us. Nicky, I'm sorry if this isn't what you wanted to hear, but I need to be honest with you and to fill you with false hope would be cruel."

Dodi got out of the car, but it wasn't until she stepped inside the house and closed the front door that Nicky drove off. Tears streamed down his face, but then he wiped his eyes with the cuff of his jumper, sniffed loudly and then smiled. He wasn't about to give up, even if it took years; he was convinced he would get his family back.

EPILOGUE

Over the next year, things gradually settled down. Nicky Junior was the perfect child, sleeping through the night and bringing his parents nothing but joy during the day. Nicky was soon up to his old tricks with his Toms, and even though Dodi had an inkling of what was going on, she didn't actually care anymore. The divorce had been finalised, and she had received the house mortgage-free and a very handsome amount of cash as a settlement. Nicky also gave her two thousand a month to cover anything the baby might need, which was more than generous. Finally, Dodi was content and happy with her life; after all, apart from a husband, she had all that she had ever dreamed of.

Unaware that his ex-wife knew what he was up to, Nicky Stanton was still convinced that he and Dodi would one day be together again. For now, he was sowing his oats, but unlike before, he always wore protection. The club had gone from strength to strength, and Nick's Place was where all the working girls wanted to work. Nicky spent time with his son a couple of times a week, and every other weekend, Dodi allowed him to have junior overnight. At first, it had been difficult for her as the house seemed so empty without a baby in it, but Nicky adored his child, so there was nothing to worry about, and she soon got used to the setup.

As for Monica Stanton, shortly after the baby had been born, Bernie Stanton passed away. It had been devastating for Nicky and his Mum, and Monica now felt lost. The last few years of her life had been spent as a carer, and as much as she had complained at times, she loved her husband and wished he were still here with her. She tried hard to get back in favour with Dodi, but her former daughter-in-law wasn't having any of it, and the only way she got to see the baby was when Nicky had him overnight. She had pleaded with her son to intervene, but that was a definite no-go; what Dodi said was how it would be, and he wouldn't rock the boat for anything. He was also aware that his ex-wife couldn't forgive the betrayal she had felt from Monica, and sadly, there would be no changing that.

Linda Smith never got to meet her grandson, though she did know about his existence. Since her husband had gone to prison, Linda had become bitter, more bitter than she had ever been in the past. She had no friends and any acquaintances she met at the bingo or down the market soon found out what she was like and quickly distanced themselves. Although she didn't try to contact Dodi, she did try to reach out to her firstborn, Emily, but her daughter wouldn't even return her calls. Linda Smith would spend the rest of her life as a lonely, bitter and sad old woman.

Robbie Evans didn't contact Nicky or Dodi again; he felt too ashamed. After her rejection and refusal to have any kind of a relationship with him, he began to drink excessively. No one was aware of the fact that, after all he had seen during his time in the army, Robbie was actually suffering from PTSD. Six months later, in the early hours of the morning and when it all finally became too much, Robbie Evans headed to Waterloo Bridge, climbed over the railings and jumped. The water was freezing cold as it engulfed his body, and he didn't fight it. As his lungs rapidly filled with the brackish brine, he gulped down as much as he could. There was no way he wanted to be saved, and as he quickly drowned, he was finally at peace. It took over a month to track down his mother, but when notified, Rita Evans never claimed the body.

Drummond's restaurant never again opened for business. The building was soon sold to a developer, and after all bank debts were cleared, there was a small amount left for Marty to start over with. Deciding to leave the city, he flew out to Spain and purchased a small bar on the Costa del Sol. It wasn't fine dining, and it took a while for him to adjust, but eventually he settled down to a slower pace of life and was earning a decent living.

As for Wally Smith, he was in his element. He saw his daughter and grandson every two

weeks, and in between that, they spoke on the phone, and Dodi sent photographs and letters. Wally would never have believed he could be happy incarcerated at Her Majesty's pleasure, but he was. Since gaining a job in the kitchen, his waistline had expanded, but he didn't mind. Becoming a born-again Christian had made him deeply regret all the terrible things he had done, and at times, especially in the small hours, the remorse was all-consuming, but he couldn't change anything, only make sure he was a better person in the future. He was now a mentor to the young inmates, and it was something he was good at. It was odd how things had turned out. He was happier than he'd ever been, and so was his daughter, but how that had come about had been at the expense and pain of others, well, what he had done to be exact, and for that, he was so very sorry.

The End

www.ingramcontent.com/pod-product-compliance
Ingram Content Group UK Ltd.
Pitfield, Milton Keynes, MK11 3LW, UK
UKHW040703280126
10359UKWH00034B/298

9 798232 641290